Sore Loser

I nailed the full house on The River with an Ace of hearts and shook my head in amazement. Smiling again, Sam turned over his two pair, Aces and Kings, and cupped his hands around the chips. He'd slid them halfway toward himself when I slowly turned up my cards. His eyes widened, then narrowed to black slits as his grin faded and he lifted his hands up off the felt. He snatched up his jacket, jammed it on and stuck a hand on the pocket where I'd slipped the note I'd written earlier. His brows drew together as he pulled it out. The dealer had distributed our pocket cards, so I peeked at them while watching Sam read my note.

> *Meet me at the aft deck after the tournament and I'll share some tips on how to win the game of modern Hold 'Em.*
>
> *—BC*

Sam stared at me a beat and then stomped off, anger radiating from him in almost tangible waves. He was mad enough now to kill, that was for sure. I just hoped Jack wouldn't let me down or I was going to be in real trouble.

The Poker Mysteries by Jackie Chance

DEATH ON THE FLOP
CASHED IN

Cashed In

JACKIE CHANCE

BERKLEY PRIME CRIME, NEW YORK

THE BERKLEY PUBLISHING GROUP
Published by the Penguin Group
Penguin Group (USA) Inc.
375 Hudson Street, New York, New York 10014, USA
Penguin Group (Canada), 90 Eglinton Avenue East, Suite 700, Toronto, Ontario M4P 2Y3, Canada
(a division of Pearson Penguin Canada Inc.)
Penguin Books Ltd., 80 Strand, London WC2R 0RL, England
Penguin Group Ireland, 25 St. Stephen's Green, Dublin 2, Ireland (a division of Penguin Books Ltd.)
Penguin Group (Australia), 250 Camberwell Road, Camberwell, Victoria 3124, Australia
(a division of Pearson Australia Group Pty. Ltd.)
Penguin Books India Pvt. Ltd., 11 Community Centre, Panchsheel Park, New Delhi—110 017, India
Penguin Group (NZ), 67 Apollo Drive, Rosedale, North Shore 0745, Auckland, New Zealand
(a division of Pearson New Zealand Ltd.)
Penguin Books (South Africa) (Pty.) Ltd., 24 Sturdee Avenue, Rosebank, Johannesburg 2196,
South Africa

Penguin Books Ltd., Registered Offices: 80 Strand, London WC2R 0RL, England

This is a work of fiction. Names, characters, places, and incidents either are the product of the author's imagination or are used fictitiously, and any resemblance to actual persons, living or dead, business establishments, events, or locales is entirely coincidental. The publisher does not have any control over and does not assume any responsibility for author or third-party websites or their content.

CASHED IN

A Berkley Prime Crime Book / published by arrangement with the author

PRINTING HISTORY
Berkley Prime Crime mass-market edition / September 2007

Copyright © 2007 by The Berkley Publishing Group.
Cover art by Karine Daisay.
Cover design by Rita Frangie.
Interior text design by Kristin del Rosario.

ISBN: 978-0-425-21768-9

BERKLEY® PRIME CRIME
Berkley Prime Crime Books are published by The Berkley Publishing Group,
a division of Penguin Group (USA) Inc.,
375 Hudson Street, New York, New York 10014.
The name BERKLEY PRIME CRIME and the BERKLEY PRIME CRIME design are trademarks belonging to Penguin Group (USA) Inc.

PRINTED IN THE UNITED STATES OF AMERICA

10 9 8 7 6 5 4 3 2 1

This is for my godparents,
my aunt and uncle,
Ann and Bob Coleman

The poker player learns that sometimes both science and common sense are wrong; that the bumblebee can fly; that, perhaps, one should never trust an expert; that there are more things in heaven and earth than are dreamt of by those with an academic bent.

—David Mamet

Prologue

You know it has been said that money creates more problems than it solves. I never believed that. Until now.

One

"**S**exy mama!"

I looked up not because I was either sexy or anyone's mama, but because I recognized the voice of my reprobate twin. He waved at me over the hordes of people between us on the ship dock then paused to wink at a truly sexy mama—an Angelina Jolieish siren complete with big lips and big boobs but skinny everywhere else, holding a Shiloh-looking baby on her hip. I glanced back down at the envelope the travel agency had sent that proved I'd paid a small fortune to be in this sweaty cast of thousands waiting to be cleared to get on a chunk of metal bobbing around in the Gulf of Mexico. This was part of the reason I now believed that money causes more problems than it solves. At first, I foresaw the three hundred and fifty thousand I'd lucked into six months ago by winning Vegas' Big Kahuna—the Lanai casino's Pro-Am Texas Hold 'Em Tournament—as a ticket to a new life. I'd just turned forty, lost my fiancé, my career and almost my life. In the rush of adrenaline following the tournament, murders and Sin City, I'd agreed to take my brother and my potential significant other, aka lifesaver, with me on a poker cruise. Already, that was going to hell—the significant other hadn't shown, my parents had, and now I had to share a room with a modern day Don Juan. Nothing could be worse than a guy on the make when that guy was your brother and, when he made his make, you had to sleep on the pool deck. This was going to be one heck of a cruise.

I watched as Ben threaded his way to me, greatly enjoying the appreciative glances of 93 percent of the women he passed (the other 7 percent being obviously vision impaired or related to him), and reviewed another reason money had created more problems than it had solved for me. It had given me the opportunity to tear up my résumé, allowing me to start my own business as an advertising consultant. To be my own boss meant more to me than most, since my old boss had been my fiancé who I'd caught doing the nasty on top of one of my ad campaigns with his executive assistant. Freedom on two fronts. I should have known better. Instead, one of my first big jobs was with an airline that hired me as a creative adjunct to my former advertising firm. Yes, you guessed it, my ex-fiancé, Toby McKnight, was head of the account. I had to see him and his twenty-year-old, gum-smacking, booty-wiggling floozie nearly every day in the heat of the campaign—the airline's, not theirs. Or maybe both, except now I was trying not to notice theirs.

Have I mentioned I have really bad karma?

And it was just getting worse.

"Bee-Bee," Ben finally sidled up to me, slid his arm around my waist and squeezed as he whispered in my ear. "I'm next in line, so I'll check out the room and catch up with you later."

I was about 1,042 in line and since he'd been 1,043 until he'd left to go to the restroom ten minutes ago, I cocked my head at him and raised my eyebrows. He shook his just-a-little-bit-too-long black hair out of his face. His green eyes twinkled. A woman walking past sighed.

"Ingrid talked me into joining her in line." He flashed a grin toward the head of the line. A six-foot-tall Scandinavian princess, surrounded by a dozen other college coeds, all shorter but no less nubile, waved at him to hurry back.

"Is Ingrid over eighteen?" I muttered, fanning myself with the ship map. It had to be one hundred degrees in the shade here at the Port of Galveston.

"What kind of question is that? She was just being kind, letting me in like that."

"Uh-huh," I muttered, frowning at the lithe Amazon.

"You old worrywart." Ben gave me a noogie. "Live a little. Have fun. Oops, I forgot. You wouldn't know fun if it slapped you on the butt."

The tanned, sexy Marlboro Man I'd been admiring in line behind me snorted in disgust. Probably at my un-fun-loving rear end. I resisted the urge to tuck my heinie behind a nearby potted palm. Ben grabbed for my braid. I was a forty-year-old worrywart on a cruise with a twin who acted liked Dennis the Menace. I might start to get depressed. And that was *before* I'd even begun to contemplate what the aforementioned heinie looked like from behind.

Ben winked and sauntered off as if he were doing the Earth a favor by being on it. Most women wouldn't argue with his supposition. God may have shorted him in maturity but more than made up for it in looks.

"Belinda!" Another unfortunately all-too-familiar voice shouted above the din.

Ack. In my peripheral vision, I could see them coming up on my right.

I turned left, trying to strike up a conversation with the Marlboro Man, but he was already talking to the bodacious blonde behind him. That noogie really turned him off. Damn Ben.

"Howard, is it really Belinda? It looks like her, but I didn't think she'd look quite so frumpy."

Frumpy? My hands reached to smooth my khaki capris. Oh dear. I'd imagined poor form but not *that* poor.

"See, Howard, she *is* our girl. Come to think of it, I think it's those ridiculous high water pants that make her look like she's packing two half-full water balloons."

I'd been hoping to avoid my parents. This was why.

"Look, Howard, she's smiling. I told you she'd be happy to see us. She just didn't hear me calling earlier, did you, pookie?"

"What?" I fanned my hot face as I forced a smile. "Of course not, Mom. Were you calling?"

Unbelievable as it may seem, it hadn't been difficult to talk me into letting my parents have my cabin on the ship. It all happened during one of Frank's half-dozen visits to Houston, a really, really nice weekend.

He was the one who'd convinced me to make a family vacation of the poker cruise. He said he liked my parents. I think he was just entertained by my reaction to them, most especially to my mom, Elva. I didn't fight it because I thought it would be a good excuse to spend a lot of time together, in his cabin. My parents would have to take mine, since the inaugural cruise of the *Sea Gambler* was full . . .

And where was Frank now?

I had no idea, actually. He'd called my cell phone and left a message this morning saying he was *so* sorry. He had a "crisis" with a job and told us not to wait on him at the port. He said he would make it up to me. Uh-huh. Frank was in the "security" business and despite the time we'd spent together since Vegas, I knew no more about what he did for a living than the first day in a Vegas bar when he'd handed me his card. He carried a gun and sometimes handcuffs. He lived in L.A. but didn't have a home phone, so I had been given only a cell number. He had an ex-wife and two kids I'd never met, who he rarely talked about. He was a recovering alcoholic who still occasionally fell off the wagon. He would leave unexpectedly on jobs and sometimes go days before returning a phone call.

Frank Gilbert didn't sound like the kind of guy that could engender trust, but somehow he did.

Or maybe I was just desperate.

Or maybe I just remembered that weekend in May all too well . . .

My first goal on this trip was to find someone to make new memories, so I could forget steaming up glass elevators. Forget slow dancing in the rain. Forget where champagne tasted best.

"Belinda, are you alright?" Mom slapped her hand on my forehead. "You are very red, and you're breathing hard."

I cleared my throat and snapped the stretchy beaded bracelet around my wrist, then used it to wrap my braid up into a bun. "It's just a little warm out here, Mom."

She eyed me suspiciously, but nodded and changed the subject. Or so she thought. "We saw Ben with his new women friends. They're quite taken with our boy." She paused proudly before nosing on ahead. She looked around at the masses surrounding us. "Where's Frank?"

Oh dear. I cleared my throat and tried for nonchalant, blowing a curl of hair out of my face to buy a bit more time.

"Well?" Elva demanded.

I forced a cheery tone. "He called and said he had an emergency. It sounds like he won't make it before we shove off."

"Humph. Sounds fishy to me. I bet he found a new girl. You should have dragged him down the aisle when you had the chance. Now you've lost the best catch you've had in years." Mom tsked. Behind her, Marlboro Man and the blonde both tsked. Super.

"When did I have the chance, Mom?" I asked, staring at the shiny head of the bald man in front of me, willing the line to move faster.

"You *were* in Vegas, weren't you?" Mom was aghast, liver-spotted hands flying around, cherry red lipsticked lips pursing and moving soundlessly with my failure.

"We were in Vegas when we'd only known each other three days." I pointed out. Why I continued to justify this vein of conversation, I don't know. A lot must be said for underage brainwashing. *Be respectful of your elders, Belinda.* I knew she'd had an ulterior motive with that life lesson drilled into my brain from birth.

"That's longer than a lot of people know each other before they get married in Sin City. Who was that star who only knew her husband something like an hour before they tied the knot?"

"Mom, they got an annulment three days later."

"So? You'd never agree to something like that. Neither would Frank. He's a guy who keeps a promise. He'd stand by you even if he had second thoughts. Get him to say 'I do' and you're in like Flynn." Mom nodded once decisively.

Great, how romantic. Anyhow, both of us were so far away from thinking about marriage that if the altar were in Boise, we were in Siberia, or maybe Mars. And what about the promise to go on the poker cruise with me? He sure hadn't fulfilled that one, had he?

"So." Mom rushed on. "Call him and tell him you'll meet him in Vegas. Get him a little tipsy and haul him in front of an Elvis preacher and get it done."

Mom didn't know about the alcoholism. Maybe I should tell her and derail her train. I didn't have the heart to do that to Frank, even though he'd ditched me. With my parents to boot. I sighed. "I'll think about it, Mom."

With that she gave a sharp, satisfied nod. "Good."

"Hey, girlie, how's that house coming along? I thought you might not make the cruise, what with having to ride herd on all those subcontractors." Dad chuckled, waiting entirely too long to change the subject.

Which brings me to yet another reason why I think money causes more problems than it solves. The house I bought. The house that may not be finished until I retire. I love old historic homes and there are some terribly cute ones with great character in University Oaks. But being properly mature and wise, I resisted because I didn't want to be constantly working on something already on its way down—if it wasn't the plumbing, it would be electrical, or the lead-based paint would start peeling, or asbestos would need eradicating. I thought I'd be smart and build a brand-new house, getting the mess all over with before I moved in. Now it's *if* I move in. So much for wise. Two weeks after they poured the foundation, the day after they began the framing, my contractor disappeared with half the money for the house. No licensed contractor worth his salt in Houston would take the job before sometime next year, so I got my contractor's license and hired the plumbers, the painters and the electricians to name a few. And what I've learned is that they show up when they are supposed to about 10 percent of the time. They do what they are supposed to about 5 percent of that time. At this rate, I've calculated the house will be finished when I am sixty-four years and two months old.

"I told them not to come back for a week," I answered. "Which probably means they will all show up every day, on time, and put the stove in the bathroom and carpet on the ceiling."

Dad chuckled. "It would go a lot faster and easier for you if you'd agree to let me go crack the whip."

I didn't miss the warning look from Mom. A regular

checkup had surprised Dad with a 90 percent blocked artery and he'd had a shunt put in his heart a month ago. "Thanks, Dad, but you need to enjoy your retirement."

He pulled a face and turned to look at an exotic Polynesian model walking through the crowd in a string bikini. Smiling to show a row of brilliant, capped teeth, she passed him a card. "Remember to shop in our gift shop on board. We have great prices on everything from lingerie to jewels—and, remember, once in international waters, everything is duty free! And I can tell"—pause for heavy lidded look down his form—"you're going to win a lot at the Hold 'Em tables, handsome, so get ready to spend it on your special lady or anyone you choose." With a wink she was gone. He looked like he wanted to chase her and, since his heart operation, I was repeatedly worried he would do just that. He'd gone from perpetually tired to perpetually peppy. I hoped Mom could keep up.

"Really, Howard, it's rude to stare."

"Is it rude to touch?"

My mouth dropped open, the blonde stifled a gasp and Marlboro Man looked like he wanted to puke. My mother just giggled and swung at his shoulder with the coral and green scarf around her neck. "You rascal."

For the first time in forty years, I could begin to see evidence of the genes that showed up in Ben. Oh, Lord, save me. It was going to be a long four days.

Two

♦ ♣ ♥ ♠

I've heard that Texas Hold 'Em was a much smaller world until just a handful of years ago. Used to be that there were just a few greats, and everyone knew who they were, sort of like Hollywood in the 40s, before TV changed the complexion of the entertainment industry. Now, the Internet has done the same for this most popular game of poker. While there are still a few Cary Grants of poker out there—the Phil Hellmuths and the Doyle Brunsons—like today's Hollywood and its plethora of flash-in-the-pan stars, there are so many so-called champion poker players around it's hard to keep track. That was fortunate for me, because although the tournament I had won had been televised and rife with melodrama, I doubted many people in the general public would recognize me. I test as an introvert on those personality quizzes; I like people I already know and love my privacy. Flying below the radar is just the way I like it.

But like I said, my karma stinks.

"Bee Cool, is that you?" I felt a hand at the crook of my elbow and looked down to my right to see a balding man with kind eyes grinning up at me.

"Ringo?" I gave him a quick hug as he pointed shyly at the top of my head. "You still have them."

My fingers reached for my silver reflective Gargoyle sunglasses, the same ones Ringo had given me when I first met him in Vegas. "Why do you sound surprised? These are my lucky charms. I couldn't have won that tournament without them."

Ringo's face glowed rosy in just a few seconds. "I saw that you were doing this tournament on board the *Gambler* and so my poker group signed up for the cruise."

"Really? You came all the way from Nova Scotia for this? How did you see I was coming?"

Ringo blinked. "The cruise line advertised it. Your picture was pasted up on the Internet with some of the other big guys— Rawhide Jones, Rick Santobella, Denton Ferris to name a few."

I'm in advertising, so on one hand, I was impressed that someone had noticed that some no-name like me had bought a ticket on their poker cruise and had thought to use it to beef up sales. On the other hand, I thought Ringo had handed me the perfect way to get my own free cabin out of these cruise ship geeks. Right now, haunted by the idea of sleeping on a pool lounge for the entire cruise to avoid Ben's hijinks, that cheered me more than the highly unauthorized use of my name angered me.

"Ringo, I don't know why you'd want to come see me play. You know I don't know what I'm doing."

"Are you kidding? You're better than the greats in the game. You just go out there and do it, you feel the game, you *are* the game instead of a master of the game. You don't use a standard strategy. You act like a Mouse one minute and a Maniac the next. You flow, you intuit, and you win."

I shook my head. I wished I thought as much about my game as he did, I might get better at it. "Ringo, it's called luck. I won one major tournament which I had unusually strong incentive to win. I might totally tank on this cruise."

We both shared a wry look at my accidentally poor play on words, then Ringo patted my hand and, as is his way, made me feel less like a goober. "You're too modest for your own good. Get out there and blast them out of the water."

He giggled and wandered off before I could offer to repay him for the sunglasses, which truly had been a godsend during my Big Kahuna tournament. All I'd really cared about was saving my brother's life, which required winning, or at least making it to the final table, and the shades really helped.

A pleasant looking man wearing a cruise ship uniform and a half smile passed me. Speaking of luck, his was bad today. I grabbed his arm and read his nametag. "Solis, from Ecuador, where can I find the Hold 'Em tournament director?"

"We're not in international waters, yet, ma'am, we can't gamble yet. Besides, the tournament doesn't begin until this evening."

"Yes, I am aware of that."

"Still you want the director?"

"Yes."

"Why do you need her?" The half smile was gone, suddenly replaced by a slitty-eyed stare.

For a moment I felt like I was back in Las Vegas, talking to a pit boss. What would the equivalent be on a cruise ship? Raft boss? Float boss? I sighed. "I just want to get something cleared up." Maybe get a free room on board for the cruise line using my name, such as it was, to build up their ship manifest.

Solis frowned suspiciously, and I lost what was left of my patience. "Look, Solis, I'm Belinda Cooley and your cruise line has been using my name and photo advertising the onboard tournament without my permission."

Solis whispered into an invisible communication device under his lapel, or maybe built into his nametag. He turned away when he saw me trying to figure it out. Geez. I guess I was in Vegas on the Gulf after all.

In approximately two seconds, a pair of unsmiling extra-large cruise employees appeared at each of my elbows. They were dressed in identical short sleeve Hawaiian-style shirts in a flower and poker motif that, I suppose, was geared to make them look friendlier. It didn't. "They will escort you to Miss Kinkaid, Miz Cooley," Solis informed me.

I had to remind myself I'd asked for this as I was propelled through the milling masses of sweaty poker fiends in completely unreasonable summer outfits, feeling like I was headed to the gestapo. As we descended in the elevator to the bowels of the ship, I fought claustrophobia.

I shot a sidelong look at the less imposing of the henchmen. For some reason, he wasn't wearing a nametag. Hmm. Maybe he just forgot to put it on this morning. "You worked on the *Sea Gambler* long?"

He grunted. Okay. I turned to the other one who looked like a cross between a pro football lineman of Samoan descent and a Viking. How much worse could it get? I suppose he could spit fire out of his mouth. No nametag on him either. Uh-oh. I forced a smile. "How about you?"

Turned out, Hans Talaupoola was a lot friendlier than he looked. He was a cruise veteran, having been in the security detail on four other ships over the past six years. Without any more prompting but an interested nod every now and then, Hans got so enthused that he imparted all sorts of fascinating inside information about our destinations.

"Wow. You ought to work on the tour desk instead of in security," I commented.

Hans beamed. "That's where I really want to work, but

they always stick me with the heavies. Sorry, Phil," he added as an aside to his partner.

Phil grunted. I was so incensed by Phil's rudeness, more for his buddy Hans' sake than for my own, that I opened my mouth to chastise him only to be interrupted by a loud buzz inside the elevator. I held by breath. Not only was I going to get stuck in an elevator but I was getting stuck in one 20,000 leagues under the sea. Ack.

"Boys," the speaker under the buttons reverberated. "You may bring Miss Cooley to me in the conference room instead of my office."

"Ten-four, Miss Kinkaid," Hans answered, pushing the number one button. We started to sink.

"That's creepy. How did she know which elevator we were in?" I looked around the metal box we stood in but couldn't see any hidden lenses.

Phil and Hans shared a look. "We gotta keep an eye on what goes on around the boat," Hans said to me.

They'd be getting an eyeful with my brother's extracurriculars, that was for sure. "Do all the cruise lines do that? There have been so many unexplained disappearances off cruise ships recently, how can that be if all the ships have 'eyes' on board?"

Phil grunted, shifty-eyed, but since that was his apparent nature, I didn't worry. But when Hans shrugged, avoiding eye contact, I got a little twinge in my stomach. The elevator door opened, they nudged me out down the hall. That was the end of that conversation.

"Miss Cooley, I understand you are upset?"

I looked behind us to see an extremely short, especially round woman with equally short and round strawberry blond hair, as she was bustling toward us in the pinkest getup I'd ever seen—cotton candy linen blouse, primrose capris, fuschia sandals. She held out her small fat hand and I responded with mine. She performed the world's briefest handshake, firm if fleeting. It was disconcerting actually, like the grip of someone ready to arm wrestle.

"As a matter of fact I am, Miss Kinkaid. I have just been told by an acquaintance of mine that you have been using my name to beef up the ship's manifest."

Her penciled-in eyebrows met over her rimless rose-lens glasses. "And why is this surprising? That is exactly what the agreement stated, that we use your name and publicity photo in our ad campaigns in exchange for a free cabin and free tournament buy-in onboard ship for this inaugural cruise."

Agreement? What agreement? I know I should've latched on to that immediately but instead went with a more vital priority. "I have a free room!"

"Yes," Miss Kinkaid had taken to using a tone reserved for the mentally handicapped. "And you have signed that room over to an Ingrid Vanderhoss. You have assigned the original room you booked to your parents, Elva and Harold, and you are bunking with your agent."

"My agent?!"

"Benjamin. Your husband, I presume."

Ack-urgh-bleck. I must have sounded like I was in need of CPR, because two men in matching poker motif shirts poked their head in the room and looked at me with concern. Kinkaid waved them away.

I cleared my throat, ended up coughing, and the two men reappeared. I forced a weak smile and they left shaking their heads. "So, ah, *my agent.* Is he the one who arranged the deal for the free room, and me in your advertising?"

Kinkaid's eyebrows did the mambo. "You didn't know? Maybe you two should consider marriage counseling to deal with your communication issues."

I shook my head and my next words stumbled on my tongue before rushing out. "He's not my husband. Ben is my brother."

Kinkaid shook her head. "Oh, well, a blood relation. There's nothing you can do about that, now can you?"

"No, unfortunately." Except for murder. That was always an option.

"I might recommend firing him as an agent, though."

I wonder how you fire someone you didn't hire. I nodded once and wagged an index finger at her. "Definitely. I'll get right on that."

Kinkaid's cell phone rang and she wandered over to the long mahogany table, spread with seating plans for the Hold 'Em tournament. I peeked over her shoulder to see if I could find my name, but there looked to be thousands. Kinkaid stuck her phone back in its rainbow-jeweled case on her belt.

"Are all the people on board registered for the tournament?"

She shrugged. "All but about a hundred or so, which is unusual and exactly what we wanted for the *Sea Gambler*, especially her maiden voyage. It's been a misnomer to call those other card player cruises 'poker cruises,' since poker is just another recreation option, like shuffleboard or snorkeling. Here on board the *Sea Gambler*, Texas Hold 'Em is everything, from the décor to the action. When one is eliminated from the tournament, never fear, because we have a whole room full of cash games going on."

"It sounds like you've hit a niche," I said, appreciating their angle from a professional advertising standpoint. Of course, what they would do with a ship decorated bow to stern in clubs, spades, diamonds and hearts when Hold 'Em lost its heat, I didn't know. Not my problem, I told myself; I had enough of my own to worry about. Since Ben had given my room to his new sancha and her buddies, I needed a place to bunk. "By the way, a friend of mine wasn't able to make it, is there any way I could have his cabin on board?"

"That really wouldn't be my area of responsibility, but I

would be happy to check on it for you." Kinkaid didn't seem especially happy about it but she did do it. Damn. Now I would owe her. How had this happened? I'd come loaded for bear. I would leave owing another person a favor. She walked to a wall phone and pushed in some numbers, consulting quietly with the person on the other end. She held her hand over the receiver and asked me for Frank's name. After a few more moments she hung up. Her closed face gave me a bad feeling.

"I'm sorry, it won't be possible for you to take Mr. Gilbert's room."

"Why not?" I asked, exasperated.

"I am not at liberty to say."

Now she was starting to sound like a member of the CIA. Geez. "Why not?" And I was beginning to sound like a parrot.

Kinkaid sighed. "Let's just say with all the recent disappearances aboard ships, we cruise lines are forced to know more about the whereabouts of our passengers. You being in Mr. Gilbert's room would violate our heightened tracing measures."

"But I paid for the room!"

"No, actually, I'm told Mr. Gilbert had the cruiseline reimburse your credit card for the full price of the fare a couple of days ago, which is of course part of the reason we can't let you in his cabin. We don't have his permission." Why the heck did he throw my gift back in my face? Jerk. Had he known he wasn't coming days ago and just not told me about it?

There was plenty of time to figure out what Frank was up to and less opportunity than ever to have my own bathroom for the next week. I peeked at my cell phone to give Frank a call to get his okay, but it was 'looking for service.'

"Good luck getting cell coverage during the voyage," she told me with raised eyebrows.

"I know!" I said, struck with an inspiration. "I'll go ahead and buy Frank's cabin back right now."

Kinkaid was already shaking her head. "It's too late once the ship has sailed, so to speak. The manifest is closed. No one can move cabins now."

I was getting lightheaded. I think I was hyperventilating. I pulled out a chair and plopped into it, shoving my head between my knees and sucking in a breath.

"Seasick?" Kinkaid asked.

"Mansick," I answered, heaving in a few more fortifying breaths.

She didn't respond and I waited until my blood pressure had stabilized before I lifted my head. When I did, Kinkaid was studying me with quixotic wonder. "Are you this volatile and unpredictable at the Hold 'Em table?"

"Umm . . ."

Truth was, I didn't have any Hold 'Em table habits. I learned to play poker a few days before the big tournament I won in Vegas. Since then I'd played a weekly home game hosted by a pro in the Woodlands, a half-dozen brick-and-mortar games in the back rooms of local bars, and been dabbling on the Internet, where I'd won a tournament or two, and figured out it was a lot different playing with your computer between you and the other folks with hands than it was playing face-to-face. Considering my records on the Internet and in person (discounting what I knew was an aberration in Vegas), I was still a lot better face-to-face, although I wasn't sure why.

Kinkaid waved her pudgy hands in the air, bubble-gum pink nails flashing. "Okay, okay. Be that way. You don't want to give away your secrets to mere plebeians."

Really, I didn't have any secrets to give away, that is, compared to guys who'd played their whole lives. I barely knew what I was doing and I would readily admit to that. I had, in fact, to several poker mag reporters who, for some reason, refused to include it in their articles. Or perhaps it was their editors who cut my quote. My friend Shana claimed it would pain those who'd devoted their lives to learning poker to know I went after it with such a disorganized, cavalier attitude. I think, like Kinkaid, they couldn't wrap their minds around the possibility that I was just lucky. In cards, not life, as was my lot, apparently.

Kinkaid was still waiting. I had to say something. I remembered how Ringo had categorized my game. "I, uh, use a lot of intuition."

Apparently, Kinkaid thought this a nonanswer. Snorting in disbelief, she nodded to herself and continued: "Since you didn't know about the publicity/cabin deal we struck with Benjamin, I assume you don't know about the other commitments either?"

Other commitments? Uh-oh. It could get worse than sharing a cabin with my self-appointed skirt-chasing twin/agent, running into my parents around every corner and having my face plastered all over creation as a poker expert?

Forget murder. Suicide was a definite possibility.

Three

♦ ♣ ♥ ♠

With my list of "commitments" (including a half-hour seminar on The Softer Secrets to Winning at Hold 'Em—who came up with that?) tucked into my cream leather and gold catchall Michael Kors bag, I marched with deadly purpose in search of Ben. Kinkaid had apprised me of "Ingrid's" cabin number (once I reminded the tournament director that it was really mine), which would be the second place I looked after checking in at our cabin. I jumped in the elevator, reviewed the map inside and chose the floor with the most bars. The elevator eased to a stop at five and a guy with blond chest hair curling out the top of a muscle shirt and tight tan legs, from his sexy running shorts all the way down to his size eleven Pumas, strode in. His obvious lack of crow's-feet told me he was at least ten years younger, and the undulating six pack visible through the huge arm holes told me he was ten times more fit, than I was. I edged my saggy rear end to the corner of the elevator. He nodded at me. I nodded back, forcing my gaze forward before I started drooling.

"Do I know you?" he asked, cocking his head as the doors slid shut.

I stole a look at him. Hmm. Though I might like to have known those biceps, I didn't yet. "I don't think so."

Frowning in puzzlement, he shook his head. "No? I guess you remind me of someone, but I think she's younger." He must have heard how that sounded because his face flushed and he stammered, "I mean, you're older than she looks. I mean—"

He was kind of cute in a rude way. Or maybe rude in a cute way. Anyhow, leave it to me to feel sorry for some guy who just insulted me. I patted him on the bicep (come on, I wasn't going to let him get away totally free) and smiled. "It's okay. I understand." *I understand you are a man, and the whole lot of you are idiots. You just can't help it . . .*

Extending his hand, he cleared his throat, regaining some composure. "I'm Ian Reno."

I put my hand in his for an extra-pleasant, firm, warm handshake. Cozy green eyes, wavy dirty blond hair flopping over his forehead. Ah, too bad he was so young. "Nice to meet you, Ian. I'm Belinda."

His mouth spread in a wide grin as he reached up and pulled my sunglasses down from the crown of my head to the bridge of my nose. I was speechless in surprise.

"I knew it," he said decisively, the unsure kid gone. "You're Bee Cool."

Oh geez. It was one thing to be semifamous. It was another to be semifamous for no good reason in saggy pants in front of a living god. At the first port of call I was off this floating nightmare.

"I watched you win that Big Kahuna in Vegas. I still don't know how you pulled that off."

I laughed at his refreshing honesty. "Neither do I, Ian. Neither do I."

"You didn't have a lot of poker experience before the tournament, did you?"

Like none. "I still don't, relatively speaking," I admitted as the doors opened to the seventh floor.

"They sure are advertising you right next to the big guns on the posters, though." Ian pressed the button to hold the elevator doors open.

I shrugged. "Blame it on my agent."

"You have an agent?" he asked, surprised.

"I have a brother who's appointed himself as such." The alarm bell sounded, warning us to close the doors. I moved to step out and he stepped forward just ahead of me, making me pause.

"Are you busy right now? Would you like to go up on deck and get a drink?" When I didn't answer right away, Ian added quickly: "You prefer either vodka and soda or straight soda, I noticed during the Lanai."

The buzzing alarm was distracting me, so I didn't comment on his sharp observation and memory. I didn't want security coming for me twice in the first hour I was on board, for heaven's sake. I nodded and Ian released the hold button, pressing the one for the lower deck. After all, what could it hurt? Ian obviously wasn't after my poker playing secrets since he considered me as lucky in cards as I did.

"It looks like you were the one who was busy," I gestured at his Pumas and sweat bands on his wrists.

"Tonight's tournament will knock out my evening workout, so I was going to run now. I'd much rather get to know you instead."

Hmm. "Even though I'm *older* than you thought?"

"That's not what I meant. I meant old in terms of maturity. In the Big Kahuna you struck me as younger because you seemed a bit out of your element, unsettled, fractured, almost as if you were trying to be someone you're not."

"Good assessment."

"Considering what happened after the tournament, I understand. Anyway, to further undo the damage my 'old' comment caused, let me explain: I find the more mature the woman, the more she is comfortable in her own skin, being her own person. The woman who's in this elevator knows exactly who she is and where she is going, hence, you seem more mature to me."

Oh dear. What a load of hogwash, and I couldn't help but buy every drop. "You're right about one thing. I know exactly where I was going just now."

Ian raised his eyebrows.

"To kill my brother."

Ian chuckled. "Likely he deserves it."

"Yes, but his demise will have to wait." I smiled as the elevator arrived on the lower deck. "Let's go have that drink."

Ian Reno was a never-been-married associate psychology professor at the University of New Mexico. Other than occasional affairs with their students, I didn't think college profs were known for carrying guns or disappearing on secret missions like security experts were. He probably answered his cell phone on a regular basis. It was also a good sign that Ian nursed his Corona with lime for the two hours we talked instead of throwing back a bottle of VO like another person we know. Not that I was comparing him to Frank. After all, I barely knew Ian and he was way too young for me anyway. And who was to say he was even attracted to me the way I couldn't help but be attracted to him.

"How would you like to go dancing after the tournament tonight?" he asked like he'd read my mind.

"How old are you, Ian?" I bit my tongue, but too late.

While he'd let his beer go warm, he'd made sure the waitress kept my Pinot Grigio topped off.

He grinned. "I don't get to join AARP for a couple of years."

"A better comparison would be, how long have you had your driver's license?"

"What difference does that make?"

"Point of reference. I want to see how comfortable you are in *your* skin."

His green eyes drew in my gaze in a contact so strong it felt physical. "Can't you tell?" he finally asked, his tenor low and soft around the edges.

Uh-oh, this much I could tell: this guy was *really* talented in the flirting game. I was *really* in trouble.

"Professor Reno!"

We both turned in our barstools, his bare thigh coming to rest against mine. Sizzle. I moved away. I could've sworn Ian hid a grin as he stuck out his hand to the coed bouncing up. And she was bouncing, all over: from her curly, silvery blond ponytailed hair, to her perky size Cs held in a crocheted halter top, to the silver ring in her exposed belly button. Giggling, she leaned past his hand and pecked him on the cheek. Ian looked bemused and shot me an apologetic glance as he gestured between the two of us. "Amber York is one of my students. Amber, I'd like you to meet Belinda—"

"Reno the Rage!" A group of a half-dozen older teenage boys and girls in swimsuits shouted from the ship's rail. They bounced up and down waving riotously. The introductions were forgotten. At least the kids didn't recognize me. I was relieved.

"We didn't know you liked poker, Prof," Amber cocked a hip and drummed her French manicure across the bare flesh above her bikini bottom.

"It's a mind game. I study minds. It's a logical interest for a psychologist."

Amber shrugged. "Sure. Cool. We just like to gamble. Well, anyway when we all saw you, we decided we'd buy you a beer and quiz you about the final. That essay question was a total pisser."

Ian threw me a questioning glance. He'd talked about his work and I could tell how much passion he had for teaching. I backward waved to send him on to the kids. He looked at Amber. "For one thing, you aren't old enough to buy me a beer."

"They don't care on board, trust me."

"Nevertheless, you can buy me a coke away from the bar and we can talk about the final for a few minutes only."

"Sure, whatever," Amber shrugged and bounced back to her rowdy friends who commandeered a table and motioned for Ian to join them.

"I'll be right back," he leaned into me as he pushed back his barstool and I breathed in CK's Obsession for Men. Yum.

"I really have to go find my brother," I said, rising and looking away as Amber bounced back to clamp onto his bicep. "Thank you for the wine . . . wines . . . and the conversation."

I collected my purse and checked the room key for the room number once more before I started out. As I weaved my way through the tables toward the elevator, Ian called out: "Thirteen years."

I lifted my hand in a casual wave but what he said didn't click until I was out of sight. Good thing. My mouth dropped open and my eyes widened at my reflection on the mirrored wall. Ian was twenty-nine years old! I was aged enough to have babysat him when he was a newborn.

Genes will be genes. I was almost as bad as my lecherous brother after all.

* * *

I couldn't find Ben, although part of the problem might have been that I had lost the intensity of my purpose. As I strolled the various decks, watching the water splash against the sides of the ship, I basked in a pleasant, loose-limbed feeling that left me no longer angry at Ben, no longer frustrated with Frank, no longer resentful of sharing a cabin with a brother instead of a lover, no longer feeling trapped into being a poker expert and no longer dodging behind potted palms in fear of my parents.

"There she is right now! Belinda!"

Uh-oh. Damned wine.

Elva grabbed my elbow and hauled me around to face her and a bushy-eyebrowed man in his fifties wearing horn-rimmed glasses, a purple and green aloha shirt, orange Bermuda shorts, knee socks and sandals.

"This is Richard Dalles," she said, waving her hands at him, then at me. "Dick, this is my daughter, the Texas Hold 'Em champion."

As Richard winced at the use of the nickname, I opened my mouth to set her straight. But I closed it a second later when she leaned into me and stage whispered, "I told him you were single!"

Whoo-hoo.

Richard had soft eyes and I suddenly felt the need to save both of us. I winked at Mom as I put my hand in the crook of Richard's elbow and led him away to a display of art to be auctioned shortly in the port-side bar. Out of the corner of my vision, I saw Elva looking like she'd won the lottery. Geez, I'd have to tell Frank how disloyal she was. If I ever saw him again.

"I'm sorry, Belinda, I'm really not trolling. I was just looking for some poker advice. When Elva mentioned she was your mother, well, I couldn't resist getting some inside scoop on your strategy."

That word again. I patted his hairy arm as we paused in

front of a ten-by-eight-foot painting of a table of Picasso-esque nudes with cards in their hands. The whole art show had a gambling theme, like the rest of the ship. I might get tired of this poker overdose. "Now I'm the one who's sorry, because I'm really not someone you want to get to help you with your Hold 'Em game."

"But—"

"But I won one big tournament. I chalk it up to luck."

"Luck is a fascinating concept though. Perhaps it isn't at fate's will after all, you ever thought of that? Maybe you, Belinda, create your own luck and that is why you got lucky in Las Vegas."

"What do you do for a living, Richard?"

"I work for NASA. I'm a mathematician."

I shook my head in amazement. "I thought life was all numbers to you guys."

"I've come to realize some things can't be explained by numbers. It was a painful epiphany for me, but one I have come to accept and actually embrace. Now I just desire to know more about them."

"Them?"

"Luck and love. Two events inexplicable by mathematics."

Humph. I thought about the recent events in my own life. "Maybe it has something to do with yin and yang. Too much of one means less of the other. That would be mathematical. You know, like those poor people who win the lottery but lose their spouses in the ensuing melee over the money. Actors who divorce because one is lucky enough to have a box office smash. The wife who sacrifices to put her loving husband through school, only to have him fall out of love with her once he gets the doctor in front of his name." I left my own personal example out—losing fiancé, winning big money, losing boyfriend, going on cruise with nightmare family. Hmm. I was overdue for the pendulum to swing back to some luck or love. Ian jumped into my mind's eye, Frank quickly replacing him, along with a big dose of Catholic guilt.

Grabbing my hands in his, Richard did a little dance in his sandals. "You are brilliant, Belinda. This is monumental. I need to narrow down a definition for luck and for love and then I can find examples galore. Perhaps then I can assign percentages to the yin and yang of it—like ten percent unluckiness calculates into fifteen percent increase in love."

I nodded encouragingly. He nodded back harder. "How's your current love life?"

Since Frank was a no-show and my only other option currently constituted robbing the cradle, I made a face. His eyes lit up as he clapped and rubbed his hands together. "Perfect. Just keep it that way and you are bound to win this *Sea Gambler* tournament."

I gave him a thumbs-up and he jigged his way past the canvases, chattering to himself. I ambled my way through the rest of the art on display, including a print of C. M. Coolidge's oil on canvas classic, *Looks Like Four of a Kind*, those six dogs playing poker. I paused at an interesting 3-D collage depicting Hold 'Em introduced to Aborigines. Ack. The next was entitled *Last to Fall*, a takeoff on Andy Warhol's Campbell's cans—except it was a deck of playing cards, lined up geometrically, faceup, out of order, but, on close inspection, missing the two of hearts. I wondered what that meant. I should have been thrilled to hear that according to Richard's new pet theory, I was bound to come out ahead on the tables here at Vegas on the Gulf, but instead, as I strolled through the *Gambler*, I just felt lonely.

Four

♦ ♣ ♥ ♠

I'd spent almost an hour on a chair on deck, staring at the slate blue ocean meeting the ice blue sky on the horizon, feeling sorry for myself, when I remembered to find a clock (I'd forgotten to wear or pack my neon Swatch; I think it was Freudian). I strolled to one of the bars adjacent to the deck and peered through glass decorated with imbedded sets of dice. It was already four o'clock. I rifled through my purse to find the cruise information envelope. Dinner was at six. The Hold 'Em tournament was to begin at eight.

And Kinkaid told me I was supposed to be at a "Meet the Real Poker Stars" reception at five. Swell.

As I made my way for the second time that afternoon to find my cabin, I half wished my luggage hadn't made it, giving me an excuse not to make the mixer. How uncomfortable would this be? I wasn't a "star," didn't enjoy being one, and if all poker stars were as arrogant and egotistical as the last one I had dealings with (Steely Stan), I could happily skip talking to any of them.

Ever.

Listening outside for sounds of Ben in action but not hearing anything, I knocked. Silence. Still, I held my breath as I slid in the key card that opened my cabin door. It was blessedly empty, save our two suitcases, and I relaxed immediately when I saw the view of the ocean past the balcony. I let the door ease shut behind me. Thank goodness I'd sprung the extra bucks for a room with a view. The cabins were so tiny, if tastefully decorated, I surely would've been claustrophobic without a window. I threw my Michael Kors onto the couch and jumped back into the sliding glass balcony door when I heard a sharp gasp behind me.

One of Ingrid's friends stood in the bathroom doorway in a skimpy minidress that showed off her unbelievably shiny tan. Her eyebrows were drawn together in vexation more than surprise. I was trying to swallow my heart back down my throat when she shook her head. "Where is Jamin?"

"A better question is: *who* is Jamin?"

"Ben-Jamin. He rocks. Get it?"

Oh boy. Speaking of rocks. "Get it," I assured her. "But I haven't seen Ben. I assumed he'd be in your room." It pained me to leave it at that but the intelligence quotient in her eyes told me that the subtleties of calling it "my" room would escape her completely.

"Jamin says you have a better room. With balcony. And lounge chair."

I glanced out at said lounge chair as the man in the next cabin leaned over his railing and stuck an arm out in a mock grab at a passing seagull. "And neighbors."

"Yes?" she said in an excited tone.

"Never mind," I said, shaking my head. I had to dress for the evening's festivities, and I wasn't going to do it in front of Stranger Barbie. "Thanks for coming by. I'll tell Ben you were here, Miss . . ."

"I'm Stella." She stuck her lower lip in a pout and shook her head as she pranced to the couch. "I'll wait."

With that she plopped down, her eyes now taking on a look like the mule my Aunt Telly owns. I sighed. "Please excuse me. I have to change."

Maybe I could change into Samantha of *Bewitched*, wiggle my nose and be back in Houston. I heaved my precious Burberry suitcase onto the bed closest the balcony and unzipped a corner. I had taken my time packing for this trip, as opposed to my helter-skelter wardrobe of Vegas. I had even thought to put what I might need to wear first on top. Of course what I *thought* I might need first did not take into account the attention of the entire ship being drawn to me as a poker star (it was a backless Donna Karan sundress and I didn't have confidence that my back ought to stand up to the scrutiny of thousands, plus I hadn't had the time Stella obviously had to buy a tan). I needed to find something more appropriate to wear for the mixer.

I had to dig past three layers but found a solid beige linen sleeveless suit with a cute belted jacket that is the classic standby, threw it over my arm and headed into the restroom.

A knock sounded at the door just as I locked the bathroom door.

"I'll get it," Stella shouted excitedly.

Oh geez. Quickly, I slipped into the suit and padded out to find shoes and accessories to make a quick getaway. Instead of my brother, the tall gorgeous Amazon named Ingrid stood talking to Stella. She reviewed my outfit and tsked.

"What?" I demanded.

"You look like a church lady."

"As opposed to . . ." I paused to wave at Stella.

Ingrid shrugged. "At least dressed like that, Stella will attract people who will offer compatible conversation. Now, you on the other hand are going to have to prop your eyelids open with some toothpicks, because the only folks who'll talk to you are those who want to address the mathematical odds of winning a hand."

Oh dear, that did sound deadly boring. I couldn't think long about probabilities at the table either. It made me sleepy. I jammed my hands on my hips. "And what do you suggest?"

Mistake. Ingrid motioned to Stella, who leaped up. I leaped out of her way so her shiny skin wouldn't touch me. I sniffed. Chocolate and marshmallows. Was that some kind of suntan oil? Yuck. She smelled like a giant s'more. Trying not to grimace, I took another step back as Ingrid and Stella threw piece after piece out of the suitcase and onto the floor, onto the couch, onto the lamp. I grabbed at the flying clothing, managing only to tangle the items worse than they'd have been if I'd left well enough alone.

"Here," Ingrid pushed a random wad of fabrics into my chest. "This is hot."

Beyond arguing, I went into the bathroom and donned a black satin and white lace camisole that I wore as a nightie, white satin pants and a short kimono-style jacket I also wore to bed.

Ingrid knocked. I cracked open the door and she threw in some black and white Jimmy Choo stiletto sandals I'd planned to wear to make my legs look longer in my swimsuit along with a rope of black glass beads.

Doubling the necklace around my neck three times so it hung unevenly just below my cleavage, I looked in the mirror as I stuck in earrings. Damn if I weren't back in Vegas after all. At least no church ladies would be seen within miles of me.

* * *

"This is Belinda 'Bee Cool' Cooley," Kinkaid announced, gesturing toward me with her microphone. I
waved from the corner of the Shuffle Lounge where I'd
been trying to hide behind the six-foot sculpture of an
Ace of Spades that reminded me of the live cards of *Alice
in Wonderland*. "Bee Cool was the surprise winner of The
Big Kahuna, the Lanai Pro-Am tournament in Las Vegas,
last winter. She went in an 'am' and came out a pro." Pause
for Kinkaid to chuckle. "Since then, she's been spending
all those big bucks and keeping a low profile in the Hold
'Em world . . . until she came aboard the *Sea Gambler*.
This is her first public appearance since her big win!"

The crowd murmured, some staring and whispering behind hands as others clapped. I shifted uncomfortably on
my Choos. I wished for the linen suit when somebody's
grandma raised her eyebrows at my too revealing camisole.

I'd been the last of the dozen "stars" to be introduced,
which had risen my hopes that I would be forgotten alto-
gether. No such luck. Now instead of forgotten I would be
the one most remembered as Kinkaid said: "Time to mix
and mingle! Have a lemonade—soft from the punchbowls,
hard from the bar. See if you can pry"—pause for Kinkaid
to glare pointedly at me—"a secret or two out of our poker
stars. One might help you win our tournament which be-
gins tonight!"

As Kinkaid handed off her mic to an underling, a quartet
on stage struck up "Luck Be A Lady Tonight." I'd planned to
pivot off the six-foot King of spades to my left and hit the
exit door four paces to my right but half a dozen mixer goers
surrounded me with arms outstretched, tournament pro-
grams in their hands. I stared, aghast for a moment. I could
never understand why someone would want any autograph,
most especially mine.

One woman whacked her husband across his shoulder. "She needs a pen, stupid."

Embarrassed, he produced one. I thanked him and began signing under my photo as the group began to fire off questions:

"What was the key to your Big Kahuna win?"

"Luck."

"Do you card count?"

"Sometimes."

"When are those times?"

"When I haven't already folded."

"How would you characterize your play?"

"Like one in a million." *Like a million people play a better game than I do.*

They all left to look for another, more satisfying, target, shaking their heads. I heard one woman stage whisper to her husband, "That one isn't going to bust loose with one secret, is she? Keeping it all tucked into that silicone-enhanced push-up bra."

Aghast, I looked at my cleavage.

"I don't know. It looks one hundred percent real to me," a voice to my right said.

Blushing, I turned to see one of my fellow "stars." He smiled and shrugged, holding out his left hand. "Rick Santobella."

I took his hand, which produced a surprisingly limp shake. He was a solid six foot two, probably two hundred seventy-five pounds. He wore his dark hair in a buzz cut, his thick neck had gone a little soft in the twenty years since he likely last held a football. He and an old cowboy named Rawhide were the only "poker stars" besides me who hadn't worn sunglasses to the indoor mixer.

"Nice to meet you. And thanks for your opinion."

"An easy one to give," he admitted, still smiling without

a hint of a leer. I relaxed as he said, "Impressive win there at the Lanai."

I waved the compliment off. "No, not really. I just lucked into it. You should've been there."

"I was there."

When I cocked my head in confusion, Rick explained: "I was in Vegas shooting an ad for Nytex playing cards and Stan was a friend of mine. I stopped by to see him play."

Shocked, I stepped back and into the metal Queen of Hearts sculpture behind me. Unbalanced, I teetered on the Choos until Rick reached out to steady me, which startled me so I grabbed the sculpture at an odd angle instead. "Uh, I'm sorry. About Stan. About beating him and everything . . ."

"Belinda, never apologize for winning. Poker Star Rule Number One. Unfortunately Stan brought on the 'everything' else that happened to him. Greed can do ugly things to a person." Rick paused introspectively. I gave him his moment, releasing the breath I'd held waiting for his answer. Whew.

"Thanks for the advice. I need all I can get. I just came on a vacation and got roped into masquerading as a star."

Rick shook a beefy finger at me. "Don't underestimate yourself. There are a lot of variables in the game and if you balance just right, you can win enough times to come out on top eighty percent of the time."

"Easy for you to say, winner of dozens of tournaments, millions of dollars. You have your own home page, your own poker blog. You make a living at this."

"You could have all that too. You have to want to do it, then get organized about it."

"I'm not sure I'd want it, even if I could pull it off."

"Well, that's the most important thing to decide. But it is a pretty cool way to make a living."

"It sure is," put in a petite blonde with a youthful olive complexion, offering a shy smile as she slid her arm around Rick's waist and he leaned down for a quick peck. Rick introduced his wife, Delia. "Except for loss of privacy. You learn to live with that, though."

"Okay, so what if I decide I want your kind of life. How do I get organized?"

"You already have the image. That's usually the hardest part."

"Image?" I asked timidly. I didn't especially want the answer. Bumbling, fumbling goofball who wears nightgowns in public?

Rick swept his arm from my feet to my head. "You've got a distinctive one-of-a-kind look—fashion, attitude. The same one you had at the Lanai, except even braver. People recognize, remember and want to emulate you."

"But this," I gestured at my outfit, "was a mistake."

Delia smiled gently. "Then keep making it. It's what makes you Bee Cool."

So if I wanted to do the World Series of Poker tour, I was going to have to close my eyes and throw things out of my closet willy-nilly as I did when I packed for Vegas or take a human s'more and her sidekick along as my fashion consultants? Scary.

"One more thing," Rick said. "You need to start getting sponsorships. Telegenic as you are, I can't believe you haven't already been contacted."

"Uh, I have, actually."

Rick and Delia both cocked their heads.

"It's nothing really. Right after the Big Kahuna, Maui Jim wanted me to wear their sunglasses in my next tournament."

"And where are they?" They both asked, looking at my head, hands, purse.

"I didn't accept." The couple sighed and shook their

heads. I rushed to explain. "I wasn't sure when I would be doing another tournament and I have this pair of Gargoyles that my friend gave me that are kind of a lucky talisman."

Poker players respect nothing if not luck and talismans. Still, Rick was a businessman. "So find a new talisman, a card marker, a rabbit's foot, copy of the Maui Jim check."

"I couldn't hurt Ringo's feelings."

I know I didn't imagine the flash of respect in Rick's eyes when he said, "Get over it. You are going to hurt feelings beating people at cards. As long as you do the right thing and—"

"The right thing is to keep Ringo's glasses."

Rick sighed as he and Delia shared a raised-eyebrow look. "Guess we have to find her a playing card company endorsement then, don't we, dear?" Delia said.

"Are you handing out endorsements now, Ricky?" An intense, whip thin man who couldn't weigh a hundred pounds jumped into our conversation. While most men at the mixer were dressed in cotton button-down, guayabera or Hawaiian shirts and light slacks appropriate for a summertime cruise in the tropics, this guy had on a black turtleneck sweater and wool trousers. Sweat pebbled his forehead and upper lip. "Got one too many and doing some charity work, are you?" he said, eyeballing me over his mirrored Dragons.

Rick sighed. "Bee, would you like to meet our colleague, Denton Ferris?" It obviously pained him to call him a colleague. In making an introduction a question, he was obviously hoping I would say no, I would prefer not to meet him.

If I had more balls I would have, because the guy gave me the creeps. Elva brainwashed me too well, however, so before I could even consider the negative, I was nodding in the positive, extending my hand. "Mr. Ferris."

"This is Bee Cool, Ferris," Rick informed him, as if it were obvious. As if I were someone. I wondered what I had done to deserve this treatment. Even though Rick and I had gotten along well from the start, this still seemed odd.

"Really?" Ferris smiled mirthlessly, revealing an unusually white set of teeth at least one mouth size too small. He ignored my hand, thank goodness, so I could drop it to my side without touching him in good conscience.

Elva's good manners reared their ugly head again, as I couldn't let the silence stretch on uncomfortably long. "That's the nickname the media gave me in my last tournament," I explained. "What's yours?"

Rick took a half turn to hide a grin as Ferris fidgeted on the balls of his feet. He muttered something.

Cocking my head, I said: "Excuse me?"

"Some of the blogs call me Ferris the Ferret," he muttered slightly louder. Rick's grin bloomed.

Ack. He did look like a ferret come to think of it, but if he were an Internet champion, how would they know that? "It must be because you are such a cunning player." I filled the silence again.

"Exactly," he snapped. "Now if we are finished with show and tell, then I want to know what you two plan on doing to protect yourselves?"

Rick, Delia and I passed around a perplexed look. "What do you mean, Ferris?" Rick finally demanded.

Ferris snorted in disdain. "I figured you would be too thick to figure it out, Santobella. One too many headlocks as a professional wrestler, no doubt."

I raised my eyebrows. Ah, that's where his thick build came from.

Rick didn't rise to the bait, although Delia looked like she wanted to rearrange Ferris's pointy little teeth.

He turned to me, grimacing at my head like I'd become Medusa. He sniffed. "And I guess you have a little too much blond in that red hair of yours."

"Uh, it's really auburn with copper highlights." I pointed out.

Rick hid a grin again, as Ferris fought to regain control of the subject. "Indeed. The point is, you two will probably be next."

"Next to win a tournament?" Rick asked lightly.

"Next to disappear without a trace."

Five

♦ ♣ ♥ ♠

While we stood in stunned silence, trying to make some sense out of the bizarre statement, Ferris looked furtively over his shoulder, spun around and scurried out the nearby door.

"Ferris, wait!" Rick finally called too late.

We shared a look and a shrug. "Do you have any idea what he was talking about?" I asked.

The Santobellas shook their heads. I glanced once more at the empty doorway and shrugged again.

A handsome, swarthy kid shyly sidled up to us. "How are you, sir?" he asked Rick as he bowed to Delia, pushing his Killer Loop sunglasses to the top of his head and revealing huge liquid dark eyes. Rick introduced me to Mahdu Singh, the teenage Hold 'Em wunderkind from New Delhi. I'd seen some magazine articles on his amazing rise to fame. He shook my hand with the awkwardness of youth.

"Have you seen Sam Hyun?" Mahdu asked Rick after a moment.

"Sam the Man is here?" Rick blurted in surprise. "Are you sure?"

Mahdu nodded.

"But why would the man who made Texas Hold 'Em a household name be on this ship and not paraded around with the rest of us?" Rick asked, clearly aghast. "I heard he wasn't playing anymore. No one has seen him in Vegas for years." Shaking his head, he turned to me to explain. "Sam won the WSOP main event back six years ago when only a couple thousand entered versus the eight thousand who entered this year. Anyhow, he won two million dollars and proceeded to lose it all the next day, along with another half million he didn't have. He tried to play his way back into the money for a while in high-profile tournaments and never could do it, breaking one of the cardinal rules of the game—he was bent on chasing the cards."

Madhu nodded thoughtfully. "When you're down, you just have to forget what you lost and consider each deal a fresh one, otherwise, the losses pull your luck down and the chase makes you too impatient to wait for the right cards that can win for you."

"Why would Sam be on this boat, of all the boats in the world?" Rick muttered to himself.

"Here's the man I loath to see," said a stylish brunette I guessed to be in her late twenties as she came up between Rick and Delia, pushing her Lancaster Diamond Butterflys to the top of her head. Now, I definitely felt like I was missing an accessory.

"Now, why would you say that?" Rick asked, leaning down to give her a hug.

"Because you always beat me!"

Smiling indulgently, Rick motioned to me. "Belinda Cooley, please meet Rhonda the Ruler Sanchez." Rhonda and Singh had already nodded familiarly at each other.

"A pleasure." Rhonda reached out in the space between

the two of us and took my hand in a shake firmer than one expected to come from her petite, well manicured hand. But the longer she stood talking to the Santobellas, the more the confident shake seemed appropriate. I thought I might have pegged her age wrong because she came across as being more mature than a twentysomething should be. I immediately thought she was someone Ian ought to meet.

Rick turned to me. "Rhonda and our daughter graduated together a couple of years ago from medical school."

"A doctor, how impressive. What is your specialty?"

"Neurology. I'm not going into practice. I am focusing on research at the UT Health Science Center."

I nodded, impressed. "Why do they call you The Ruler?"

Rick and Delia both chuckled. "Because when she sits at the table, she is in total control in about ten seconds, all the players under her spell. If she could harness Lady Luck too, she would have it made."

She shot an odd look at Rick. "But *you* are the one who seems to have figured out the secret of Lady Luck."

"Hardly," Rick answered breezily.

I changed the subject before the chink in the conversation could expand. "So, maybe we should ask Rhonda if she knows anything about Ferris's comment?"

Rhonda tensed, her glossed lips drawing into a fine line. Delia shifted from flowered sandal to flowered sandal. Rick shook his head. "Ferris is a crackpot."

"Psycho freak is more like it," Rhonda put in acidly.

"Are they talking bad about you again, sis?" Ben sidled up on my left, slid an arm around my waist and kissed my cheek, breaking the tension and setting fire to female fantasies. Rhonda's eyes lit up. Delia melted. I wanted to backhand him, but instead I smiled and introduced him around the group. Ben always knew the best ways to wriggle out of trouble. Approaching me in public when I wanted to kill him was of course perfectly plotted. Then we would have to sit together at dinner in front of Mom and Dad where, again, I would have to bite my tongue. Grr.

"So who's the psycho freak if not you, Bee Bee?" Ben asked, winking at Rhonda.

"One of our fellow poker stars," I answered. "He seemed to think that Rick and I were about to disappear . . ."

"I just heard about that and came to make sure you'd packed your pepper spray to ward off bad guys."

"What are you talking about?" The four of us asked at once.

"One of the passengers apparently is an insurance investigator and has found a link between a rash of unexplained disappearances at sea. Another passenger overheard him quizzing some of the cruise staff about it."

"What's the link?"

"All those who disappeared played poker."

"Since eighty-five percent of America plays poker now, that is as much of a link as they all had blue eyes." Rick pointed out.

Ben shook his head. "They all won at poker. Even if they weren't all considered famous, like you all, they each had lifetime poker winnings totaling more than a quarter million dollars."

"Maybe the motive was robbery, then." Rick said. "And that wouldn't be a problem here, because Kinkaid just explained to me before the reception that they will be keeping track of our winnings at the casino and in cash games on a plastic key card like the Vegas casinos use. The difference is, it's going to work like a credit card. We get the balance at the end of the cruise, with the cruise line hoping the balance is in their favor, I'm sure. The only cash anyone should have on this cruise is just for shopping at port."

Ben shrugged. "From what I heard, there's no proof any of the passengers who disappeared were robbed. One lady's purse disappeared but it could have gone over the side with her. Some wallets were missing, apparently, but they could have been lifted by the cruise staff after the fact. Some wallets were found sitting where the missing person was last seen."

"So maybe the killer is after money but gets interrupted," Delia put in, worry now clouding her eyes.

"Poker players are gamblers. Maybe these folks got in over their heads and on the wrong side of an impatient lender," Rick said.

"The mob?" I asked.

Ben shrugged. "Maybe it's not about borrowed money, maybe it's about won money. What's that saying—for love or money. Maybe it's emotion—the other big killer in the world. Could it be jealousy? Maybe it's somebody knocking out the competition."

That halted the conversation for a moment because if that were the case we all were potential suspects, along with the mysterious Sam Hyun. Hmm. I suddenly felt guilty even though I had no reason to be.

"Now who's got that bright idea?" A tall, skeletonian senior citizen in a guayabera and Stetson asked. He shook hands all around, then pushed his dipping snuff into his weathered cheek before he continued. "I wish I'd thought of that, considering my tough competition on board this raft."

Rick introduced me and Singh to Rawhide Jones, winner of the first ever World Series of Poker almost forty years ago. He doffed his hat for me so gallantly I had to stop myself from curtsying. He shook Singh's hand so hard the poor kid was left rubbing his arm.

I instantly liked the man, mostly for his vulnerable bald head surrounded by thinning gray hair and his warm brown eyes that sparkled with vigor and happiness. "Why do they call you Rawhide?" I couldn't resist asking.

"Don't I look like a long piece of it?" He grinned, rippling up a hundred wrinkles around each side of his mouth. "I swear my wife has to beat the dogs off on a regular basis."

"Dogs in heat maybe, you sly old coot," Rick corrected. "Come on, Rawhide. Tell Bee the real story."

"Not now, boy," he answered, waving off Rick's demand. "I interrupted y'all. Continue with what promises to be an enlightening conversation."

There was a pause, where we searched for where we'd left off. Ben, who was obviously in his infamous focus mode about the disappearances, broke the silence. "Rawhide, there's talk that poker winners are the target of some kind of cruise ship hitman."

"Ben," Rick cautioned, turning to Rawhide. "There's no proof these people are being killed. There have just been a rash of disappearances at sea and some investigator, as yet unnamed, has supposedly found a link that they all played Texas Hold 'Em, and they all had a decent win history."

"How do the people disappear?" Delia blurted out, grabbing Ben's arm. It looked like Ben had fed at least one overactive imagination.

"Different ways, which is why no one has ever made a connection between them before." Ben began counting on his fingers. "Some disappear while the ship is at sea, explained away as falling overboard. A couple of them left traces of blood, but no body was ever found. One left a suicide note, the writing of which apparently didn't match the passenger's. One lady left an evening bag with a broken strap next to the deck railing. One man was going to meet his wife and young sons and disappeared going from one deck to two below in broad daylight. Several never got back on the ship when at a foreign port, explained away as they wanted to disappear."

"Maybe that's the case, young man," Rawhide put in. "They all socked enough poker money away in a Grand Cayman account and simply wanted to get outta Dodge."

Delia swallowed loudly and asked: "Did all disappear from the same cruise line?"

Ben shook his head. "No, at least half a dozen different cruise lines. And all different ships. Different ports. Different seas."

"But haven't any of the cruise lines investigated the disappearances?" I asked.

Ben shrugged. "According to my secondhand report, each instance had a plausible explanation. The woman with the handbag had a history of depression, perhaps the bag got caught as she jumped overboard. The man who disappeared between decks had epilepsy and could've had an attack that sent him over the railing."

We all paused to look at the four-foot railing, which before seemed more than tall enough to keep us aboard. Now it seemed suddenly ominous.

Ben continued. "One man who disappeared while at port had been seen by other passengers arguing with his wife that day."

Rawhide whistled. "Gol-durn. That happened to me and Sally'd be in the slammer and not for being after my poker winnings. Good thing she stayed home this trip."

We all laughed, everyone but Delia. "But we all have arguments from time to time," Delia said softly, glancing nervously at her husband. "That shouldn't be reason enough to explain a desertion."

"I think we are being melodramatic," Rhonda announced. "Statistics can prove any theory. This is the same concept. You fish long enough for a connection, you will find one. Remember Rick's 'blue eyes' comment. It's ridiculous. We need to drop this macabre theme, get on with dinner and our favorite game." She'd been so quiet during the intense discussion, I had almost forgotten she still stood with us.

Before any of us could comment, Kinkaid pulled up next

to us in a pink tafetta ruffled minidress that made her look like an upside-down overfrosted cupcake. "What macabre theme?"

We shot furtive guilty looks around the group, before Ben, who's never felt guilty in his life and didn't know Kinkaid on sight anyway, said, "Cruise ships seem to be eating poker players for breakfast these days."

Leave it to Ben to be ever tactful. Kinkaid lost the color in her face, leaving her cream blush standing out like two round pink stains on a white canvas. She cleared her throat in an effort to compose herself, then thrust an arm-wrestling hand forward. "I haven't met you yet. I'm Alyce Kinkaid."

Ben brought her knuckles to his lips. "Jamin Cooley at your service." Oh, come on.

Instead of succumbing to Ben's charm, Kinkaid pulled his hand down into a hearty shake. I remembered her bone crusher as Ben winced. I had to like the woman a little more. "Not the same Ben-jamin Cooley who is Bee Cool's agent?" Ben looked uncharacteristically ashamed for an instant before nodding. The rest of the "stars" stared at me, perhaps impressed, most likely amazed. I waved off both as Kinkaid continued sternly. "I certainly hope you enjoy our cruise, Benjamin, but I have to ask you to be careful of your comments. In this age of terrorism, we have the same concerns as airlines do, and our travelers' safety comes first. I have to caution you that if you make any more inflammatory or threatening comments I will have you put ashore at our first port."

Delia gasped and Rawhide interjected: "Miz Kinkaid, you're recollecting me of my toy fox terrier Rex going after a possum in the barn. Ben wasn't trying to stir nothing up. And, by the by, neither was the possum, he was just going after dinner."

Kinkaid nodded once. "And just like Rex, I am just doing my job, Mr. Jones."

Rawhide raised his eyebrows and the bill of his straw Stetson in acknowledgement of her touché.

Rick said: "Miss Kinkaid, I think you're trying to scare us into being quiet. We all could ask you to address the topic Ben brought up—considering poker winners are going poof and we happen to qualify."

A ramrod had gone into Kinkaid's spine and apparently super glue on her lips, as they barely opened to issue the next statement. "We've heard about that theory and our investigators don't find it a plausible connection. Still, in an effort to make you all more comfortable, we are stepping up our security."

"How?" Delia and Rhonda both asked.

Kinkaid smiled tightly. "If I told you that, I would compromise our efforts, wouldn't I? If any of you don't feel safe, I will arrange for your transport home as soon as we dock tomorrow in Key West. But if you ask me, the whole thing is the result of paranoia."

Ben's tail was now firmly tucked between his legs and I was enjoying it. Before she swished off, Kinkaid reminded us all to be a little early to the tournament so we could get our table assignments first.

"Did you get the name of that insurance investigator?" Rick asked Ben.

Ben shook his head. "All I know is he has a handlebar mustache, wears a bowtie and has a propensity for bowling shoes because they don't make noise when he walks."

Rick nodded. "Ought to be easy to pick out of a crowd."

"What do you want to bet that investigator will be the one who disappears next?" Singh asked quietly.

That was a bet none of us wanted to touch.

* * *

"**S**ince when did you get in the *agenting* business, *Jamin*?" I leaned in and whispered to Ben as we walked toward the dining room. He flicked me a dark look, before he was distracted by a bodacious blonde in a see-through white gauze dress.

"I'm just looking out for you, Bee Bee," he said with an impish grin at the blonde who winked, waved and wiggled.

"You thought I wanted to give up my anonymity? You thought I wanted to be thrown in with a bunch of poker experts like I know what I am doing? You thought I was dying to be accosted by strangers around every corner wanting my advice on how to win? You thought I would be so bored on the cruise I would look forward to spending a couple of hours giving a seminar on the Softer Secrets of Winning at Hold 'Em?"

"Ooo, that sounds erotic. I might even come to that one," Ben winked.

I glared.

"Come on, Bee Bee, at least this will keep you so busy you can't sulk about Frank not showing . . ." he put in with arched eyebrows.

"I am going to kill you, Ben!" My voice rose a few decibels out of whisper range. A couple of people stared.

"Oh, Bee Bee, you don't play well anyway. This just gives you some work to do for fun. Besides, just think of what a boring cruise you would have had if it weren't for me."

"How wonderful that sounds. A boring cruise in my own room that you gave away to some group of girls who will end up spending most of the time in our room anyway—"

"Well, you're right about part of that, at least one girl will be spending most of the time in our room."

"I knew it." I stopped and stomped one Jimmy Choo before marching on through the crowd headed into the dining room. "I'm doomed to sleep on a pool lounge while you have some sort of ménage à quad—"

"No." Ben had a look that was completely unfamiliar to him. It was so rare, I stopped and stared as he continued reluctantly. "Ingrid and I switched. I'm staying in the comped room with the other girls. She wants to stay with you. She says you are more fun than I am"—ouch, that hurt him—"and she insists you need her help."

I finally placed the look. Ben was sulking. I'd stolen one of his play toys. Only I didn't want it. "Ben, I don't want Ingrid in my room. I want her in my room less than I want *you* in my room. Besides I can't think of what kind of help she can give me."

"Well, there is that one position . . ." Ben mused.

I shot him a warning look, opening my mouth. He put his hand up in defense. "Just joking. You probably already know it anyway."

I huffed. He grinned. From the table in dead center of the big room, just under the incredibly overdone crystal chandelier, my mother in a too snug, orange, eyelet dress, stood up and started waving frantically. Half the room looked our way. Ben leaned in and whispered, "Ingrid says she will be your fashion consultant on the cruise. And considering how well she did with your getup tonight, I'd say she is going to make it memorable for everyone on board."

Just when I thought this vacation really couldn't get any worse. And this was only day one.

Six

♦ ♣ ♥ ♠

Dinner was better than I expected in some ways and worse in others. Frank's empty chair kept staring at me, but so did Ian Reno (even hotter in real clothes) from across the room. The good and the bad of those facts kept flip-flopping, depending on if Frank's chair was staring at me with reproach like I was a two-timer while Ian was staring at me like I was dessert, or if Frank's chair was staring at me like he was a poor working man called to make a living while Ian stared at me like I was the world's worst fashion disaster.

Meanwhile, the conversation buzzed around me. Somehow (I try not to figure out how my brother gets things done), Ben had managed to get Ingrid, Stella and the last muskateer, Callie Rogers, at our table for eight. Dad, who was to my right, entertained Callie with the turkey calls he'd perfected for hunting. Ingrid, who was to my left, and my mother of all people, spent most of their time with their heads together discussing my fashion choices for the rest of the trip, living proof it can always get worse. Across from me, Ben flirted with Stella so mercilessly I thought she might be arranged over the strawberries Romanoff before it was all over. It was a no-brainer that these two would be sharing one of the beds in my comped room. Maybe I should take pity on Callie and invite her to join me and Ingrid.

I tried to concentrate on the food, which was exquisite—portabella bisque, buffalo mozzarella and tomato salad, apricot-cured lamb chops, garlic couscous and snow peas—and my poker strategy for that night, which I thought should be tight. I really didn't know what to expect from the floor—were cruise Hold 'Em players mostly brick-and-mortar tournament players who just chose a cruise as one of several possible venues in which to play a game they lived and breathed? Or were they Internet poker addicts? Or were they vacationers who barely knew their way around a deck of cards but thought poker sounded sexy?

It would make a difference. I would have to be ready to adjust to circumstances, but I expected to be able to play tight at the top of the tourney in order to be able to play looser if I was still alive in it at the end.

Now I could relax. I hadn't given much thought to my strategy before, expecting to wing it and learn a lot along the way, considering it was only my second major tournament and I would be invisible to everyone but Frank, who wouldn't care. With my sudden and unexpected high profile, the pressure was on to make somewhat of a good impression, or at the very least, not embarrass myself.

"Are you excited, B-Bee, uh, Belinda?"

I'd been so lost in thought, the whispering voice startled me. I looked around at the table and found everyone engaged in conversation. No one looked at me expectantly. *Huh?* Was I so stressed out I was hearing voices?

"Nervous, then, m-maybe? But not enough to affect your appetite. *Obviously*."

The voice, a high tenor or perhaps low alto, with a slight stutter, seemed to come from behind. I looked over my left shoulder, then my right and jumped to see a man crouched below my elbow. He flashed a gap-toothed grin. "Well, which is it? None of the above?"

"What are you doing down there?" I whispered.

"Important work."

Frightening notion. What important work was to be done crawling around under tables? I really didn't want to think about that. I glanced around my table to see if anyone else was noticing my strange encounter. Of course not. "What important work constitutes harassing vacationers about eating too much?"

"That's n-not it, I was just being observant there. We j-journalists are always supposed to be observant."

"Why are you being observant under the table? Seems like you could see a lot more from up here," I whispered. Why was I whispering? Because *he* was whispering, of course. I suddenly realized I had a bad habit of fitting myself to life instead of fitting life to me. Maybe that was the root of all my troubles.

He tugged at my pants leg, reminding me of my most pressing issue at the moment. "I have a p-problem."

"Join the club. I have more than one." I chipped in, first on the list being accosted by a whispering stranger at my feet. I imagined what kind of problem he could have—did he wet his pants? No, he said he was a journalist. Maybe he needed to pass me some secret evidence in an undercover investigation? Deep Throat at work.

"You don't have *my* problem," he challenged.

"Try me."

"I have s-social anxiety disorder."

"Huh?"

"I am p-pathologically shy, severely socially introverted, c-chronically debilitated by shyness."

I barked out a laugh. I couldn't help it. He glared. Everyone around the table shot me looks. I glanced down and shut up. This was going to be hard to explain.

"Look, we all feel that way sometimes. I test as an introvert on those personality tests. I don't really like crowds or strangers."

"You don't get it. I sweat, blush, tremble, get dizzy, feel my heart racing and my mouth go dry just with the thought of sharing the same six feet with someone."

Okay. Maybe he had it a little worse than I did. "I thought you said you were a journalist."

"I do mostly investigative pieces where I don't have to talk to people face-to-face. There's a lot of meeting in confessionals and things like that."

"I see."

I was talking to a pathologically shy journalist under the table at dinner on a cruise with my parents, with my secret "agent" brother, with his walking s'more lover and fashion consultant friend, *without* my boyfriend and *with* a possible poker player abductor on board. Okay, I know I was doing what Rhonda accused us of, but really, who else was being accosted by someone with a social phobia? Why me?

I looked around the room again. No one. On the bright side, according to the luck and love theory Richard and I hammered out, I was bound to win at Hold 'Em tonight. If I ever made it.

"Hey!" My shy friend nudged my knee. "Don't patronize me. I have real problems."

"Look, you think you have problems?" I whispered. "You're just shy. Try being an old maid, redheaded forty-year-old woman who's been thrown over by a fiancé and a boyfriend in the last six months, been almost killed by smut film smugglers, been pandered about by a brother who is masquerading as her agent and now has to deal with her parents on the same cruise."

He looked a bit taken aback at that. "Okay. You might have me there."

"I thought so." I sighed. "So now that you are over yourself, tell me why you're under my table?"

"I'm doing a piece for *Cadillac of Poker* magazine."

I nodded. The magazine had tried to interview me after Vegas and I wouldn't go along with the sensationalist concept they threw out so they ditched me. I really didn't blame the editors. I just didn't want to be seen in a nine-by-thirteen glossy on a bed of cards and cash in the string of my bikini and five-inch platforms on my feet (they had a deal with Skechers), and, I almost forgot, wearing a Stetson. I might have grandchildren one day. Heck, I might even have children one day, and one of them might want to become president. I had to plan ahead.

"What's the piece?"

"The emotions Hold 'Em players experience during a poker cruise."

I pulled a face. "Kind of specialized, isn't it?"

"In the editorial meeting, they just got to thinking about the whole cruise/summer vacation thing and how it affects a competitive player. I mean, you go to Vegas, you are there to gamble and win. It's easy to stay focused in that culture. Now, you go on a cruise, and you are tempted by the sun, sand, surf, the shopping at the ports, the whole lazy, do-what-you-feel-like thing. Plus some people have to drag along nonplayers and that's a drain on the psyche. It's a complicated issue."

"Good luck to you, then, uh . . ." I couldn't remember him introducing himself, so I stuck out my hand.

He grabbed my hand, pumped it and squeezed a couple of times. "Name's Jack Smack."

I snorted. "It is not."

He shoved his chin in the air. "It's my poker handle. I adopted it in real life to help overcome the SAD."

SAD for shy people. Great acronym. I struggled to hold a straight face. "Oh? Are you playing in this tournament, Mr. Smack?"

"You can't do that."

"I can't do what?"

"Call me mister. It's just Smack or Jack or Jack the Smack. Mister takes away the trash punch."

"The trash punch?" I raised my voice in surprise.

"Belinda," Elva corrected me in a stage whisper. "This is a nice dinner not a fraternity party. There is no punch. You can ask for wine."

"What do you know about fraternity parties?" I demanded in shock as Elva giggled. I wasn't sure I knew my parents after all.

"Why were you telling the floor you wanted punch anyway?" Ben asked.

"I was talking to Jack Smack." I motioned to my right and looked down. Of course, The Smack was gone.

Silence was passed around the table like the plague. Everyone stared at me. "We need to take her temperature," Elva finally declared. "She's hallucinating. She may have Montezuma's revenge. How's your intestinal health, pookie?"

"Elva, we aren't even in Mexico yet," Howard pointed out.

Callie and Stella giggled. Ben rolled his eyes. I peeked under the table. No Jack. I scanned the floors near the tables around us. No social phobics in sight. I signaled our waiter, who'd introduced himself as Armond from the British Virgin Islands. "I need coffee. Black."

*   *   *

Dinner wound down about seven thirty, the tournament started at eight, and I was supposed to be early. That left me only five minutes to run to the cabin to repair my makeup and take a Valium. Too bad I didn't have any.

The whole Jack Smack incident made me forget completely about Ian. He caught me by the arm as I made for the elevator along with dozens of other tournament hopefuls discussing strategy. "Hey, are we still on for dancing after the tournament? The Betcha Club on the top deck has a salsa band."

I blinked. Ooo, Ian was especially cute in clothes close-up. And, salsa was so sexy. Restraint, Bee, he was a baby.

"I would hate to have to wait for you," I said with a grin.

"Oh, aren't we diplomatic. You know *I* will be the one waiting for you, the poker star." He put a hand lightly on my waist and leaned in to whisper. "And I don't mind waiting. You're worth it."

Now, Frank would have said no such thing. Frank was sexy in nuance, in suggestion, in testosterone. But I have to say that obvious was working for me right now, since Ian was the one standing here and Frank wasn't. I could feel my mad at him rising up again in the center of my chest. I coughed, hoping to shake it out. I hated feeling so angry.

"Okay," I finally said, trying to brush off thoughts of Frank. "You're on. I'll meet you at the club after I play my last card. Maybe we'll get lucky and sit near each other in the tournament."

A commotion at the other end of the dining room cut into my sad attempt to flirt. I'd been out of the game too long. I didn't count Frank because I fought more than I flirted with him.

"Help! Help! He was looking up my skirt. He's a freak!"

We turned to see a woman in her fifties jumping up from her dinner table, swishing her black lamé skirt around like it was crawling with a thousand fire ants. The maitre d' reached under the table and pulled Jack Smack out by the arm. The dozens of diners who hadn't yet made it out of the dining room doors paused, murmuring and pointing. Without thinking I rushed to the gathering crowd and called out, "It's not his fault. He's shy. I mean, he's been diagnosed as a social phobic—you know, a pathological introvert."

"He's a freak!" the woman shrieked.

A tall earnest young man stepped out from the crowd. "Listen, ma'am, I am a lawyer with the ACLU. It is not politically correct to name-call the emotionally challenged. In fact, it is grounds for slander. The Anxiety Disorders Association of America would get behind this abuse."

"I didn't call him a freak because he's a nutcase, I called him a freak because he's a Peeping Tom! He was under the table! He was looking up my skirt!"

The ACLU lawyer shut up and melted back into the crowd. Guess criminal litigation for sexual assault wasn't his specialty.

"This, I am afraid, is grounds for removal from the ship, sir." The maitre d' said to Jack whose face was glowing red with shame. He was beginning to tremble. Sweat was rolling down the sides of his face.

"I'm sure this is just a misunderstanding. He's shy and sometimes people don't know he's there because he's quiet," I blurted. "Jack's a freelance journalist, on a story, I'll vouch for him. I'm sure he was under the table because he'd dropped his pen, right Jack?" What the heck was wrong with me? Jack might be the modern-day Ripper for all I knew. Although he didn't look much like one, with his big puppy dog eyes, sucking his gap teeth as he nodded with pitiful obedience, gasping for breath, glancing from me to the maitre d' and back.

"Miss Cooley?" The maitre d' asked with his tone whether I wanted to go out on this particular shaky limb.

I nodded. Mopping his brow with the cuff of his dress shirt, Jack looked like he might crawl up and kiss me. I shot him a warning look. He bowed his head humbly as the maitre d' began to give him a lecture about proper behavior at the dinner hour.

"There you are!" Kinkaid hissed as she grabbed my arm. "We were expecting you to be early to the tournament."

"I'm sorry," I said. "There was a problem—"

"We have a problem of our own," Kinkaid snapped. "Rick Santobella is missing."

Seven

♦ ♣ ♥ ♠

"**W**hat do you mean Rick is missing?" I asked Kinkaid as she propelled me with a turbo grip on my triceps through the crowd and into the elevator. Her glare must have been enough to ward off anyone wanting to join us, for when the doors closed, we were alone.

"We were waiting for you and Rick," she said, pausing heavily, "when Delia came running up, asking us if we had seen her husband. During dinner, he remembered he'd forgotten his lucky marker at the cabin. Apparently, he is on a diet, so chose to get it during dessert. He never returned. Delia went to the cabin and he wasn't there, so she assumed he'd gone ahead to the tournament."

I could feel my heart rate accelerate, beating in the hollow of my throat. "He's probably been waylaid by a fan and lost track of time."

"We can only hope that's the case. Thanks to your brother, and the nonsense he was spreading earlier, all my high-profile players are panicking. We'll be lucky to get the tournament off the ground tonight. I am counting on you, especially, to hold it together."

Heartwarming of her to be so worried about Rick. "Why me?"

Kinkaid turned to me, stunned. "Because you work in advertising, that's why. You understand appearances are everything."

I did? I thought people paid me to come up with creative ways to sell things.

"Use some flash and dash. Cover up the trouble. You have the experience, so I expect you to open up the cards tonight."

"What do you mean?" It was time to let my panic of crowds take control.

"You will have the mic to order the first pocket cards to be dealt."

"I don't think we ought to play. Under the circumstances."

"There's where you're wrong, Belinda." Kinkaid explained. "If we play, eighty percent of the ship will be occupied, and my security team will have a much easier time hunting for Rick than if all those thousands of people are wandering around on board with nothing to do, getting in our way."

I hadn't thought about that. "What's your plan to find him?"

"That's our problem, not yours."

The elevator stopped and the doors opened onto the second floor where I could see the glittering ballroom set up with hundreds of poker tables. Players filtered in, some pausing first at the bar set up just outside the door to grab a drink before checking in at the registration tables. Kinkaid propelled me forward again into the loudly charged preplay atmosphere, which would morph by the last day of the tournament into one of quiet competitive tension.

"Bee." Delia jumped up from an overstuffed chair in the

hallway. A woman in the security detail uniform of poker shirt and slacks, looking like Don Ho in drag, followed behind her as she ran up and gave me a hug. "I'm so glad she found you! You're okay?" I nodded as she continued breathlessly. "But what about Rick? Where could he be? What I am going to do? I knew this was going to happen."

I patted her on the arm. "Miss Kinkaid assures me the cruise line is doing all it can. Meanwhile, while they have security checking for him, you should go to the places he might have gone—"

"He was coming back to dinner!"

"I know." I felt so helpless. "Why don't you go back to the cabin and see if you can find anything that might give you a clue to where he is. Maybe you overlooked a note or—"

"We have the cabin sealed for security purposes," Kinkaid interrupted.

I turned to Kinkaid and raised my eyebrows and my voice just enough to make her nervous. "Surely you don't suspect Delia of having something to do with Rick's disappearance."

Of course they probably did, since most cops suspected family members first and likely the security on board was run by an ex-cop. Still, I thought I might intimidate Kinkaid into letting Delia do something.

Kinkaid was fidgeting with the rainbow phone case on her waist, praying no doubt for a call to interrupt. "No, certainly we don't suspect Mrs. Santobella."

"Good, then it won't be a problem for her to go back to the cabin for another look around? Certainly a wife might notice something out of place that a total stranger searching the room wouldn't."

"I'll arrange it," Kinkaid snapped, snatching her phone and pressing a speed dial number. Delia turned her big brown eyes on me in gratitude.

"Let me know what you find out," I said.

Delia nodded as Kinkaid whispered instructions to the sentry. As they disappeared down the elevator, Kinkaid turned to me. "You certainly are meddling in things you have no business in."

"And you are volunteering me for things I don't want to do. I suppose that makes us even?"

Kinkaid pursed her shiny pink lips, ran her fingers through her fluffy hair and pointed toward the stage where sat the podium shaped like a huge hundred-dollar chip. "I'll welcome everyone, then you take the mic and order the first deal, after that march on down to the empty chair at table sixty-six and play Hold 'Em. Good luck."

Table sixty-six—Ack. I hope Richard's theory would hold true and I would win loads at the tournament. I walked toward Ian at table twelve. He winked and gave me a thumbs-up. Ringo sat two tables over and motioned me urgently to him.

I strode over. "Hey, Ringo. What's up?"

"Where are your Gargoyles?" he asked.

I felt on the top of my head then remembered I had left them in my cabin, expecting to have time to return to freshen up before the cards went into play. I swallowed hard, suddenly nervous. "Uh-oh, I didn't have time to go get them."

Ringo whipped his shades off his face and put them into my hands. "Take these."

"Ringo! I can't keep taking your sunglasses from you. What will you do?"

Ringo grinned irresistibly. "My eyes lie better than yours do."

Kinkaid stuck me in the small of the back with a sharp fingernail. "Get going, Miss Cooley. We have a whole room waiting for us."

Delivering a grateful look to Ringo, who winked, I glanced at the glasses before I slipped them onto the top of my head. Wraparound mirrored Anarchys. At least they were consistent with the theme of the cruise so far.

Some cruise tournaments operate like a bunch of satellite events leading up to one main endgame tournament, for which the winners of the satellites qualify—sort of like a mini–World Series of Poker. The no-limit $100/$200 tournament on the *Sea Gambler* with its twenty-five hundred dollar buy-in was different in that it was one long strung-out big event. Instead of a crescendo of excitement building each night, this tournament advertised itself as full throttle excitement from the first deal. It looked to me like there were at least 150 tables in the room, with ten players each. Everyone had the opportunity to rebuy once. Those who were eliminated from the tournament could stay and watch or they could go to the side poker room and play on one of tables there that dealt games from four in the afternoon until four in the morning when we were at sea.

The buzz of conversation began to quiet as Kinkaid clicked up the stairs to the podium. I lagged behind her, hoping I wouldn't have to spend as much time standing on-stage behind a giant chip with thousands staring at me. I nodded as I passed two familiar faces at the last table.

I did a double take.

Elva and Howard?

I put it in reverse and leaned down to whisper in my father's ear. "I think you're in the wrong place, Dad. This is the Hold 'Em tournament."

"Then we're in the right place, girlie."

"I didn't know you guys played poker."

"I play bridge every Wednesday after my rose club," Mom said defensively.

Dad winked. There was a lot of that going around.

"Don't worry. I won my share of five-card stud when I was in college."

"Uh, Dad, Texas Hold 'Em is a little different game than five-card stud and bridge," I began. "Don't you think you ought to learn how to play before you fork over big bucks to buy in?"

"What? Do you think you're the only person who can go into a game not knowing how to play and win?" Elva huffed. She turned to Dad and raised her eyebrows. "I think Miss Ma'am here is acting a little big for her britches, don't you?"

Oh dear. I was going to have to kill Frank if I ever saw him again for talking me into this. Dad winked. Three of the eight other people at the table tried to hide their smiles. The other five were laughing out loud. Super.

The speakers whined as Kinkaid moved the mic down to her mouth. "Welcome everyone. It doesn't get more glamorous than this, does it?"

Uh-huh, Kinkaid. I was just thinking that.

"I mean, think about it—you are on one of the most gorgeous, state-of-the-art ships on the sea, headed to exotic paradises and about to play what is known around the globe as the Cadillac of card games—Texas Hold 'Em." Kinkaid had just noticed that I was still down on the floor and shot me a killer look which propelled me toward the stage. I guess my parents were on their own, headed to the poorhouse.

"I am Alyce Kinkaid, director of this no-limit championship tournament that boasts prize money of more than a million dollars. We pay to a hundred places and besides big money there is a secret prize for numero uno. Remember, the rules are traditional and a copy of them is available at each table. We will take a ten minute break every two hours. We call the game until the next night without notice, so play your best from the get-go. Now to call out the first deal with

her favorite poker quote is one of our celebrity champs—
Belinda "Bee Cool" Cooley. Have fun and good luck!"

Applause and hoots of excitement filled the room as I
made for the microphone. Favorite poker quote? Was this
some kind of joke? Could the woman not have at least
warned me? Suddenly the sound system began to play
Kenny Rogers' "The Gambler," the lyrics of which were, of
course, the only poker quote that had sprung to my panicked
mind. Ack. What was I going to do?

I reached the podium and paused, looking to all the
world like I was enjoying the hoots and hollers, when in
fact I was scared to death. Suddenly I remembered what
Frank had told me the last time he'd come to visit me in
Houston. We'd gone to play a brick-and-mortar game at
the back of the neighborhood sports bar. When we'd walked
in, the poker room was nothing but guys. I'd begun shaking
my head and Frank, reading my mind as he has a knack for
doing, leaned into me and whispered the famous David
Shoup poker quote and added: "He's right, this is your best
environment to play. You can clean up here." He'd been
right. I'd gone home with forty-one hundred dollars.

I cleared my throat. The crowd quieted. Kenny's song
dropped to background noise. "Thank you, Miss Kinkaid. I
realize all of you come from different walks of life as well as
bring differing degrees of poker experience into the game.
The beauty of Hold 'Em is that neither the most skilled nor
the luckiest always wins. But one thing will doom you every
time, even more than bad luck. I would like to send you all
into the tournament with this from David Shoup: 'The com-
monest mistake in history is underestimating your opponent;
it happens at the poker table all the time.' "

Applause filled the room again.

Kenny's song swelled . . . *"know when to run. You never
count your money when you're sittin' at the table. There'll
be time enough for countin' when the dealin's done. . . . "*

Kinkaid smiled tightly at me in reluctant approval and motioned for all the dealers to begin. I could see Ian give me another subtle thumbs-up. I dipped my head in acknowledgment and made for table sixty-six.

On my way, I saw an empty seat at table three and knew it must be Rick's. He still hadn't shown.

Six hours later, I was heads up with a middle school English teacher who had nerves of steel. I guess trying to teach teenage hellions not to use "like" every other word will toughen a person's nervous system—convenient for tournament Hold 'Em. I, on the other hand, rarely feel cool under pressure even though my fans seem to think I look cool. I think they need glasses. Prescription ones. I jittered, on edge as I watched Delia Santobella repeatedly peek into the big room, no doubt praying Rick would materialize at any moment.

Normally in tournament Hold 'Em, players were moved to different tables as the number at their tables diminished, but I think Kinkaid and her minions were so distracted by Rick's disappearance that she was slow on finding the tables low on players. That left me with the wrath of Semion High.

The Flop was Ace of spades, Jack of clubs, eight of clubs. I had a King of clubs and nine of clubs—setting me up for a straight draw, which I hate, or a flush draw, which I hate only slightly less, or a straight flush, which I find almost as unbelievable as the perfect man. I love trips and pairs and full houses. They seem so clean and easy, attainable. My opponent was hard to read, so much so I had thought she was the sucker at the table for the first twelve hands. After that, she took out at least four players, big wake-up call to me before I went broke. I belatedly remembered my earlier sage advice to the room. Fortunately,

I was the big blind in this hand and had to wait for her bet. She looked tempted to go all in. I could see her counting her chips in her head. I figured she had two clubs also or perhaps pocket Aces.

I knew I should fold as I calculated the odds of my draws. Out of the corner of my eye, I saw Hans rush up to Kinkaid, who was patrolling the room, and whisper in her ear. She spun around, looked at table forty-three where three people still played. Hans nodded. They marched over to the table and spoke to the dealer. He nodded and looked at his watch. Kinkaid motioned to Hans and then they both hustled out of the room.

"Miss Cooley?" The dealer verbally nudged me.

I looked around. Both the dealer and the teacher stared at me. Uh-oh. I looked at the chips pushed forward on the table in front of my opponent. Not all her chips, but damned close. I might have to go all in to stay in the game, as I calculated that I probably had a couple hundred less in chips than she did. I looked back at the doorway where Kinkaid and Hans had disappeared. A couple of the poker chip/flower shirt uniformed cruise dudes were trying to un-obtrusively stand guard, but it was pretty obvious to me. What was going on? Had they found Rick? If so, why did they go over to table forty-three if his table had been number three?

"We can't wait any longer for your bet, Bee Cool," the dealer announced.

The teacher took a sip of her Scotch and soda, giving me the stony stare she must have perfected on a thousand middle school renegades. And suddenly I felt like acting like one of them. My limited Hold 'Em knowledge told me to fold and take my five hundred dollar hit. The renegade in me said, "All in."

The teacher choked on a cube of ice. The dealer gri-maced in pain for me, I thought, not the teacher. A couple of the folks watching from outside the boundary whooped as I pushed all my chips forward, then began stacking them to get a count. The teacher began stacking her chips too, matching my stacks with her own and pushing them to the center of the table. In the end, she was left with about two hundred fifty dollars in front of her. Shaking his head, the dealer turned over an Ace of hearts on Fourth Street. Damn. The teacher bit back a smile. She had pocket Aces for sure. The dealer sighed as he slid the next card off the deck.

He flipped it over. Two of clubs. The teacher shrugged. It was muck to her, as she already had her trips. The dealer looked expectantly at me, but I waited for propriety. The teacher turned over her pocket pair of Aces. I showed my flush.

Just then we heard a muffled, "Oh no!" from the doorway, where Delia grabbed a cruise employee's arm and covered her mouth with her other hand as she stared into the room, toward the table where Kinkaid had paid a visit.

I looked back at table forty-three and tried to remember if I saw anything unusual there earlier. That's when I saw the marker still sitting in front of one of the empty seats. It looked like a piece of rawhide.

Eight

◆ ♣ ♥ ♠

"Delia," I demanded, dragging her into the hallway on my way to the bathroom. I only had eight minutes to get back to the table. "What's wrong? Is it Rick?"

"This time it's Rawhide. He's disappeared."

"From table forty-three," I mused.

She nodded, dark eyes hooded with worry.

"How?" I asked.

"We don't know. Miss Kinkaid said he requested permission to go to the restroom in an unscheduled break. The dealer told him he would fold his hands and post his blinds until he returned. He never did. That's not like him."

"That's not like any gambler," I reflected. "How long has he been gone?"

"About an hour. First we thought he might have sat back down at a different table, but he's so distinctive and no one remembers seeing him since he was moved from table twenty-seven to table forty-three about two and a half hours ago. We've got our security force combing the ship. He'll turn up," Kinkaid finished with certainty as she swished past us on her way to a dealer who had his hand up in the air.

"Sure," Delia murmured, glaring at her. "Like Rick's turned up. I tell you, Bee, she's trying to brush this under the rug."

"I suppose that's her job, minimizing the damage that might interfere with her tournament's success."

"Whose side are you on?" Delia demanded softly, which was worse than a shriek.

"Yours, Delia." She looked at me suspiciously, so I felt forced to continue. "If for no other reason than self-preservation—we've been at sea sixteen hours, two people have disappeared, both are high-profile poker players and I fall into that category. All I'm saying is—we need to see things from Kinkaid's perspective in order to figure out how to motivate her to do more."

"I'm sorry, Bee." She bowed her head, looking small and alone. "I'm just tired and frustrated and scared."

I patted her arm. "I know, Delia, you need to get some rest."

She shook her head. "But how can I with Rick . . ." She paused, swallowing hard. "Out there somewhere."

"Look, Delia, I think Rick's on board. If he is, then he'll be found. If he's not, well, he's gone. There isn't a whole lot you can do about that, right?"

Tears welling in her eyes, Delia nodded, swallowing hard. "Except imagine his pain. His fear."

"Tomorrow when we make port, we will demand that the captain get the authorities to search the ship, bow to stern, for Rick and Rawhide."

Delia extracted a handkerchief from her silver sequined clutch and pressed it to the tip of her nose. "Thank you, Bee. I'm sorry I'm so emotional."

Suddenly I remembered how hysterical I'd been when

Frank disappeared in Vegas, and I'd only known him a couple of days. Geez. If we'd been married for decades like the Santobellas, I'd probably be comatose with what she was going through now. I sighed and swallowed around a lump in my throat. Now I missed Frank again. Dammit.

"Are you okay, Bee?" Delia asked, watching me closely.

"Don't worry about me. You go back to your cabin. Maybe Rick will be there waiting."

She offered a watery smile and shuffled off, desultorily.

Glancing at my watch I saw I now had two minutes to return to the table. The devil in polyester was there waiting, watching me with eagle eyes, no doubt hoping she could will me to get lost on the way to the bathroom like Rawhide. Hmm. Could it really be someone trying to knock off the competition? It certainly looked like it. Two down and ten to go.

*T*he rest of the evening's play was rather anticlimactic. One of the tournament flunkies finally figured out our table had gone to heads up and quickly moved us, twenty minutes too late for my opponent. Worse luck for her that the bonehead put us at the same table again. I apparently had psyched the teacher out with my accidentally brave all in and she played scared the rest of the game. Of course having few chips didn't help her. She really needed to play aggressively to get back into the game, but didn't. It wasn't even challenging. She finally lucked into a few good hands that I folded before The Flop, so she only gained blinds. Finally the cards turned for me. I wiped her out with trips—a pair of tens in my pocket and a ten on The River. She'd gone all in with a pair of Aces. It was hard to argue with playing her hand, so if Richard's theory held true, she would be lucky in love.

As I slid the Anarchys to the top of my head, she

congratulated me. "You have a unique style, rather chaotic but effective. Where did you learn to play?"

"I'm still learning," I admitted as I shook her outstretched hand. "But a friend taught me the game."

"Someone special, I can tell."

I remembered Ringo's observation that my eyes couldn't lie. Good thing I'd had the sunglasses tonight after all. "I thought he was, anyway."

"Oh." She grinned. "One of *those*, huh?"

I chuckled. "You have one of *those*?"

"Oh, I've had many, but I don't have one now. I got married a year ago. Steven is the bomb."

The kids were rubbing off on her a little. Smiling, I looked again at her hands. I usually try to categorize my opponents from the get-go. I'd pegged her as a spinster, could I have missed the ring? No, her ring finger was bare. "You don't wear a ring?"

"Not when I'm playing poker; it's too distracting. I see it and I start thinking of him and then, well, I can't concentrate on the game."

Chalk one up for Richard's theory. The way she was glowing, she was way too lucky in love to have won Hold 'Em. "I think you're the one due the congratulations, then," I said.

She giggled as a man snuck up behind her, wrapping his arms around her waist and kissing her neck. "I guess you're right."

Sighing, I watched as they walked away.

The dealer called us back into action as I glanced at the doorway to see Kinkaid consulting with Hans and a man I didn't recognize. Two of the other three people at the table who I'd read at the first flop fell off predictably. One older man was getting tired as the clock neared two in the morning, proving one important element of tournament poker: it truly is a marathon. Being stubborn with stamina is a distinct advantage. A twentysomething salesman who was lucky to still be in after playing like an ultra Maniac finally went all in when I had the nuts. He'd read me wrong, mostly because he read me as a 36D instead of a 125 IQ. I love playing against those kind of guys. That left me and a wily middle-aged department store shoe buyer from Pittsburgh at the table with only a few minutes to go. I wasn't looking forward to playing heads up with this character, whom I guessed drove to Atlantic City for the big game every weekend.

One piece of luck fell my way when Kinkaid called the tournament for the night and moved us to a new table for the continuation. The dealer passed the chip count to Kinkaid who had materialized to approve it. "I guess you listened to your own advice, tonight," she said to me.

"Just in time."

Kinkaid dismissed the dealer for the night. I collected my faded wooden marker and tried to stop thinking about the man who'd given it to me. "You need to keep quiet about the disappearances, Belinda."

"Why?"

"Haven't you ever read *Mutiny on the Bounty*? We are living on an isolated floating society with no way off when we are at sea. We don't want mass panic among the thousands on board. That would only make it more difficult to find Mr. Santobella and Mr. Jones, now wouldn't it?"

The isolated society thing shook me a bit. *Titanic, Inferno, Earthquake*, the disaster movies of my youth popped into my mind's eye. Perhaps even worse, I imagined a *Gilligan's Island* sort of existence with my mom, Ben, Stella, Ingrid and Jack Smack. Ack, back to the image of the disaster films, those suddenly seemed less scary. I couldn't think of anyone I knew on the cruise who would be much help in a crisis except my Dad and Rick. Maybe Rhonda, but I didn't know her that well. I suddenly had trouble swallowing. I cleared my throat and forced myself to think like Frank, the former cop.

"It seems to me the more people know about Rick and Rawhide the more eyes you'd have looking for clues."

"That's true, Miss Cooley." Hans appeared at my left elbow. "But investigators will tell you that more eyes don't necessarily mean better clues, just more of them—most of which only muddy the waters and waste our time. The fewer people know about this the better it will be for the gentlemen in the long run."

I opened my mouth to argue further, but an arm snaked around my waist and a voice to my right spoke first, "If you can excuse us, Miss Cooley and I have a date."

Oops, I'd forgotten all about Ian Reno. I suppressed a shiver at the contact of his fingers at the strip of skin at my midriff. Poor effort, evidently, for he felt my response and slid his finger along the waistband of my satin slacks, torturing me further. My mind might be full of Frank, but my body was listening to Ian. There was something to be said for the howl of pure animal attraction and this was the loudest I'd ever fallen victim to.

Kinkaid's eyebrows rose and Hans gave Ian the once-over. I introduced everyone around. The two cruise ship employees gladly bid us good night, no doubt glad to be rid of meddling me. As they walked off, I stepped out of Ian's grasp and looked at my watch—one forty in the morning. "Isn't it too late?"

"Too late for what? The dance club stays open until four. I thought we'd go to the post-tournament chocolate fountain, dip a few strawberries, sip a little champagne, then hit the club for some salsa dancing."

"Oh, well," I stammered, the mention of champagne reminding me of the last time I drank it with Frank, making me feel guilty. "See, I'm usually in bed by now."

Ian's gaze held mine. His smile spread slowly. "Sure. We can do that instead."

My face flushed. I felt like an awkward teenager. "No, that's not what I meant. I'm usually *sleeping*. Y'know, snore, snore. Alone. In pajamas." I dropped my gaze. Ack. Why couldn't I be smooth and cosmopolitan about this? Because my brother got all those genes, leaving me with the uptight and nerdy ones.

"Of course, they are Victoria's Secret pj's," I added, suddenly not wanting him to think I went to bed in neck-to-toe flannel. His eyebrows rose, forcing me to add, "Not the see-through ones, just the lacy ones."

Ian tipped my chin up with a finger that caressed my chin. "I think you are hard up for some fun, Bee Cool."

Uh-oh. I don't know why I was dragging my feet. Ian Reno was attractive. Okay, better than attractive. He was hot. He was a professional with a fascinating career. He was for some reason interested in me. The only drawback was he was just slightly younger than I was, and so what? Demi and Ashton had made that cool a long time ago.

There was the issue of Frank, but, I told myself with resolution, Frank had made that a nonissue by his nonappearance on the cruise.

I heard a thump behind us and saw a man hopping on one foot, his back to us. He had apparently stumbled over a lawn chair on deck, and was hurrying away, obviously embarrassed. A sense of déjà vu washed over me and I cocked my head, wondering what had inspired it.

"Well?" Ian murmured.

Turning back, I smiled slowly at him. "I think you're right."

Ian blinked, a little taken aback. Maybe I was calling his bluff.

I continued, not ready to be *that* brave. "I think it's time to grab some of my favorite junk food and hit the club."

Recovering from his surprise quickly, Ian nodded and dropped his hand to caress the small of my back. "You're on. Come with me."

As we strolled to the Rendezvous Room for the luscious dessert layout, I asked Ian about his poker play that night. He explained the cards hadn't fallen his way, but he'd been fortunate to have moved tables often, then been able to read the players well enough, and quickly enough, to outplay them. "I'm still in it, mostly, I believe, due to my theory."

Did everyone on the boat have a theory? "And what's that?"

"I think luck plays a role, a high enough IQ to do basic math is vital, but mostly Hold 'Em's a game of psychology."

"Giving you psychologists an automatic edge," I pointed out as we paused at the rail. I leaned against it and stared down at the churning silver sea.

"Not necessarily. You'd be surprised at how book learning does not always translate into life experience and inherent talent," he admitted, body radiating an intensity that told me he loved his job, or at the very least this topic. "Some people are born with sensory abilities that give them the edge when it comes to reading all the intangibles— body language, pauses in play, choices in play. Volumes are written on how to do this but I think they are a waste of time. Yes, you can read all the laws of averages in shifting of the eyes, bouncing of legs, sweat patterns, lip tension, pauses in bets and play them. But in each individual game, if you can assimilate the laws of averages and then override them when your brain tells you the woman next to you is really a Maniac when she plays like a Rock, then you win that game, don't you? That's what makes a Hold 'Em champion."

"Whoa. That means there is a lot of thinking going on. I sort of feel my game. Maybe I am doing it all wrong."

Ian grabbed my elbow. "That's what I am talking about,

Belinda! You are a textbook example of my theory. You intuit instead of intellectualizing."

Did he just call me an observant idiot?

"So how do you go about proving your theory?" I asked, instead of forcing him to extrapolate further on my lack of mathematical ability. "Lock a bunch of poker players in a room and throw tests at them?"

"That's one way," he said, staring at the nearly full moon riding on the edge of the ocean above its undulating reflection.

I waited for him to offer another option, but he remained silent, deep in thought.

"Why don't you do a study? Get a federal grant. They pass those out for every ridiculous reason and your theory at least is one that would be of interest to the general public."

"It's an idea." He glanced from the moon to me, offering a brief smile which disappeared as he looked back at the moon. "But, you see, federal grants have many restrictions that would force me to compromise my standards, perhaps preventing a clear outcome . . ."

Ian certainly was passionate about the psychology of poker. I'd always found passion in any form irresistible. I waited a moment for him to elaborate but he seemed to get more immersed in thought the longer we stood there. I watched his jaw clenching, his eyes glittering, his mind churning, no doubt calculating the different ways to conduct the proper study to prove his theory. I touched the top of his hands, which he had clasped tightly in front of him, elbows on the railing.

"I think you're onto something. You should pursue it."

"Maybe I already am." He smiled warmly, pushing off the railing and drawing my hand into his elbow. "Now, Miss Cooley, I'm dying to take a dip in the chocolate fountain. How about you?"

"A quick one," I said, distracted by a shot of guilt. How

could I go have fun when Rick was MIA? "And then I really should check on . . ." Oops, I had sort of promised Kinkaid I wouldn't blab. But this was Ian, after all, if anyone understood the psychology of a mutiny on the *Bounty*, it would be a psychology professor. I suppose I could tell him.

"Check on whom?" Ian asked.

I gave him an abbreviated version of the two disappearances. He listened with his brows drawn together sharply. Finally, as I paused to take a breath, he stopped me with a shake of his head. "I think you are overreacting. Could it be that both men just took a break or are shacked up with a pretty woman they met on board and will turn up? In life things are usually less dramatic than they seem. And, much as you don't want to, you have to consider that perhaps both men just don't want to be found."

I swallowed, feeling instantly stupid. Since he didn't give much credence to the ominous kidnapping theory, odds were he wouldn't repeat this to anyone. Still, I felt the need to tell him about Kinkaid's insistence that we keep the information top secret. I felt like I was in high school as I struggled for the right words to ask him not to tell the college coeds. "Ian, please—"

A high pitched soprano behind us interrupted suddenly. "I know what happened."

Nine

♦ ♣ ♥ ♠

Amber bounced up between us in a halter dress with the shortest skirt I have ever seen.

Ian threw me a smug look before focusing back on Amber. "You know where they are?"

She looked over her bare shoulder, apparently on the watch out for someone. "I think I know who did it. You know Paul."

Ian nodded and filled me in. "Paul Pennington is the tall, shaggy-haired blond kid you saw with Amber and the others at the pool. He's in one of my classes too."

Amber tiptoed to the window and peered around a column, decided the coast was clear, then tiptoed back. "Paul discovered online poker earlier this year and is a total addict. We were going out for a while and, like, he plays constantly, trying to win back what he loses, missing classes, tanking tests. Like, he'd stay up all night trying to get ahead, but as soon as he would, he'd think he could win more and keep playing. Mirror image when he's losing. He thinks, like, if he keeps playing he will eventually win. Total addict. He told Jerry last week that he's, like, desperate. He's spent all his student loan money, maxed out his credit cards and his parents are going to go psycho."

"How did he afford coming on this cruise?" I asked.

"It's why we're all on this cruise. He bought the seven of us cabins after he won some big online tournament in March. I feel bad. I promised to pay him back, but he said that little bit wouldn't make a difference. Freckle on the ass of a 400 pound woman, was his exact quote."

"Nice image," I muttered. "But what does this have to do with Rick and Rawhide?"

She looked around again, then leaned in to whisper, "I think he robbed them and threw them overboard!"

Ian raised his eyebrows and cocked his head. "Really?"

I shook my head. "For one thing, I doubt that skinny rail could overpower an ex-wrestler that outweighs him by at least a hundred pounds. Besides, there's no reason why either of them would be a target for large amounts of cash. The tournament's not over. We just play for chips and a seat right now."

She blew out a breath that feathered her long bangs around her eyes. "Paul heard five guys talking right after we'd boarded the ship. They were planning on having a private ring game outside the tournament. He recognized four of them after he went to the poker stars' reception."

I shrugged. "So? They could be playing for seashells for all we know."

She shook her head. "They said they were playing no-limit 10/20."

"There you go." I threw up my hands in relief. "Nobody playing in one little 10/20 cash game carries enough to kill over."

"Unless the ten and twenty are in thousands of dollars."

A scary lump rose in my throat. Ian whistled. "Who were the poker stars involved?"

"Rick Santobella, Rawhide Jones, Mahdu Singh and Denton Ferris."

"Kill them all," Ian said quietly, eyes back on the moon floating on the horizon, "and win the ring game by default."

While I hated to incur the wrath of Kinkaid for being a big mouth, I knew I had to get Amber to at least talk to Hans and his security cronies. I suggested it, but Amber wasn't budging. "No way I am going to get Paul in trouble."

"Why tell us then?"

She blinked back some little girl tears. "I heard you telling Prof about the disappearances and I got totally, like, freaked. Then I got to thinking Prof is a shrink and might be able to figure out a way to talk Paul out of hurting anyone else."

I patted her arm. I never thought I'd make a good mother, but I guess I had some maternal instincts after all if I could feel sorry for a girl who likely considered her boob job her greatest accomplishment.

Ian's face had taken on a serious professorial demeanor. "I'll do what I can, but I certainly can't make any promises, Amber, especially if I have to pretend to be unaware of his gambling addiction. I recommend you do what Belinda suggested and go to the ship's authorities."

It was a heavy decision for a kid who'd not yet escaped the peer pressure years. I leaned over and gave her shoulders a squeeze, and got a watery smile in return. Boy, was I going soft. I think my brother had made me a codependent for PWMBDs (People Who Make Bad Decisions). Dashing her tears away with the back of her hand, Amber sighed and slowly shook her head, a hank of bangs getting caught in the corner of one wet eye. I resisted a strange urge to draw it free. She sniffed as she turned away. "I just hope, like, nobody else gets hurt."

It seemed to me as she walked instead of bounced away that she'd grown years older in the last fifteen minutes.

"That really dampened the mood, didn't it?" Ian asked, startling me.

I hadn't realized I had been so lost in introspection. "What do you think?"

"I'd still go 'all in' on both men will reappear," he said, putting his hand at the small of my back, titillating my nerves again despite the "dampened mood" and trying to guide me out of the dark and into the sparkling interior of the ship.

I wasn't so sure, and he must have read it in my look, because he paused a step, adding more weightily, "However, I will find a careful way to talk to Paul. His financial desperation combined with the robbery opportunity certainly would be a plausible motive for murder. Of course we don't know anyone has been killed or if Paul has the propensity to be a killer. And, besides that, the boy needs some kind of help if he is an addict."

I couldn't be in less of a mood to go dancing, but Ian didn't brook my several attempts at getting out of it as we found our way to the Rendezvous Room. "There is absolutely nothing you can do about this but worry, Belinda, and that isn't healthy."

I stared with guilty fascination at the two huge chocolate fountains—one dark and one white—balanced on either side of the room. They were surrounded by people holding skewers bearing strawberries, honeydew melon chunks and bananas. I heard at least a half dozen moaning in pleasure as they chewed. I love nothing more on this planet than chocolate, but somehow tonight it seemed sacrilegious to be feasting on such gross plenty as security combed the ship, looking for my two new friends. I turned away. Ian caught me at a table stacked with dark chocolate–dipped biscotti, cherry-laced marble fudge and milk chocolate–frosted macadamia brownies. He wafted a mint chocolate candy under my nose. How did he know my ultimate weakness?

He tickled my lips with the sliver of chocolate. I opened my mouth and he slid it in. Yum.

"Did you know that chocolate is the ultimate brain food?" he said as I purred, rolling the minty smoothness around on my tongue. Ian explained: "*Psychology Today* did an article recently that cocoa has the most antioxidants of any food. Antioxidants protect the brain more than any other part of the body—therefore eat chocolate, the darker the better, be smarter and more emotionally balanced."

I smiled. "I think I need a couple of pounds tonight."

He grabbed my hand, leading me to the dark chocolate fountain. We dipped fruit until I reached a first: I actually got tired of eating chocolate.

I licked my fingertips. "Do you always have an answer for everything?"

Ian shook his head. "But you'll know when I don't, because then I ask a question, like all good psychologists do."

"Is it: How do you feel about that?"

"I see you've been through therapy?"

"No, but considering what my friends and family regularly put me through, I probably need it."

"Hey, I take offense at that," Ben said as he goosed me. I jumped and so did Ian. Just as I was about to worry about Ben's recent proclivities (wouldn't put anything weirdly sexual past my twin), Ian pulled a vibrating Blackberry out of his pocket, his lips tightening to a thin line.

He looked at the two of us, shaking Ben's hand as I made a hasty introduction. "I apologize, Belinda, I have to check an e-mail," Ian said. I felt a jolt of relief. We had amazing chemistry but I really wasn't sure where this was going or even if I wanted to go wherever that might be.

"I didn't realize we could get messages out here on the water." Ben put in, raising his eyebrows at Ian.

I ignored him, touching Ian's sleeve. "Is something wrong?"

"A minor issue with work," he said, trying to act relaxed but remaining tight-lipped.

"But you're on vacation, dude!" Ben said, with a mischievous glint in his eyes.

"For some, work is life," Ian said as he brought my fingers to his lips for a kiss. "I promise to make it up to you."

As he hurried off, Ben leaned in, mockingly repeating in a deep baritone. " 'For some work is life.' " Where did you find that asshole, Bee Bee?"

"This is just like you were with Toby, Ben. You always hate the guys I hang out with if they are hotter than you are."

"I just hate the guys you latch onto if they are bigger assholes than I am, Bee Bee." Ben winked. "And I was right about Toby, wasn't I?"

I'd talked myself into this corner so couldn't do much but huff off. Ben followed as I stopped at a table full of chocolate-covered everything, including, I noticed, grasshoppers. Ook. Ben snatched one up and popped it in his mouth, no doubt just to gross me out. I struggled not to show him it worked, reaching down and grabbing a candy from the next silver tray, long and shaped like a half moon, a brazil nut. I noticed Ben grinning as I bit down. The nut tasted oddly squishy and segmented.

"Brave of you, my girl. I've never tried a chocolate-covered mealworm, but I understand they are a delicacy in Malaysia," an elderly man standing next to us offered.

Gag. Scrambling for a napkin, I couldn't bring it to my mouth soon enough. Ben held the side of the table to steady himself he was laughing so hard. Half a dozen people left the fountains to wander over to see what the excitement was all about.

"Not good?" The senior citizen squinted at me.

"I don't recommend it," I choked out, wadding the napkin with the offending insect into a ball and looking frantically for a place to dump it.

"Ah, perhaps it would be more palatable with white chocolate." He nodded thoughtfully and wandered off. A couple of preteens covered their mouths with giggles as they looked from the rest of the mealworms to me and back.

"So, I'd guess you are still in the tournament," Richard said, sidling up with a wink. Ben looked curiously from me to my square-headed acquaintance and back, not sure of what to make of this relationship. I was tempted to kiss the top of Richard's head just to freak my brother out.

"I am; the mealworm tip you off?" I asked, winking back.

Ben, now thoroughly confused, opened his mouth and closed it. I had so rarely in our forty years together seen my twin speechless that I blurted out a brief explanation of Richard's theory on life, love and luck. Ben cocked a disbelieving eyebrow as he listened. As I wound down, he shook his head, causing his hair to flop down over one eye and a gorgeously elegant woman walking by to gasp. Ben threw her a grin before telling Richard, "No way is that theory working for me. Since I've never been in love, by now I should've won millions at Hold 'Em, or at least on lottery tickets."

"How do you know you've never been in love?" Richard asked.

Ben opened and closed his mouth. The brunette who reminded me of a young Jacqueline Kennedy paused. Ben cleared his throat. Speechless twice in five minutes? It was a new personal record. I grinned.

"I think I would *know* when I was in love," Ben finally argued.

Richard shook his head. "Guy like you, avoiding commitments as strongly as you need to breathe, wouldn't recognize love if it bit you in the gluteus maximus."

The Jackie-O looked tempted to try that method until a tall blond man claimed her by the elbow, drawing her away and glaring at Ben, who was oblivious.

"So you're saying that every time I've lost gambling, I've won a heart?"

"Or lost yours to another," Richard put in slyly.

Ben fidgeted. This was way too deep for the love 'em and leave 'em man. "Guess I have to swear off women any time I put up a blind, huh?"

"That's a little too simplistic," Richard said. "It could be you already are in love with someone in the background of your life and she loves you, just one or both of you don't know it yet. Then, your tactic wouldn't work."

Ben shot me a frustrated caged animal look. "Who is this dude, some kind of shrink?"

"No, that was the other guy," I shot back. "This one is a mathematician."

Snorting, Ben waved him off. "What do you know about emotions, dude?"

"More than you do, at least I can recognize them well enough to measure them."

I laughed out loud at his comeback.

Ben backed away from the table. "Where do you find these freaks, Bee Bee?"

I shrugged, perversely enjoying Ben's intense discomfort. "They find me."

"Figures. You're bound to win the whole tournament then, sis."

"How'd you do?" I called as he paused in the doorway.

"I was smokin'! Now, if you'll excuse me, I'm going to rake it in on some cash games."

"Hope he doesn't sink too much into those." Richard winked at me. "He's in love. He just doesn't know it."

While I wanted to believe Richard's theory, I just couldn't think of anyone I knew that Ben might have fallen for other than the human s'more. While Richard devoured a couple of pounds of chocolate-covered cranberries, I wracked my brain for other possibilities. Maybe Jill, the cute teller with dimples at his bank who repeatedly refused his offers of dates. Maybe Teresa Guilbeau from fourth grade. I think he still talked about her.

"There you are!" I turned as a hand clamped onto my ponytail.

"Mom?" I asked, my voice disappearing into a croak of surprise.

Elva stood there in a robe, smelling and looking like she'd been bathing in olive oil. Dad stood behind her wearing a grin, his belt missing three loops on his khakis and his shirt buttoned one hole off center. I'm sure I didn't want to know.

"We had hired a masseuse to come in to give us private lessons, you know. We're old, we need all the help we can get for our aching joints," she began in full lecture mode. "And leave it to you to ruin it just as things were getting interesting."

Uh-oh. *TMI*. "Mom? I was just standing here, talking with Richard, minding my own business—"

"And that, my dear, is the problem. Someone is looking for you and you're off being irresponsible, incommunicado on this huge hulk of a ship and I have to get decent and go hunting for you . . ."

I reviewed her getup. *This was decent?* "Mom, you could've just left a message at—"

"He insisted it was important!" she interrupted.

My heart skipped a beat. "Is it Frank?"

She shook her head impatiently, waving one hand in the air to silence me. "You wouldn't be so lucky. This is some gentleman named Rick. I suppose one of your new conquests. He had an Italian last name I couldn't make out before he hung up the phone, although it sounded familiar. He was rather rude if you ask me but of course you won't, because what do I know. I'm just your mother."

I'd already grabbed Elva by the elbow and guided her out the door, quizzing her in detail about Rick's call.

Ten

♦ ♣ ♥ ♠

My heart was pounding so hard by the time I found a house phone that I was afraid I wouldn't hear Rick, even if he was still there to answer. When she'd asked, he'd told Mom that he was praying I could help him with a problem. He'd hung up before she could ask where I could reach him.

I thought I knew.

As I played what he'd said over and over in my mind, I realized that the flippant use of the term "pray" might be the way Ingrid or Stella or Ben would use the word but not Rick. When he was praying, I'd bet he was down on his knees.

The ship's directory was under the glass on the table, just below the house phone. I found the number for the chapel and dialed. "Hello?" a man's voice answered tentatively.

I paused, having not made a plan if I couldn't recognize Rick's voice, which of course would be nearly impossible since I had never talked to him over the phone.

"Rick, it's Belinda."

Sneaky, I know.

I heard air blow through the lines and nearly hung up. I might have gotten a perverted minister instead of my poker pal. The air blew again, and this time I recognized a sigh. "Bee Cool, can you come help me?"

"Rick, where have you been? Why do you need help?" I imagined him amidst stained glass, polished oak pews and glowing candles, hands clasped around a Bible, on his knees. "Are you suicidal?"

"I will be if you don't get here soon!"

Click. A buzz signaled the end of the connection. I dialed again and the line was busy.

Great. I looked back at the directory under glass, my eyes first finding security then the poker tournament office.

I considered dialing both, pawning this off on Hans or Kinkaid. Then I considered dialing the Santobellas' room where Delia was surely asleep by now, as emotionally exhausted as she had been hours ago. This was her husband and her problem, after all. Yet, something stopped me. The begging in his tone, maybe. A sense of danger niggling at the base of my spine. Mostly, the fact that I wasn't sure if this was really Rick, which, of course, was probably the best reason for calling in reinforcements. If someone was pretending to be Rick, it was probably the bad guys who nabbed him.

Where was Frank when I needed him?

I called the next best man, who was a far cry from Frank in a crisis, but all I had. "Yo." he answered. I could hear a pleading voice in the background.

"Ben, I need you to help me."

"No way, no how, sis. You already helped enough with your boyfriends' head trips. I don't need any more help tonight except the help Stella's giving me right now. Excuse me."

"But—" Click.

I could have been in the process of having my arm sawed off and my brother wouldn't be interrupted from his extracurricular activities. I sighed and wished for Frank again. I could call Ian, I supposed, although I didn't quite trust him enough. Then I remembered someone aboard I did trust.

Good old Ringo appeared, sleepy eyed, but with his five long hairs carefully combed over his bald spot, outside the chapel at 3:37 a.m., no questions asked. I'd hated to wake him, especially with the lame excuse of returning his Anarchys in the middle of the night. I didn't want to get him involved in any danger that might accompany my meeting with mystery-man-maybe-Rick but I thought if I got the chance to scream as he headed down the hall, he could call for my rescue.

"Now you can use these if you play any cash games tomorrow morning," I said breezily.

"Bee Cool, the ring games don't open until after noon."

"Is that right? Well, gosh darn, I didn't have to get you out of bed then, but I will sleep better knowing they are back with their rightful owner. Now let me pay you for my lucky Gargoyles."

He patted me on the shoulder, reviewing me like I was his addled yet favorite great aunt. "It gives me more pleasure to see you wear them than to wear them myself, Bee Cool. I feel part of a success I could never be."

"Oh, Ringo, that's not true, your day will come."

"How can you sound so sure?"

"Dating someone special?" I asked, noting he wore no wedding band.

Ringo shook his head sadly. "Not for years."

"Then it's your time at the poker tables," I assured him

cheerily, reaching into my purse and pulling out Richard's card. "Find this guy on board. He'll give you some hope."

Ringo nodded, reviewing the card. "Okay. Can I walk you to your room?"

"Uh . . ." I glanced at the chapel door and put my hand on the handle. "You go on. I'm going to have some alone time first."

"I can wait for you." Ringo offered eagerly.

"No, that's okay," I paused. "But, if you hear me scream or anything, go ahead and call security."

"Why would you scream?" Ringo asked, aghast.

"Uh, sometimes I have a flashback to a terrible thing that happened to me years ago, and I get uncontrollable. It's better to just let security get me back to my cabin where I can chill out."

"Are you sure?" His eyes twice as big as usual behind his bifocals, imagination working overtime.

"It's, y'know, embarrassing. I'd just rather you not see me that way." I dropped my head.

Ringo patted my arm. "I understand."

Sighing dramatically, I nodded, waved Ringo on and didn't open the chapel door until he began to reluctantly work his way down the hall.

I waited a beat, pulled the door open and slipped in. It was half dark inside, with faux stained glass throwing colored shades on plastic pews laminated to look like oak. Electric candles instead of wax and flame lit the altar, reminding me again I was on Vegas on the Gulf. I realized I was holding my breath. I was just getting dizzy as a finger tapped my shoulder. I spun around, nearly fell as the room wavered, sunk into a pew and sucked in a couple of breaths. Rick patted my back. "Are you okay?"

I put my index finger over my lips to shush him. "You scared me," I whispered.

"I'm sorry but I just talked to you, who were you expecting?" He asked as he sat down next to me.

"I didn't know that was really you on the phone. You disappeared. I've never heard your voice over the phone before. We didn't know if you'd been kidnapped or killed."

Rick's face reddened. He tore his gaze loose from mine and looked down at hands he clasped and unclasped. "Nothing like that."

For the first time I noticed the shiny patch of matted hair on the top of his head. I touched it and he winced. My fingers came away with sticky dark goo—blood. "Rick, what happened?"

"I left the dinner table to avoid the temptation of those desserts, and decided to take the time to explore the ship. I was on the Trips Deck when a woman came up to me. She recognized me from the Bellagio tournament I won last month and asked me if I couldn't give her a couple of tips on the game." He'd started to flush again. I guessed the woman might have been admiring more than Rick's game.

"What was her name?"

"Jane."

"Sure." I said and he flushed redder. "Was Jane coming on to you?"

He looked away, at a stained glass window unfortunately of the Garden of Eden. Oops. He dropped his gaze to his hands again. Clasp. Unclasp. "Maybe a little. She was very attractive, dressed really provocatively, except for her hat and sunglasses. I thought she was trying to be one of us. You maybe."

"So you wouldn't recognize her again?" Except her bra size, probably. I reserved judgment. He was guilty enough with no help from me.

He shook his head. "Probably not. She did have Marilyn Monroe hair, though, I remember that."

Which might have been a wig. "So what happened?"

"She had a deck of cards with her. We decided to sit down at the Fourth Street restaurant for a few minutes."

"Which was a ghost town because it was the first night dinner and nobody misses that."

He nodded again sheepishly. No telling what happened there. "We went over some advanced strategy. And then . . ."

I waited a beat. He watched the pulsing light of the electric candles, searching for something in his mind. "And then?" I prompted.

"And then I don't remember. I woke up in the maid's closet on the fourth deck under a stack of dirty towels. And I came here."

"Why the chapel?" I asked Rick.

"What better place to hide on a boat full of gamblers?"

"Every official on the ship is looking for you, not to mention your wife. Why do you want to hide?"

"Because I need to come up with a story."

Uh-oh. "Why did you call me instead of Delia?"

"Because I want you to be my alibi."

Eleven
◆ ♣ ♥ ♠

I didn't want to be anybody's alibi. I had enough problems of my own to take on more. I sucked in a fortifying breath before I spoke in my best calm, rational voice. "Rick, why do you think you need an alibi?"

"I don't know what went down with this Jane woman. Anything could have happened."

"Well, obviously, you had a chat, threw around some cards, you got clocked by a heavy object and dragged into a broom closet, left for dead." I examined his head again and saw it was worse than I first thought. "You need stitches." I stared at his pupils. "You have a concussion. We have to see the ship's doctor."

He grabbed my wrist and forced me to sit again. "First we have to get our stories straight."

"Your story is the one you just told me. My story is the story I just heard. What's to get straight?"

"No, I can't mention the woman. Delia will kill me."

"Some stranger might have just tried to do that. So why

don't we try to find her first and deal with the murderous person you're married to second?" I suggested, striving for patience.

"No, you don't understand, I can't tell my wife about this other woman. See, I was unfaithful once."

Dirty laundry. What a mess.

"What aren't you telling me?" I demanded.

"Maybe I wasn't dragged into the closet. Maybe it was my idea or her idea and we ended up there. Maybe I slipped and fell while I was doing something I wasn't supposed to and she panicked and ran away."

Men. I sighed, closed my eyes and rubbed my now aching temples. I opened my eyes and drilled him with a look reserved for my troublemaking best friend. "You remember sleeping with her?"

The shocked widening of his eyes gave me the answer before he opened his mouth. "No! I remember fantasizing about it." He paused, embarrassed. "I remember us playing cards. I don't remember anything after that until I woke up in the closet."

I have a cruel streak, I have to admit. For that was the time I could have told him about Rawhide disappearing too. That Jane might have had something more nefarious on her mind than poker tips and a quickie. Instead, I let the sweat developing on his forehead come to full bloom and slide down his face in rivulets. Finally I asked, "So what is your plan? How do you want to use me?"

His face flushed again at my words. "It's not like that. You have kind eyes and a good heart. It just seemed to me you were—"

"A sucker?" I snapped.

"A savior," he breathed.

Oh please.

"Listen, Rick, besides the fact that any lie you will tell will be falsified by the video cameras they have on board,

Rawhide is missing too. That complicates any story you might want to tell, except a true one."

"What!?" Rick wiped the rolling sweat with a shirt sleeve and paused, thoughtful. "Rawhide is a notorious lady's man. Jane could've moved on to him after she finished with me."

Damn, I'd hate it if Ian were right. "But why conk you on the head in the maid's closet unless you got fresh without her consent? What is her motive? You weren't robbed, were you?"

Rick shook his head, reaching around to feel the wallet in his pocket that he obviously had checked already. "No. Maybe she's just crazy or a psychopath."

"A serial black widow who just preys on Texas Hold 'Em champions? Maybe the wunderkind from New Delhi hired her to knock the two of you out of the tournament so he could be poker's Tiger Woods." Rick looked way too sold on this random notion so I added reasonably, "Seems a little farfetched."

Rick wilted. "Oh."

I played out possible scenarios in my mind. I just didn't think like a criminal very well. Finally I said: "Perhaps she was just bait."

"For what?"

"I wish I knew." I mused. "But whatever it was, you foiled them."

In the end I was forced to equivocate a bit. Rick's story to security and Kinkaid was that he woke up in the closet, not remembering anything, including who he was (hoping his amnesia was an acceptable excuse for whatever stories the video cameras told), wandered the halls, saw my photo on one of the tournament posters, ended up in the chapel for guidance (right) and called my parents' room that the operator still had listed as mine. I met him in the chapel, talked him into telling all to the authorities and calling his wife (that part being true and probably the least believed).

An emotionally drained, sleep deprived and, at least once, scorned Delia was suspicious. "Nice of you to be there when Rick needed someone," she said, with her woman's intuition on full alert, even if it was misguidedly pointed straight at me.

I sighed. It was five a.m. by now and I had been fully grilled by Hans and the silent, perplexing presence of Phil. Rick was at the physician getting his head sewed back together. "I'm just grateful you can relax now that your husband is safe and enjoy your cruise," I told Delia.

"Fat chance," she snapped.

"What do you mean?" I asked.

"I mean that I will have my eyes on you. Using my confidence against me to get my husband is disgusting. If you think he is going to forward your poker career, like Phil Laak and Jennifer Tilley, the Unabomber and Unabombshell Two, then think again."

"I really don't think of myself as having a poker career to forward, Delia, it's more like one lucky break—"

"Don't give me that self-deprecating caca," the sweet-faced little woman said, shocking me speechless with her venom. "That might work with men, but not with me. You are smart and talented and you should use it to win Hold 'Em games not to manipulate men."

Wow. "Thanks." I said, more surprised by her compliments than offended by her insults.

"Don't thank me, I could be your worst nightmare," she spewed. The happy middle-aged couple I'd seen not twelve hours ago had morphed into something else entirely. I hoped there was a life lesson in here for me for all this suffering— appearances are not what they seem? Mind my own business? Beware of poker playing ex-wrestlers and their seemingly mild-mannered wives? She jutted her chin in the air. "How would you like yourself splashed all over the cover of *Card Player* with a full exposé of your affair with my husband?"

Actually, as an ad exec, I had to say that if I were trying to further a poker career that would be the best thing for me. The old adage of any publicity is good publicity is often true, unfortunately, definitely more often than it should be. However, since I really wasn't that organized or mercenary or, face it, brilliantly opportunistic, I shook my head. "Delia, I am not having an affair with anyone, least of all your husband."

No good deed goes unpunished. She narrowed her eyes. "Even if I believed that, there is the other reason to suspect you."

I raised my eyebrows. "Yes?"

"Bad things have a habit of happening around you, don't they? Six months ago, Stan gets killed, now Rick is almost killed. Who is the common denominator? You."

She was right, of course. I didn't think she was in the mood to hear me whine about bad karma and my theory on money and trouble right now so I just held her righteous gaze.

Delia narrowed her eyes at me. "I'll remember that."

So would I.

I awoke at just after noon to the ring of the telephone next to my bed. I was tempted to ignore it except I thought it might be my mother and if I ignored her she would be knocking at the door in a matter of minutes. I assumed Ingrid, who'd been blessedly asleep when I'd come in, was long gone doing what stunning Amazonian model types do on tropical cruises. I reached out of the covers pulled over my head and found the receiver.

"Ar-oh?" I croaked into it.

"Belinda?" A pleasant-sounding tenor that rang a familiar bell asked.

"Ye-oo." My back seized up as I tried to sit up in bed. I was going to have to start working out regularly or taking Geritol or something. I hadn't been battered by anything but Delia's words last night, but my body ached like it had met a truck on the interstate.

"It's Ian," my caller clarified. The image of Mr. Hot sprang into the cabin, kick-starting my brain and my beauty regimen as I bolted up against the pillows and began finger combing my hair. He continued. "Tell me: Is anything wrong? I've been looking all over this ship for you. I pegged you for an early riser."

So I'd been right. He had been fitting me into one of his psychology holes the whole time he'd been with me. Hmm. I thought of that plastic puzzle game my goddaughter played as a baby, fitting different shaped pieces into the right opening. Was I a hexagon or a pentagon? Nothing too symmetrical, I had a couple of misshapen sides for sure. Maybe those would prevent him from categorizing me. I'm not certain why I wanted to throw him for a loop except that I am a bit perverse that way.

"I'm fine, just sleeping in a bit. I had a late night."

"Oh?" His voice piqued with obvious jealousy. "After I left you?"

"Yes. Rick turned up."

"Really?" Ian didn't sound particularly surprised, but perhaps he was just being guarded in case he hadn't been right. Of course he had been partially right, about the disappearance having something to do with a woman, but I couldn't tell Ian that.

My caller cleared his throat over the line, "Is he . . . ?"

"Rick's alive, although injured. Bashed on the head, or, as one of the security officers suggested later, he slipped and hit his head."

"Sounds plausible. What about Rawhide?"

"I haven't heard anything." I peered at the message light on the phone. It was blinking. "I probably ought to call Kinkaid and check on him."

"Wait, before you go to do that, why don't we agree to meet for lunch at the Fourth Street restaurant?"

Hmm. Where Rick last remembered being before his unfortunate incident. "That would be nice, when?"

"Surely half an hour would give a pretty lady like you enough time?"

Dream on, dude. I'd barely be out of my jammies by then. I knew I was being conned, but apparently it was still working. I smiled at my reflection in the mirror on the opposite wall. "In order for you to maintain your current fantasy about me, I think I need an hour."

Ian laughed. It came across as a little forced to me, but I guessed it was because he was a man who usually got his way. Or maybe it was because he usually dated girls half my age who could get ready for a date in fifteen minutes or less. "See you then," he said before he hung up.

Replacing the receiver, I swung my legs to the side of the bed and jumped up only to find myself sprawled, belly down, over Ingrid's bed a moment later. Whoa. I was more geriatric than I thought!

"Forgive me for the intrusion, passengers," a deep baritone intoned from a small intercom speaker on the ceiling. "This is Captain Santiago at the helm. I hope all of you are having a pleasant cruise so far. I know some of you may have noticed a lurch or two in our normally smooth sailing. There is a tropical disturbance that's blown up in the Gulf of Mexico that we are trying to go around. It surprised us by increasing in intensity overnight more than meteorologists expected, so we are catching just the edges of it. Our plans to dock today have been postponed, since it's not safe to do so at this time. The good news about this is, the tables in the poker room are open and will remain so until we leave international waters again, so you might get some extra game time in. We should experience these rough waters for only a few hours or so, so try your best to be careful moving around the ship until dinnertime."

This was going to be cool. I peeled myself off the bed and tested my footing in a semicrouch. Was I going to have to walk around the ship like an orangutan for the afternoon? I waited for a few minutes and the ship didn't tilt, so I made for the bathroom and sure enough, it gave another lurch. My shoulder smacked into the wall and I catapulted myself for the doorknob to the bathroom, except the door opened before I could get there and I ended up headfirst in the toilet.

"Bee!" A hand grabbed the straps of my nightgown and hauled me upright. Spitting and spewing, I blinked at my rescuer. "What are you doing here, Ingrid?"

"This is my room."

I sighed. The day had already gone downhill fast enough so that clarifying that one detail wasn't high on my pisser list. She began patting my face with a towel.

"Really, Ingrid, I meant, why are you still here in this boring old room instead of enjoying all the excitement this fantastic cruise ship has to offer?"

The corners of her giant azure eyes turned down and she cocked her head like my dad's golden retriever when you told him he couldn't go for a ride in the Chevy. "How could I do that? I can't abandon you, I'm your fashionista," she said.

Huh? "My what?"

"We could say clothier, or personal dresser, but fashionista, now that has a ring, so I went with it."

"But I don't need a fashionista . . ."

"You are rich. You are famous. You are going to be in *People* magazine. You need a fashionista."

Ingrid was delusional. "First of all, I'm not rich so I can't afford any staff with 'ista' on the end. Second, I might be famous on this cruise but that's it. And third, I'm not going to be in *People*."

Ingrid was nodding as she reviewed my clothing choices, which I noticed, had all been neatly hung up in a color coordinated rainbow in the closet. Keeping her back to me, she held up fingers while she talked. "First, we can work something out like a percentage deal on your wins so you aren't out of pocket any cash. Second, you are big-famous but small-headed and that is good for being your friend but not good for being successful in today's poker world. Number three, you *are* going to be in *People* magazine because I have the appointment down on your calendar for two days after the cruise lands."

The cruise *lands*? It sounded like a spaceship coming from Mars, which after this conversation felt about right. "What calendar?"

"I have a calendar of your activities." She waved at a leopard print daytimer on the nightstand. "Including your facial and massage which is scheduled for one o'clock. You'd better get a move on."

"I have a lunch date for one o'clock. So what's moving is the spa appointment." Which, incidentally, I didn't ask for.

Turning from the closet with an arm full of a collection of my clothes, she huffed. "You stars! So demanding."

Why did I feel like my life was out of control? I fought for patience first. "Ingrid?" I asked sweetly.

She turned to me, wrapping the long fingers of her left hand around her tanned, taut hip above her silver spandex capris and putting the other out to hurry me up.

"Why does *People* want to interview me?"

"Because . . ." She paused for heavy emphasis. "You are one hot momma two-time Texas Hold 'Em champion with a fashionista and an attitude."

I tried not to snort in disbelief. For some reason I thought it would offend Ingrid. What? My life was out of control. "Someone at *People* can't count. I've only won one Hold 'Em tournament."

"Ben told them two."

My twin again. "Well, by the time they interview me I'll have murdered him. Maybe they can write about that instead."

Twelve

♦ ♣ ♥ ♠

Ingrid apparently had spent the morning, while I slept, cruising the ship, but for fashion not for fun. I don't know where she was getting the money (from Ben, I guessed, in some twisted plot of revenge from when we were fourteen, and Shana and I shaved his legs in his sleep), but she had spent a couple hundred dollars to come up with the worst fashion disaster I had ever seen much less worn. It was a spaghetti strap minidress of a thousand leather chamois dyed in a rainbow of colors hanging in a collage of four-by-six-inch pieces. Some colorful wooden chunky jewelry really dressed it up. Now all I needed was a bone in my nose. I swear I looked like a cavewoman. I would have been way better off with my saggy capri pants.

Ingrid threw me some leather flats decorated with shells that laced up around my ankles. Just when I thought it couldn't get any worse.

Walking past the mirror on our floor, I winced, trying not to look at myself.

At the elevator, I pressed the up button and waited. I felt a presence but looked behind me and saw nothing but an empty hallway. A few minutes later, the elevator still hadn't arrived. I was tapping my toe impatiently when the potted ficus to my right shook and out popped a man. "Ack!" I screamed before I recognized him. "Jack! I'm sorry; I didn't see you."

"Don't be s-sorry, Bee. I am a master at staying out of sight."

I remembered my urge to hide behind a palm when we were boarding. I guess Jack wasn't so strange, just exaggerated in his phobia.

"Oh, Jack, why did you hide so long? It's just you and me here."

"Sometimes it just t-takes me a while to work up the c-courage to ask what I need to ask."

"What if you don't have anything to ask? What if you're just going to say 'hey'?"

He shook his head and sighed. "Then I don't come out of the plant. If I don't have a conversational agenda, then I can't t-talk to people at all. That's why I went into journalism. It gives me the excuse to interact. I thought it would help me get over the shyness."

"Well, I'm proud of you for trying."

"You know, Bee, you are a good person," he said. I rolled my eyes, and he guffawed. "I really do have to thank you, Bee."

I gave him a shoulder squeeze. "Maybe by the end of the cruise you can just see me and say 'hey'." Nodding, he grinned. "So until then, tell me what you wanted to talk to me about."

The elevator came. Jack went wide-eyed with panic. I waved the couple in it to go on without us. He relaxed.

"T-tell me what's going on with all these poker star disappearances so I can have an exclusive and really break into investigative journalism. I m-mean, a story like this, I could hit network."

"You want to be on *TV*?"

"My d-dream is to be a correspondent on network television."

"Hmm, that might be a stretch, but if you set your mind to it, you'll do it."

"D-do you think the c-cameras could hide hyperventilating and profuse sweating?"

"Maybe once you get there you'll be beyond all those handicaps." I shook a finger at him. "However, there is one handicap I know you'll have trouble overcoming in order to get on TV."

Jack bowed his head. "I knew it. I'm t-too ugly."

"Nope. You're too modest. I work with enough TV personalities to know that your ego is way too small to survive in that business. Start growing your head right now."

Jack offered a small smile. "I c-can do a lot of things but I can't do that. I'll just have to be an anomaly."

I laughed and hip bumped him. "You are destined for stardom with that attitude."

"And then there's the s-s-stuttering . . ."

"I've noticed, Jack, that you only stutter when you are trying to make conversation, not when you are really after a story."

He brightened, his hazel eyes gleaming with hope. "Really?"

"Yep, ignore it and you'll beat it. Now, what can I tell you?"

"I need whatever you know about the mystery insurance investigator, Rawhide and Rick Santobella and anyone else who's gone MIA."

"I know nothing about the investigator, except that he favors bowling shoes and bow ties. You'd have to talk to

Ben about the guy, although I'm not sure he knows much more."

"What about the players vanishing like David Copperfield is on board?"

"I guess there's no proof Rawhide vanished," I said, cagily. "And Rick went AWOL for a time but is fine now."

"Yeah, I heard you two were getting it on, which is why he missed the tournament."

Spinning, I sucked in a breath so hard and so fast I nearly swallowed my tongue. Jack Smack chuckled, holding both his big hands up. "Glad you don't pack heat, or I'd be d-dead. Don't worry, I didn't believe it. Partly because I think you're too good a person to commit adultery, and partly because I saw you at the tables all night and didn't think you were the type to do the n-nasty in a bathroom stall during your ten minute pee break."

I shuddered, and Jack nodded. "I knew it. D-definitely a s-silk sheet, champagne and r-roses girl."

Somehow, Jack's quirky charm drew out a smile when just moments before I thought I would vomit. "I suppose the gossipmongers have me shacked up with Rawhide now?"

Jack shook his head. "Nope. Scuttlebutt is he was depressed about his wife's cancer and he now is sh-shark food."

I pulled a face and suddenly found it hard to swallow. "That's worse than hearing I'm a scarlet woman."

Jack was watching at me with his big puppy dog eyes. "You are t-too s-sweet for your own good, you know."

"You've never met me over the felt." I winked.

Jack bumped me with an elbow. "And I won't. N-not ever. I couldn't play my way out of hell if the d-devil gave me a single chance."

I was about to answer him but was distracted by someone down the hall. In my peripheral vision, I'd noticed a figure loitering at the end of the hallway and now I turned to look. The hall was empty. Shaking off an eerie feeling as a case of paranoia, I turned back to Jack.

"I really liked Rawhide, purely on intuition. I don't know his real name and can only assume he gets his nickname from his choice of card marker. Other than that, I couldn't be much help shedding light on what might have happened to him. I know less than you do."

"No one knows his real name, although he once s-supposedly told someone it was John Jones. Some say he is an ex–Texas Ranger. Some say he's an ex-con. Could be both, which would give him plenty of enemies, but I'm betting it's somewhere in between."

"I thought you weren't a betting man," I teased.

"Aw, I'll bet for facts, not ch-chips." Jack grinned.

"Some facts you don't have to guess at. If I were you, I'd talk to Hans with security, surely they've looked at the ship videos and found out exactly what happened to both men."

Jack shook his head. "The cruise line put a gag order on all their employees. Nobody official's talking."

I nodded, remembering how panicked Kinkaid had been. I wondered if Hans would tell me something on the side. "Where is the ship registered?"

"Nicaragua."

Oh swell. I'm sure their justice system relied on sound democratic principles and wads of cash. They would be the ones responsible for any investigation. The American Embassy could get involved but it would be messy and likely unfulfilling. We wouldn't be docking in the Keys today so the odds of getting American authorities involved were dwindling.

Jack cocked his head at me. "It doesn't make much sense, though. The rumor mill is writing off one man as s-screwing around, falling and hitting his head. The second disappearance is being spun as more lethal, although possibly accidental. What's your take?"

I really didn't want to sic Jack on Paul, the gambling addict college student, without more evidence that he was involved, and I couldn't tell him about Rick's mystery lady and the broom closet either, so I just scrunched my face up thoughtfully and shook my head. "Coincidence?"

"Do you believe in c-coincidences?" Jack waggled his eyebrows.

Frank didn't believe in coincidences. I tried not to think about that. Or rather, about him. I shrugged, trying for nonchalant. "I don't know what else they could be."

"S-Start thinking like a journalist, and you'll think of a dozen elses they could be from a j-jealous rival to a mafia hit."

"Sounds like you're thinking like Oliver Stone instead of Anderson Cooper," I said, letting my smile soften my words.

"You can t-tease me all you want, Bee Cool, but you just be careful. If this is an organized hit of the poker stars on board, you need to remember you are on that list."

How could I forget?

Ian Reno was one of those wrinkle-free people—you know the type, whose clothes always looked freshly pressed and whose psyches were so carefree (or was it confident?) that their faces probably would age without a crease too. I wished I knew how they did that because I had a line between my eyebrows that would soon rival the Grand Canyon. Maybe Ian's secrets were a good dry cleaner, a skilled plastic surgeon and no twin brother, but I didn't think it was that easy.

He smiled when he saw me walking toward where he waited at the entrance to the restaurant, drawing me in to kiss my cheek. He smelled like he did yesterday, of Obsession. So hip. So *young*.

"You look," he reviewed my get up with a carefully neutral expression, "cool."

I raised my eyebrows. "You're kind. I think I need to fire my fashionista."

"Your what?" he blurted. For some sadistic reason it occurred to me that Frank would've had a sarcastic comeback that would've made me laugh while Ian just looked uncomfortable.

I waved noncommittally in the air, hoping to wave Frank out of my mind too. Ian seemed happy to let that conversation go, guiding me with a hand on the small of my back to the buffet line. I paused and swallowed a gasp at the amount of food displayed in front of us. My best friend, Shana, who'd been on cruises with many a boyfriend, had warned me that the food on cruises were feasts of plenty. This was more than plenty. This was gluttonous, reminiscent of the Romans.

There were two entire tables longer than my apartment filled with salads, fruit and appetizers. Alongside that was a chef at a nacho bar. A pizza maker tossed dough at the pizza bar. Four tables held the side dishes and main dishes with a sous chef frying mushrooms and onions and red peppers to garnish the made-to-order steaks. Eight smaller tables set in a semicircle were overflowing with desserts with a chef at a table in the middle scorching fresh crème brûlée.

And this was lunch. Good thing I'd missed breakfast or I would need a whole new, larger, wardrobe by tomorrow morning. Of course, Ingrid was trying to oblige me. I guess I'd have to start making her take measurements after every meal. Surely I would be filling in those Capri pants a little better by the time we made our first port.

"Mind boggling, isn't it?" Ian asked.

"Unbelievable that the ship doesn't sink under the weight of all this food."

"Where do we start?" he asked, reviewing the tables with a glance.

I really didn't want to seem like an oinker in front of the uberstud, but having not eaten for going on eighteen hours, I was starving. I let my answer be my stampede to the plates at the salad table. I filled mine up so fast, I didn't even get halfway down the first table before I had to stop, and then endure the embarrassing wait while he picked through the soybeans and tofu. A health food nut. Maybe that was his secret to being smooth. Hmm. I don't think I could make the sacrifice, even to avoid wrinkles and cellulite.

After he found a home for his last alfalfa sprout, I let him lead us to a table that was uncomfortably close to the flow of dining traffic. I considered asking him to move but dismissed the thought as paranoid.

"Did you talk to Paul?" I asked between bites of some awesome bleu cheese and pesto lobster cream pasta salad.

He paused, chewing on a mouthful of lentils. "He was nervous and, frankly, quite disturbed. We met at the coffee bar, and he drank five double espressos."

That was enough to make me pause between a garlic breadstick and the cheese souffle. "In what time period?

"A half hour."

Ack. "Poor kid. He's really messed up."

"He may be," Ian admitted. "He is an addict. No doubt about that. He has himself in complete financial disarray. Apparently his parents are type-As who expect a lot and forgive little. Home pressure is high for this guy."

"But do you see Paul as a potential murderer?"

That seemed to take him aback for a moment. "I have to say that everyone is a *potential* killer. Not everyone is a *likely* killer. Love and money are common motivators. A mother may kill without any other psychological pathology on her part when her offspring's threatened. That doesn't make her a psychopath."

"Okay, you've muted it all to an acceptable level. Anyone can kill with a proper motivation."

"That's a simplification, so I offer a qualified yes."

Geez, Professor. "So do you know how far in the hole this kid is?" I asked.

"Almost two hundred thousand dollars."

"Whoa! That's a lot for a teenager. Where is he getting all this money?"

"For a while from his student loans, now from credit card advances."

"That's scary, that a kid can get that much money so easily. What are these card companies thinking? So now Paul is not only addicted to gambling, he's addicted to credit cards as well."

Ian nodded and dove a fork into his dry grilled salmon. I'd lost my appetite thinking about the mess Paul was in. "But," I mused aloud, "I doubt Paul went on all those other cruises where they say poker players disappeared. If someone was really after poker players with the intent to rob them, it wouldn't be this kid."

Ian shrugged, wiping the corners of his superclean mouth with a napkin, then leaned over to dab at my left lapel where I'd dribbled some cream sauce. I knew I should consider it a sweet gesture, but it bothered me. "Copycat crime," he said, placing the napkin on the table, apparently satisfied that this was as clean as he was going to get me. "Happens all the time. Besides, no one knows that these events are connected. They might be nothing more than disturbing coincidence."

That word again. "You're a scientist and you believe in coincidence?"

"Of course. I gamble don't I? What's luck other than fortunate coincidence? Many scientific findings are the result of properly interpreting coincidence. Many seemingly random things actually have been proven to have a purpose."

"Then that would make them the antithesis of coincidental, wouldn't it?"

Ian cocked his head and smiled. "It all depends on from what direction you look at life. One man's coincidence is another's expectation."

Ack. This discussion was beginning to give me a headache. I knew less than I did when we started. Perhaps that was Ian's strategy, dazzle me with his brilliance until I was blinded by the bullshit. I sighed. That wasn't fair. I was just restless and cranky. Perhaps chocolate would help. "Shall we get some dessert?"

Ian put a stilling hand on my forearm. That current of sexual awareness rippled through me as it did whenever he touched me. I wondered how I could simultaneously find him intellectually irritating and physically attractive. Weird. "You seem a little wiped out from last night. Stay here and let me get it for you. What would you like?"

"Whatever you choose," I answered, distracted by a tall, broad middle-aged Asian man, graying at the temples, who protected his plate of food like locusts were descending. He glanced around furtively before he hurried to a corner table and sat down alone with his back to the room.

Could this be Sam the Man?

I glanced from Ian, who was scoping out the dessert options thoroughly enough for it to be the Last Supper, back to the maybe-Sam. I couldn't resist. I jumped up and tip-toed over to his table, sliding into the seat opposite him. He had his head tucked low, shoveling food in faster than he could possibly chew and swallow.

"Hi," I chirped, trying to sound like an airhead. "Are you famous?"

"Are you stupid?"

"Why do you ask that?"

"Exactly."

Talk about a non sequitur conversation. I decided to cut

to the chase. I wasn't much for the indirect, I wasn't patient enough.

"You're Sam Hyun."

"You're Belinda Cooley." He never looked up, never stopped chewing. Talk about a poker face.

A cold sliver of fear snaked down my spine. "How do you know who I am?"

"Exactly."

I swallowed hard. "You are a legend of Texas Hold 'Em. Winner of eight bracelets, you made the game a household word."

"That's not how you know me. Someone told you who I was."

"You and Rawhide, you've been playing the game longer than many of today's stars have been alive."

"Rawhide is a con artist. I am a card player." His words cut the air between us. He clenched his fists, but still looked down at his plate as he bit out the rest. "You wouldn't recognize the difference because you are like millions today who play Hold 'Em on the damned Internet, drop into some luck and think you know it all."

His animosity should have cautioned me. "Actually, there you are wrong. I know I don't know much about the game. Never claimed to."

Finally, Sam the Man raised his head and narrowed his eyes at me. "What are you up to?"

"Exactly."

The corners of his mouth might have twitched. Or I might have imagined it. "I'm on vacation."

"No ulterior motive?" I asked.

"Yes. One."

"That is?" I asked, trying not to hold my breath as I waited for the answer.

"To play cards and win."

My mouth dropped open in shock. "You're going low profile in the tournament?"

"I figure I eliminate enough of you stars and I might, finally, win one," he said, ducking his head and concentrating back on his meal like I'd never interrupted.

After two solid minutes of watching Sam shovel chicken mole into his mouth without a breath, I returned to our table to find a steaming plate of bread pudding bathed in chocolate sauce at my place, a plate of fruit in front of the other chair and no Ian. As I pulled the pudding closer to me, I noticed a bit of cruise line stationery peeking from the bottom of the plate. I slid it out. On the sheet, written in small block print, in ballpoint ink were the words: Play cards, not detective. Stay out of trouble or you could be gone too.

I looked up in alarm just as a tall man strode by my table. Without meeting my gaze, the Marlboro Man from the line yesterday nodded in acknowledgement and kept walking. Denton Ferris scurried by on the other side. Ian was nowhere to be found.

Thirteen

♦ ♣ ♥ ♠

My head was so full of the mystery note, Sam's possibly incriminating statement, Marlboro Man's nod and Ian's disappearance that I almost ran over my mother in the hallway outside the restaurant.

Not a good move.

"Belinda Elizabeth Cooley!" she shouted, staring at the stain on my lapel. I suddenly thought she and Ian would get along great. "You ought to be ashamed of yourself. What if I were an old decrepit woman who you nearly mowed down?"

"Versus a semiold, almost-decrepit woman?"

My dad threw me a wink.

"Don't be cheeky," Elva snapped. "You are already on my bad list for not checking on us during the play last night. Just go on and play poker like no one else matters in your life. Like it doesn't matter to you that your poor father and I come on this cruise to spend time with our only daughter and we never see her and she lets us get eliminated from the tournament in the first hour, then when we *finally* find something to occupy us, your friend has to interrupt." Deep sigh. Rolling of eyes.

I raised my eyebrows and looked at Howard. He shrugged.

"Didn't catch any cards, huh, Dad?" I asked sympathetically.

"Not a one, girlie. When you're dealt a Dolly Parton and the guy next to you gets pocket rockets, you know it's going to be a bad night."

I flashed him a thumbs-up, impressed with his lingo on a 9/5 deal for a pocket.

"I wanted to play in some hot ring games anyway. I'll do much better in those. I know when to fold 'em." He paused and threw me another wink. "I heard about a secret big money ring game with some of the pros. Might talk myself into that one."

I froze. Uh-oh. That was the one I'd heard about. The one that might be reason enough to commit murder. "Dad," I admonished. "You don't carry that kind of cash around with you."

"What do you know about what I carry around with me, girlie?" He leaned over and pinched Elva on the rump. She giggled.

Ack. "Okay, Dad." He was probably just talking big, but just in case, I added, "Check with me before you go so I can give you some tips." *And talk you out of it.*

"You got it!"

As they turned to go, Mom looked askance at my outfit. "Really, Belinda, you shouldn't try so hard to recapture your youth."

I opened my mouth and shut it, realizing arguing or even clarifying was futile. Instead, I used a foolproof distraction technique. "How's Ben?"

"Oh Benjamin," Elva took on that dreamy proud momma look she always got when she thought about her favorite child. "He and those cute girlfriends of his went for a dip in the pool. He's still in the tournament, you know. He'll be sure to qualify for that Main Event. He promises he'll take us to watch him in Las Vegas. At least *someone* cares about including his parents in his life."

I think I was the one who paid for their cruise but in fairness to Mom, I did it reluctantly, and I am sure Ben made it sound like he'd orchestrated the whole thing. Ben was like that. I sighed, figuring for the millionth time in my life that the facts weren't worth clarifying. Dad patted me on the shoulder, probably figuring the same thing. Elva heard what Elva wanted to believe. When she retold the story of what happened in Las Vegas, *I'd* gotten Ben kidnapped and somehow *he'd* managed, doped up and comatose, to save *my* life. Humph.

Shaking my head, I smiled and gave Howard a squeeze. "Having a good time, Dad?"

"The best! Key West here we come. Your mom and I are going kayaking on a manatee hunt."

"I wouldn't count on docking there, Dad, because of that storm. They'll probably just cruise on toward our next port."

"Well, if we do, we promise to come back with pictures of the big critters."

"Just promise to come back in one piece!"

Dad winked at me just as someone slid an arm around my waist. "There you are. I was worried about you. And here you just found better company."

I turned to Ian and smiled apologetically. "This is my family." I introduced Ian around to Dad and Mom, who was giving her best thousand-degree once-over, head to toe and back again, pausing at his ring finger, as Dad made small talk. Ian put his hand at the small of my back, and I got the message he wanted out of there.

While I didn't blame him, I also couldn't extract myself just yet. I eased out of his reach.

As Dad wound down about his research into manatees and

began talking to Mom about hiking the ruins in Cozumel, I turned to Ian. "What are your plans for the rest of the day?" I asked.

"I was hoping you were free this afternoon." he whispered.

"Um, my, uh, fash—friend made an appointment at the spa for me to have a Dead Sea mud facial and sea kelp body wrap," I told him quietly, knowing if Mom heard about it, she would insist on a two for one offer.

"Too bad. I guess I'll have to drag out my stack of *Psychology Today*s and get caught up on professional reading while you pamper yourself."

Mom sure heard that. Her head snapped around, leaving her conversation with Dad. "You are a psychologist?"

"Indeed." Ian made a half bow. "An associate psychology professor at University of New Mexico."

"Good for you, my boy," Dad said heartily.

I looked at my watch. "I need to run."

"We'll meet then for a drink at the Betcha Club before dinner?" Ian asked, or really assumed, although I'd rather think he asked.

I nodded and he said good-bye to my parents. Elva leaned in, as we watched him go, to say, "Don't you know, Belinda, all shrinks are crazy and Roswell is the alien capital of the world. Two strikes against him."

"The university is in Albuquerque," I pointed out.

"You don't know where he grew up, now, do you?" Elva demanded.

"Handsome boy," Dad said helpfully in a complete non sequitur.

"Boy being the operative term there, Howard. I think he's quite a bit younger than you, Belinda."

"I don't know why Ben can run around with girls barely out of diapers, and I have a drink with a man a few years younger and it's an unpardonable sin."

Elva sighed and looked to the skies for divine intervention. "Belinda, you shouldn't get so worked up about things. I was just giving you some motherly advice. You don't have to take it, certainly. You're a grown woman, after all. I just love you and care about you, pookie." Sniff.

She won on redirect as always, not addressing my question, yet simultaneously shutting me up and making me feel guilty. My mother would have made an excellent defense trial attorney. I swear she could have gotten Ted Bundy off scot-free.

"Poor Frank," she said sadly as Dad dragged her off, with a wave at me. "Discarded and forgotten."

I was still steaming as I stomped to the elevators and reviewed the ship's map. The spa was up one floor, so I decided to wear off some of my anger by climbing the stairs. Halfway up, I almost ran over Solis, the cruise ship employee who'd helped me the first day. "Hi Solis, how's it going?"

"Miss Cooley. I watched you play last night. You're good."

"Mostly just lucky, but thank you," I answered, putting my hand in my purse and feeling for some bills. "I hope you all with the cruise line are having some luck too, finding my friend Rawhide Jones?"

Curtains pulled across Solis' eyes as they narrowed. "I don't know."

I extracted the first bill my fingers found and slipped it into his hand on the staircase railing. He looked down and gasped about the same time I did. A C-note?! I thought it was a twenty. I had to get a little smoother about this detective business or I was going to go broke asking a couple of questions.

After looking around, Solis leaned in. "They found his hat. Cowboy hat."

"Where?" I whispered back.

"In the railing on the fourth deck. Stuffed there. Before he jumped, or after someone pushed him . . ."

I shivered, and Solis crossed himself.

"What about the video cameras on the ship?" I whispered. "Don't they show what happened?"

Solis shook his head. "They were all covered up. Where Mr. Rick was. Where the cowboy's hat was. It's all black on tape."

Whoa. I stifled another shiver. "I guess Rawhide didn't jump then," I observed. "Unless he took extra time to prevent an audience."

"No worries, Miz Bee. The new security, they'll catch them."

"Who's the new security?"

Solis opened his mouth just as a round pink tornado flew down the stairs—Kinkaid in hot pink capris and a matching marabou-collar sleeveless sweater. She threw a look at Solis that sent him back about three strides. He tucked away the hundred and nodded to me as he hurried away. She grabbed my forearm. "There you are. I've been looking everywhere for you. We have to have a little discussion about ethics and morals when you are representing the game we are sponsoring on board this ship."

"Look, I didn't do anything—"

"But you *are* about to rob the cradle. I just saw your mom and she told me all about your new beau." Kinkaid paused to giggle, leaning in and whispering, "You go, girl!"

Okay. Weird. "Um, thanks."

"Now off you go. Can't keep that sea kelp and your masseuse waiting." Mom and her big mouth. Humph. Could a girl have no secrets?

I smiled and waved. It wasn't until I was almost at the spa that I remembered I hadn't mentioned getting a massage to Mom.

* * *

A lovely brunette of indeterminate age with the most flawless complexion I had ever seen drew me into a room where the sounds of dolphins in conversation reverberated. I must have made a face because Valka cocked her head and asked me if I would rather hear whales, seagulls, waves or sea snails.

"Sea snails?"

"It is especially subliminal."

"Huh." I liked dolphins—they were cute—but they were doing a lot of high-pitched squeaking at the moment. "I'll go for waves."

She nodded and, handing me a plush towel, instructed me to disrobe while she went to change the noise theme. She disappeared out the door opposite to the one we'd come in. There was a padded table in the middle of the room and an array of jars of some of the most icky looking muck I'd ever seen. It reminded me a bit of the colors for fall two years ago—baby poo yellow, toad wart green and Oklahoma mud orange. I wondered which jar held the sea kelp. The opposite wall was glass, with a floor-to-ceiling view of the sea and the sky. Liberating really, until I got close and it looked like the sea was really really far down and then it was a bit scary. Dolphins were drowned out by waves. I slipped out of my clothes, feeling self-conscious, especially when Valka returned.

Valka messed around with a tub in the corner of the room. Then she laid on the table what looked to me like oversize Saran Wrap and ordered me to recline on top of it. Once I was facedown, she whipped the towel off me like an NFL trainer. It was definitely a good thing I couldn't see the layers of kelp because they felt disgusting. Although they'd been warmed, they were very wet, very gooshy and very slippery.

"It's ticklish." I tried not to wiggle.

"Be still," she ordered.

I tried. "Uh, Valka, how long do I have to keep this crap on?"

"One and one half hours. And it is not crap. It is antioxidant, that means anticrap."

I was going to have to be squishy in the anticrap for *that* long? It'd better tighten up the cellulite is all I could say.

She flipped me over like a giant tuna on a boat deck and began kelping me on the topside. Ick. I closed my eyes. I couldn't believe I was undergoing such needless torture. I really didn't care that much about my oxidants, after all. I didn't even make the appointment, for goodness' sake. Then, I remembered my Dad's favorite saying, "What doesn't kill you is certainly good for you." I think he meant it about some life experience more substantial than kelp on my rump, but I'd use it here anyway.

Valka then proceeded to cleanse my face with a series of implements that felt like fine coral, acid and sandpaper, respectively. Then she clapped her hands. "Now, the Dead Sea mud."

Goody.

The mud was warm and more soothing than the kelp. The only negative was it smelled to high heaven. I was afraid I would throw up my lunch.

"Stop wrinkling your nose," she commanded.

"Blech," I argued.

"After all the synthetic products you live in and around, you just aren't accustomed to the clean smell of nature. Open your mind. This is cleansing. Relax." She paused and I heard her sliding open a window. "Here, I will introduce the sun-drenched sea air to help you."

I opened my mind, took a deep breath, tried to relax and cringed. The waves emanating from the walls were pounding harder and harder and harder. I was feeling a bit pummeled. A piece of kelp slid off my thigh and onto the floor. "Uh, Valka? Could I go with the whales now? We're in a perfect storm in here. Not too relaxing."

Valka sighed weightily, washed the mud off her hands in the basin, closed up the kelp and walked to the far door, pausing with a hand on the knob. "I will go change it and you just do deep breathing. Close your eyes. Feel nature. Feel the kelp and the mud drawing the poisons out of your body. Feel your body healing. I will be back later."

I know dolphins are smart but whales are more relaxing, fins down. Their deeper voices booming and whooshing lulled me into a state where I could somehow assimilate all I'd been through in the last twenty-four hours. It didn't bring me to any conclusions, but I did get it organized in my mind.

I looked up just as I was about to drift off to sleep and noticed something out of place amidst the synthetic vine curling up the corner of the room to the ceiling. It took me a moment to recognize a hidden video camera. My first thought was that my brother, who was surely paying for my funky clothes and all this pampering, had installed something to record his money's worth by putting me all over the Internet. My second thought was Hans telling me the cruise line had to keep an eye on their passengers. Was some guy in a video room watching me get covered with seaweed? My third thought was Solis telling me the cameras near Rawhide's hat and Rick's attack had been covered. Then I saw a carefully placed hank of sea kelp hung over the lens.

Uh-oh.

Before I could figure out how to move, handicapped by kelp, Saran Wrap, Dead Sea mud and whale ergonomics, something fell over my face and everything went dark.

Fourteen

♦ ♣ ♥ ♠

I should have been scared, but instead I was just pissed off. Serene to psycho in 1.2 seconds. I yanked at the piece of material over my face and tried to sit up. The material wasn't coming off easily, adhered to my head by something stubborn—duct tape, I'd bet. Or perhaps the mud had glued it to my face. I oozed off the table anyway, hitting a body, which yelped. I felt hands grabbing at me, my slippery antioxidant suddenly my ally. I'd have thought the kelp would be falling willy-nilly in my angered gyrations, but I suspected Valka had mixed in some herbal glue to make it stick.

I sensed two people in the room, but the song of whales in full mating disoriented me as I banged into the jars against the wall. One fell to the floor with a sloshy thump and I grabbed at one on the wall and yanked off the top, brandishing it as a weapon. I hoped it was the baby poop–colored goo, and furthermore, that it smelled even worse than it looked. I heard a groan, then a muffled voice that could've been an alto or a tenor say: "Just throw her out the window."

Ack. I wondered if sharks liked kelp and Dead Sea mud. I *knew* that open window was a bad idea. Damn Valka.

A hand tried to grab at me again and I flung the contents of the jar in the direction where the attached body should be. I heard a tortured gurgling and suddenly worried that I had burned the bad guy with acid. But then my preservation instinct kicked in—I threw the entire jar at him, apparently onto another vital body part because there was a distinct "oof." Then I slid past the other bad guy, letting the breeze from the open window orient me, and dove for where the door to freedom should be. I knocked over two pieces of art on the wall before hitting the knob. I wrenched open the door and felt my head snap back as someone grabbed at my hair and the tail of the towel around my face. I ran forward anyway, wrenching the towel off my head, and taking half my hair out with the duct tape that had held it on. With a small yelp of pain, I kept going down the labyrinth hallway.

I ran past the startled receptionist, down the corridor and straight into a six-foot hunk of man.

"Whoa, mermaid," he said, hands on my shoulders. "You're pretty far from the water. It's out there." He pointed over the side of the railing.

I struggled against him. "I don't want to die."

He laughed. "There might be a lot of things on my mind right now, mermaid, but killing you isn't one of them."

I looked up into the face of the Marlboro Man.

Ack. Of course. Just my luck. I would win tonight in cards if I lived long enough to play because I was embarrassing myself beyond imagination. "What's on your mind?" I asked weakly.

He laughed, a nice, solid trustworthy laugh, and doffed his button-down short sleeved shirt, pulling it out of his jeans and unbuttoning it with amazing quickness. He put it around my shoulders and let me button it down.

His chest, I noticed as I buttoned, was awesome. Smooth, tan, muscular six-pack that he clearly worked for. Total stud muffin. Brad Pitt perfect. He was gallant, an awesome specimen. And I still missed Frank. Dammit.

"What's wrong?" he asked.

"Where do I start?"

"Wherever you want to," he began patiently, then the phalanx of spa staff descended on us.

"Miss Cooley," a woman whose nametag said she was Spa Manager Gretchen spoke with a patronizing tone, putting her arm around my shoulder and trying to direct me back through the spa doors. I stopped outside. "We are so sorry you got upset. You should have told one of us you were claustrophobic."

"I'm not claustrophobic!"

"She just didn't like the kelp," Valka told her boss, shaking her head at me. "You should not have such a closed mind. The toxins you lock in your body will kill you."

"What's going to kill me are the men you let in the room who wanted to fling me out the window!"

"Men?" The Marlboro Man asked in a quiet, hard voice. His face darkened, and he looked really upset, more than he should for a mere stranger. I was touched, but before I could say thank you, he pushed through the spa doors and disappeared.

Meanwhile, Gretchen, Valka and the two other spa women who'd appeared shared a look that said I was crazy. Valka tsked. "I should not have turned on the whales."

"The whales?" Gretchen blurted. Valka nodded. Gretchen turned to me. "We need to get rid of the whale song. We've had some trouble with it causing hallucinations."

"I didn't hallucinate being blindfolded, groped and threatened to be thrown into the sea."

"Groped, sure, she wishes," one of the spa assistants, Moira, muttered.

"Look," I said. "Call security. If Valka didn't let the bad guys out the back door, then they are still in the spa somewhere."

Valka straightened her spine until she was four inches taller. "I let no one in or out!"

"Okay," I said as Gretchen called security. "Let's go find them, then. I will show you what happened."

"Don't you want to wait until your boyfriend comes back?" Moira asked.

"He's not my boyfriend. I don't even know his name," I realized aloud. "He just caught me as I ran out and let me borrow a shirt."

"How do you know he's not one of your bad guys?" Gretchen asked.

"They were chasing me. He was in front of me."

All four women shared a raised eyebrow, then led the way back to the spa. I scanned the labyrinth hallway for the blindfold with half my head of hair with it, but it was empty. I started to get an icky feeling in the pit of my stomach. As we opened the door, I could see the place was a mess—and there was no proof I just hadn't made it all myself.

"It's okay, the video camera will show what happened," Gretchen said.

They looked up and saw the lens covered in what I was still wearing. Four sets of eyes slowly looked back at me. Hans peeked in the door and reported the spa was empty except for one woman undergoing cellulite reduction therapy in another room who hadn't seen anyone but Moira. No evidence of any intruders. He threw me a sympathetic look.

"No towel blindfold and duct tape with auburn hair in it, by chance?" I asked.

Hans shook his head. "Have you checked your purse? Were you robbed?"

I reached under the table and opened the magnetic clasp on my Michael Kors. Travelers checks, check. Passport, check. Cabin key, check. Note? I riffled through cosmetics. No note. "Something's gone."

"Your money?" Hans stepped forward. "Your room key?"

"No, those and my identification are all there. A note is missing."

"What kind of note?"

"A threatening note I just got at lunch."

Hans frowned. "What did it say?"

"It warned me not to play detective or I'd be gone too."

Hans rubbed his forehead. "That's the only thing missing?"

I nodded.

"Maybe the situations with Mr. Santobella and Mr. Jones have made you a bit overwrought. You were up all night, after all. I suggest you head back to your cabin and get a little rest. I'll look into the note and intruders once you can give me a description."

"I didn't see them."

"Were they men or women?"

"Either."

There was much eye rolling. Hans sighed heavily. They obviously all thought I was a fruit loop. Great. The spa staff began to disperse.

It was hopeless to try to make them believe me. I began to gather my clothes.

"We won't be charging you for the damage, Miss Cooley," Gretchen said, obviously reluctantly. "Also, we are willing to begin your spa treatment over again . . ."

"Oh, that's not necessary," I said as I slipped my shoes on.

Moira, who'd begun to clean up, reached around the

back of the potted vine and picked up something, holding it out to me. "You must have dropped this."

In her hand was a rainbow-jeweled phone case. Hmm. Maybe the bad guys weren't all guys after all.

There was no record of Kinkaid ever taking a spa treatment, although the receptionist admitted that cruise officials didn't have to make appointments and often made private arrangements with staff for a quickie spa visit. None of those on duty at the time admitted to working on Kinkaid, but I supposed if she and Valka were in on some conspiracy she wouldn't admit it.

I was beginning to feel as ridiculous as the spa staff wanted me to feel as I tucked the phone case into the zippered compartment of my purse and took my now semi-sticky self out on the deck. I had rinsed my face clean, drew my hair back in a ponytail to hide the hunks missing and picked most of the wads of seaweed off, hoping Marlboro Man's shirt would look like a swimsuit cover-up, making it appear I had spent the afternoon in the pool instead of getting kelped and almost killed.

Marlboro Man had never reappeared. I wished I'd thought to ask his name. Still, I had to remind myself that, after the note, I couldn't trust anyone on board except for the three members of my family. As kind as he'd been and as much as my instincts told me he was safe, the Marlboro Man did have incredible timing today—he'd been walking by the table just as I read the note, and later, just as I fled my attackers.

I thought about the people who had known I was going to the spa—Ingrid, Kinkaid . . .

"I thought you said you were busy all afternoon?"

And, of course, Ian.

I turned as he reached me, giving me an intense once-over, pausing longest at the shirt. "Busy with some afternoon delight, I suppose, when all this time I thought you were getting a massage at the spa."

Although I was flattered that he was jealous, he certainly had no right to be and that irritated me. "I was—a sea kelp wrap and Dead Sea mud facial."

"I thought you were supposed to look refreshed and relaxed after a trip to the spa. You look like you've been put through the wringer." He squinted at my legs. "And I think they forgot to get some of the kelp off your right calf . . ."

"My visit got cut short."

"Which is why you are wearing another man's shirt?"

"How do you know this belongs to a man? I could have an affinity for Ralph Lauren button-downs."

"Ten sizes too big? I'm a psychologist, remember, Belinda," Ian said. "Plus, I've seen your sense of style and it isn't masculine in the least."

"Don't think you've got me all figured out, Ian Reno, because I will prove you wrong," I said, crossing my arms over my chest and eschewing the elevator for the stairs. Halfway up I realized it was a bad idea since I had absolutely no underwear on and the shirt was indeed that much too big. The Marlboro Man had shoulders to rival Arnold Schwarzenegger. Too bad Ringo hadn't saved me. His shirt would've fit me.

I think Ian was enjoying the view from about fifteen stairs behind me because he wasn't rushing. I put the Michael Kors at my rump. I was almost at the next deck when I saw a familiar pair of blue jean–clad legs saunter by. Marlboro Man! I turned on the gas.

"Hey, Belinda, slow down," Ian called behind me.

Marlboro Man, wearing a new blue button-down, had disappeared around the corner of a billboard advertising the Hold 'Em tournament. He tapped my photo with an index finger as he went by. I bumped into a woman who gave me a queer look (who could blame her) before jumping out of my way. I rounded the billboard and saw Marlboro Man making his way through the double glass doors leading to the outside deck. I opened my mouth to call out, but stopped myself. What could I say? Hey, dude? Yo, cowboy?

Ian caught up with me and saw me watching Marlboro Man, who'd stopped on deck next to the railing to talk to a man in a white and gold cruise ship uniform. "That's him, isn't it? My competition."

"That's him," I muttered distractedly. Both mens' backs were to me, but their posture denoted an intensity in their conversation, although neither man gestured or moved much at all.

"You were chasing him so hard, why didn't you call to him to wait for you?"

I looked at Ian, still trying to figure out why the cruise employee Marlboro Man was talking to seemed so familiar. "Because I don't know his name," I answered distractedly.

Fifteen

♦ ♣ ♥ ♠

By the time I worked up the nerve to go interrupt Marlboro Man's conversation, he and the ship employee had moved off in separate directions. As much as I wanted to know MM's name, I was curious about the employee too. If I caught up with him, I could always ask the name of the big cowboy who he'd just been talking to. There was something about the way the employee strode with purpose that said power, in a way that seemed at odds for a person who wore his name on his lapel. But before I could get within ten feet of him, he ducked into an employees-only door that clicked shut.

"Damn, damn, damn." I muttered.

"What is going on, Belinda?" Ian demanded.

I looked at him in surprise. I'd forgotten I had a shadow.

I sniffed. Something smelled suspiciously like a familiar soap. I thought Ian wore Obsession. I sniffed again. "Do you wash with Dove?"

Ian cocked his head at me, drawing his eyebrows together.

"No. What does that have to do with anything? What is going on?"

"I wish I knew." I shook my head. I must be going crazy, missing Frank so much I thought I smelled his soap. Silly.

"Do you think your boyfriend's gay?" Ian asked, putting an understanding hand on my arm. "There was obviously something between those two out there. Is that what this is about, your hurt pride?"

"Noooo." I paused for a breath of patience. "First off, that's not my boyfriend. Obviously, since I told you I don't even know his name."

"That's just the story you told me."

"That also happens to be the *true* story. I want to talk to him because I suspect he went looking for the guys who attacked me in the spa, and I want to know what he found out."

Ian gasped, grabbing my shoulders, looking into my eyes as if they would tell him more than my mouth would. "You were attacked? Are you okay?"

I nodded. "I'm just pissed off and slightly embarrassed." I paused to flash a fake smile at a couple who were eyeballing me in disdain. They hurried away.

I'd expected Ian to jump on the overwrought bandwagon but he didn't. "What do you think is going on?"

I shrugged. "Someone has it out for me. I got a threatening note under my dessert plate at lunch. After you ditched me."

"You ditched me, remember?"

I couldn't really argue since I'd been off talking to Sam at that point, and I didn't want to tell Ian about it, so I shrugged and tried to look apologetic.

"How do you know it's not this mystery man who left you the note?" Ian asked, crossing his arms over his chest, eyebrows raised.

"I don't. I don't at all."

* * *

After a shower in which I had to employ the entire contents of three shower gel containers to rid myself of the kelp residue, I dressed in my new Live in CYN bikini and looked in the mirror. Ack! For the first time on the cruise I was glad Frank wasn't there. I peered closer at my reflection. I think the kelp had accentuated my cellulite instead of ridding me of it. Maybe it was some kind of time-release thing.

Damned attackers. I was mad enough to kill them. Painfully.

I considered changing to my Venus one piece but decided that only a wetsuit would fix the problem, so I donned a cover-up and sat down at the phone. During my endless shower, I'd decided I had to get to know a little more about my fashionista roommate as well as Valka. As both were blond, either one of them could be the woman who lured Rick into the closet. I needed a better description from the source.

I dialed the Santobellas' room and Delia answered. Her voice stiffened when I identified myself. I asked after Rick's health. "He's resting," she said. "And still has amnesia, so can't confess yet to what you two did."

"Can I talk to him for just a second?" Couldn't hurt to try.

"No!" she shouted. "How stupid do you think I am?"

After that, the conversation deteriorated into a flow of invectives in Spanish. I said good-bye while she was sucking in a breath and hung up.

Okay, that went well. Apparently I'd have to move on without Rick's help. I needed to hide my purse with its important piece of evidence before I left. Hmm. I gauged the spaces that would fit my Michael Kors. Big bags were in and were fantastic to look at, but they were hell to hide. Finally, I took one of my pillows out of its pillow case, got a hand towel and wrapped my purse in it, stuffed the wrapped purse in the case, sat it next to its mate and plumped it to look as even as possible. Now what to do with the pillow? It refused to fit in any unobtrusive space. After fifteen minutes I gave up and did what everyone else on board apparently did with unwanted items—I let myself onto the balcony and threw it overboard, thinking some sea anemone would sleep better tonight.

Feeling slightly guilty, I left the room and walked down the hall toward the elevator, feeling a presence behind me all the way. As I reached the elevators, I turned around and looked. Security after me for pillow ditching? Someone disappeared into a room down the hall near mine. One white pant leg and a cruise uniform shoe was all I saw. I guess I was in the clear. I breathed deeply and tried to relax.

Dove soap again. Warm and musky overtones. Frank.

I peeked down the empty hall again and swore under my breath. My imagination was obviously working overtime.

The elevator appeared and I rode it to the Flop Deck where the adults-only Vegas pool was located. I hadn't seen it, but according to the cruise literature, poker was being dealt from cash tables in the pool itself. If I knew my twin at all, I'd bet he was going all in on the coolest version of Texas Hold 'Em yet—cards, cash, alcohol and mostly naked, all wet women. As I turned the corner I could see I won that pot. Ben sat in the water from the waist down, playing footsies with a beautiful Japanese girl in a string bikini sitting across from him while to his right Stella jock-eyed for attention and to his left a woman my mother's age rubbed her thigh against his. These were the world's smallest poker tables, forcing people to touch each other as they floated and played.

I think Hugh Hefner had designed this venue.

"Not your thing, I guess," Callie commented from the

pool steps, sliding a hank of her silver blond hair behind her ear. I could see she was trying not to watch but was unable to resist. The whole scene did sort of invite one to be a voyeur. Waitresses in bikinis made of playing cards swam around the lagoon-style pool with floating trays full of fruit and umbrella-garnished frozen drinks. Waterfalls crashed. Bodies undulated. Voices whooped with wins and moaned with losses. At least I think that was a loss Ben was moaning about.

"It's that obvious?" I asked, trying not to grimace.

She grinned and nodded.

"Did I gag out loud?" I asked.

Grinning wider, she shook her head.

I shrugged. "Different strokes, I suppose." Hearing myself, I made a face at my poor and unintentional joke.

"You got that right."

For the first time, I noticed Paul Pennington wearing some wildly colored toucan swim trunks at an adjacent table pushing all his chips forward on a three of spades, seven of clubs, nine of hearts flop. I cringed, hoping the poor boy had pocket Aces and knew his table. He took a swig of his piña colada and pulled hard on his straw when a King of diamonds fell on Fourth Street. Uh-oh. With four others matching his bet, he was in trouble here. The River was a six of hearts which gave one guy a straight and another woman trips. Paul threw his pocket deuces at the dealer so hard she fended them off with her hands. Then he dove to the bottom of the pool and stayed there. I looked at his chips they were stacking and calculated near three thousand dollars.

A lot to wager in a silly poolside game.

The kid was seriously sick.

But soon I started worrying more about the fact that he might drown himself over it.

I turned to Callie. "I wonder if the cruise planners anticipated people getting suicidal amidst the combination of gambling, alcohol and water eight feet deep. Do you see a lifeguard?"

She looked around and shook her head. No one at the table seemed concerned as they bet the next hand. I waited, glancing at the bottom of the pool where Paul lay like a flounder. Finally, my patience broke. Flinging my cover-up to a deck chair, I dove to the bottom, grabbed Paul by the back of his swim trunks and lugged him to the surface.

He spewed out water for a moment as a handful of people in the pool looked over at us curiously, including Ben.

"That's one way to pick up men, Bee Bee!" He shouted, then leaned in to the older woman next to him and said proudly, blithely unaware I was trying to save a life, "That's my sister. Obviously takes after me."

Paul looked at me sullenly. "I wasn't finished yet."

"With what?" I asked. "Your daily underwater meditations?"

"Drowning myself," he said.

Uh-huh. "Why would you want to do that?"

"Why do most people want to off themselves?" Paul slapped the water with his palm. "Because my life bites."

"Mine does too sometimes, but I don't want to die."

He narrowed his eyes at me. "Hey, aren't you that chick who won that big tournament in Vegas?"

"There are lots of tournaments in Vegas. I won one once."

Paul snorted. "Yeah, no wonder you don't want to die. You just won a quarter million dollars."

I wasn't going to correct him because now he was eye-balling me like the fatted calf. Remind me not to give him access to my checking account when walking with him near the ship's railing. "Money isn't everything," I said, quickly adding, "Besides, there wasn't much left after the IRS got through with it."

"They take a big chunk?"

"Gambling tax is twenty-five percent."

"Shit, then maybe I should do the other job instead of trying to win back the money I owe," Paul said under his breath.

"You got a job offer?" I said brightly, as if he meant me to hear what he'd said. "Congratulations."

Paul looked up, apparently surprised that he'd spoken aloud. "Yeah, some guy I know is doing a special research project and he needs an assistant. I'm not too sure I can do what he wants done, but it pays well."

"Go for it," I advised.

He bobbed his head. "Later," he said, shoving his way past Callie, making for the steps. He turned around. "Listen, my name is Paul Pennington if you want to hang out sometime."

Sure, meet you at the back of the boat with my debit card and a flotation device. I smiled and waved and decided to swim a lap.

"What a jerk. He didn't even thank you for saving his life, did he?" Callie asked, swimming up behind me.

"I didn't expect him to." I settled on a ledge next to the waterfall and Callie joined me.

"You're nice. I can see why Ingrid wants to hang out with you."

Yeah, right. "Why *does* Ingrid want to hang out with an old woman like me?"

"No, you're really cool for being old." She paused, blushing. "I mean, you're cool like Michelle Pfeiffer or Nicole Kidman. I want to be like them and like you when I get o—to be your age."

"Thanks." I muttered. "So Ingrid just hopes my Kidman-Pfeifferness rubs off on her so she can emulate it decades from now?"

Callie shrugged. "I don't know, really. She gets obsessive compulsive. I guess she decided to obsess on you."

"So you're good friends?"

"She's my friend but I haven't known her that long. She transferred to our school midsemester."

"From where?"

"Some school I'd never heard of. She has a Washington D.C. driver's license. Her parents live in Southern California. That's where she's from."

"How do y'all know Ben?"

"Oh, Stella and I didn't, not until yesterday. Ingrid and Ben knew each other before. Ingrid invited us to come with her on the cruise because Ben was going on it."

I watched Ben rubbing Stella's back. Where did Ingrid fit in? "Ben and Ingrid are lovers then?"

"Oh no." Callie shook her head decisively. "They're just friends. Stella made sure before she went for him. Ingrid was really clear about it too that she and Ben are just pals. Ben's not her type." Something wasn't right here. Ben was such an irresistible bad boy, he's everyone's type, at least once. Besides which, Ben didn't have women friends. He had girlfriends and lovers and ex-lovers and would-be lovers but no one with estrogen was ever his "friend."

"Hmm. What's Ingrid's major?"

"Psychology."

Before I could think too hard about that, Ben hollered, obviously friendlier with the tequila bottle than he had been earlier. "Bee Bee, come float some cards my way. We're on the water, in the water, playing poker." He thought that was hilarious as did the rest of his table. Even the dealer smiled.

"I think I need to leave before my embarrassment quotient rises any higher."

"He's so cute," Callie murmured, watching Ben undulate the muscles under the giraffe tattoo under his belly button for Stella.

"Unless you're related to him." I threw over my shoulder as I eased my way past Ben's table to the pool steps.

"Come on," Ben called. "This dealer is a pocket princess and queen of the fancy flop. You can't lose, Bee Bee. Live a little."

I did want to talk to Stella about Ingrid. I surveyed the table and gauged that everyone sitting at it was sufficiently inhibited by alcohol. I could outplay them as long as I caught a few good cards.

When the man sitting next to Stella got up and said, "I'm outta here," the deal was sealed.

All I had to do was let the dealer swipe my room key to get chips. Way too easy for kids like Paul, I thought. The table was plastic made to look like wood, with a green surface that was Astroturf. Weird. I sat down on the stool that was concreted into the pool bottom and tried hard to keep my leg from floating into the knee of the man sitting to my left, who was definitely taking up more than his share of the pool. I tried to scoot my cemented stool and nearly fell off. This was uncomfortable.

"Where's Ingrid?" I asked Stella.

"You don't know where your fashionista is?" Ben asked, falsely aghast.

"I haven't seen her since noon."

Ben raised his eyebrows. "You mean you have no one to blame but yourself for that bikini?"

"Very funny."

Everyone at the table thought so. I was beginning to think this was a bad idea. The dealer pitched us our pocket cards. I slid the Gargoyles down over my eyes and peeked. Pair of tens—spade and club.

Not great, not bad, depending on The Flop. I was in late position, which was a terrific place to start. I waited until the table got around to me. Everyone had stayed in, calling the big blind. I guessed most were going to play every hand no matter what they had.

I decided to raise. It was a $5/$10 game so it wouldn't cost me much to shake them up a bit. The raise definitely threw them. All except Ben took another look at their pocket cards. A bunch of fish. Ben grinned at me.

Everyone called my raise, just like a bunch of limit Internet players. The Flop was five of spades, three of spades, Jack of hearts. I was probably already beaten by someone with a higher pair or someone who'd stayed in with a Jack or someone one short of a spade flush. That was the problem with playing with people who didn't know what they were doing—someone usually got lucky. I'm sure that's what my opponents in the Lanai tournament were still saying about me. The problem was, you couldn't get lucky every time, but you could be beaten by someone else every time. I could probably outlast enough of them to win money, but I wasn't sure I had the patience to sit at this table that long. Besides my fingers were already getting pruny. Once I talked to Stella, I was out of there.

Sure enough, I called my way through the rest of the hand and got beat. The Turn was an Ace of diamonds, which normally would have sent me folding. A Queen spade fell on Fifth Street, giving Stella trips, but Ben held the spade flush I had feared.

As Ben swept the chips his way, chortling happily, I leaned over to Stella. "Too bad. You might have had it."

She giggled. "You think?"

I nodded. "Trips are a good hand."

She paused in midsuck on her straw. "We're on a trip, right?"

Okay, bartender, cut her off. "Yes, indeed we are. On a major trip."

"Cool."

"So, where did Ingrid run off to this afternoon?" I asked

Stella as the dealer threw us our pocket cards on the next
hand.

Shrugging, Stella took another slurp of her banana
daiquiri. "She said something about chains . . ."

"And whips?" Ben put in, waggling his eyebrows.

Stella jostled him with her shoulder. He peered down
at her cleavage. I felt like I was at a Playboy bunny party.
"Chains, like necklaces, earrings, bracelets, zippers and stuff
like that, Ben," Stella slurred, talking with her hands waving around her neck and ears. "She's looking for jewelry
for Bee's outfit for tonight."

Uh-oh, sounded like I was going to look like a biker
chick. "Ben," I asked in my best warning voice. "Are you
giving Ingrid money to dress me?"

Ben put his hands in the air, palms forward. "Hey, hey,
no way. I would never be that good to you."

"He's joking," Stella giggled.

"No, he's not," I assured her. "Has Ingrid always had a
big interest in fashion?"

"I don't think so. She's always looked good, but anybody that beautiful would, wouldn't they? She works, but
doesn't like to talk about what she does. Callie thinks she's
a masseuse, I think she's a call girl, but maybe she really
just works at a boutique. Maybe some cheezy one that she'd
be embarrassed to tell us about like Forever 21."

"Let's go, people," the dealer urged. "Place your bets."

I peeked at my pocket and found a two of diamonds,
seven of clubs. Even if I was trying to act like a fish, I
couldn't stick with this one. I folded.

"Nobody folds at this table," the Japanese girl playing
footsies with Ben announced.

"I noticed," I observed drily.

Ben went all in in a crazy jackal move. The Flop was
two deuces and a four of spades. For some reason everyone

was matching Ben's bet which was totally crazy since I had one of the other two deuces. Fourth Street was an 8 of diamonds. The fourth deuce fell on The River. Damn damn damn.

Ben took everyone's money with a King kicker. I couldn't believe it.

"See?" The footsie girl looked at me. "That's why you don't fold at this table."

Sixteen
♦ ♣ ♥ ♠

As I walked back to my cabin, I realized that looking for answers had just complicated the puzzle instead of clarifying it, not to mention making someone angry enough to want to make me "gone." I couldn't prove the spa invaders had anything to do with the note, but since I didn't routinely make people mad enough to want to make me disappear, I had to assume so. I stopped at the Internet lobby to e-mail Frank, filling him in on the goings-on, asking his advice on how to proceed with my investigation and which authorities I needed to get involved.

I felt eyes on me again as I walked down the hallway to my cabin. Paranoia was uncomfortable, I told myself. But since I was fresh from almost being flung out the window at ten stories, my sense of self-preservation overpowered my intellect, and I looked over my shoulder. The hallway was empty, although I heard a door down the hall click shut. "Jack?" I called. No one popped out of the decorative greenery.

Sighing, I let myself into the cabin to pure, blissful quiet. I had an overwhelming urge to lie down on the bed and sleep for days. The vacation I'd hoped would be an opportunity to relax had been nothing but a headache since before we boarded the *Sea Gambler*. It was four o'clock, leaving me only an hour before my Softer Secrets workshop. I could take a little rest. Or I could dress and get out of the cabin before my fashionista returned with chains and zippers for me to wear. That was a better idea.

Besides deciding what to say in my workshop, I still needed to cement my plan for returning Kinkaid's phone case. Her phone wasn't in it, that would've been way too much fun and way too easy to prove she had been in Valka's room at the spa sometime in the last twelve hours. I remembered seeing her pull her phone out of its glittering case last night during the tournament but I didn't think to look for it when I encountered her in the stairway this afternoon. I'd decided to find her on the pretense of asking about the progress on finding Rawhide, and ask not so casually if she was missing her phone case. I wanted her to suspect I might know where it was and worry. Desperation made people do telling things.

I rang the desk and asked for Jack Smack's cabin. He wasn't in, but I left a message that I wanted to meet him for a drink before dinner to ask him about Sam the Man. It was only after I hung up that I remembered I was supposed to meet Ian at that time also. Oh well, I'd make it work.

After my third shower of the day, I threw on a lime and lemon swirl pattern cotton dress with crocheted bolero and my favorite Manolos. I grabbed my Prada clutch with the oversize sequins and sat down at the couch to transfer the vital items out of my Michael Kors. Sliding it out of its pillowcase, I paused and frowned. I thought I'd put the purse in with the back facing front. Now the front was facing front. I shrugged, deciding I was getting forgetful.

I removed my MAC lip gloss, bronzer, glitter powder and my purse-size Guerlain perfume. I slid my cabin key in the keeper pocket of the clutch. Then, I unzipped the side pocket of the Kors and reached for the jeweled phone case. Nothing.

What?

My fingers grappled in the empty space, trying to make the evidence reappear with double the effort. No such luck. I turned the purse over and shook out the contents. Lots of junk. No rainbow-jeweled phone case.

Flinging the comforter back, I searched the bed linens. No jeweled case. I searched the floor. Nothing. Frantic, I opened the closet and looked inside the shoes and pockets. No case. I ran my hands over Ingrid's bed, in her pillows. Nothing.

"What are you looking for?"

I jumped. Ingrid stood behind me, putting down two shopping bags. I don't know how she'd gotten into the room without me hearing her. I'd have to wonder about that later. "Something is missing," I finally answered.

"And you think I took it?"

"No, I think someone's been in our room."

"How much money did they take?"

Money? I hadn't even thought of that. I returned to the pile on my bed and plucked out my wallet. Opening it, I counted my traveler's checks and credit cards. Everything was there. "No money."

"No money? What did they get then—your good jewelry, maybe gold, diamonds, pearls?"

I shook my head. The only good jewelry I'd ever owned had been my five-carat marquis-cut diamond engagement ring that I'd returned in a fit of rage, having seen my fiancé in flagrante delicto with someone other than me. Stupid move. I could've sold the rock and paid for the rewiring of my house, or better yet, bought a midlife crisis Miata. Important life lesson—don't let your heart rule your mind. Or, don't let your pride throw a hundred thousand dollars at a man's crotch.

"What is it then, Bee?" Ingrid demanded.

I didn't trust Ingrid, so couldn't fess up to having Kinkaid's phone case, although I couldn't come up with a plausible reason why either of them would be conspiring to fling poker players off the ship either. I'd work on that one more later as well.

"Oh, no big deal," I said, collecting all the things on the bed and stuffing them back into the Michael Kors. "I probably just misplaced it."

"Maybe we should call security if you think someone unauthorized has been in the room."

"No," I snapped. Hans seemed like a cool guy, but Phil was a dolt and there's no telling how creepy their boss, the head of security, was. He was nameless and faceless even in the midst of Rick's and Rawhide's disappearances. Someone had known I ditched my pillow because of a security cam, or they'd come into the room and just gotten lucky. I scanned the ceiling and light fixtures for likely lenses and counted the times I'd wandered around the room naked. "It's okay."

Ingrid cocked her head at me, skeptical but fortunately distracted enough by my dress not to pursue it. "What do you have on?"

"A sundress," I answered.

"No. No. No." She shook her head to punctuate each word. "That is cute. We don't do cute. That is not the Bee Cool image we are trying to portray."

I stood and floated the tiered skirt out. "But why not? I am being cool in it."

Ingrid tsked. "You are sexy and untouchable. Bee Cool is too hot to handle. This is what I just told the *People* magazine researcher who e-mailed today for some background info."

Oh dear. Stay calm. "Whom did they e-mail?"

"Ask her at Bee Cool Hold 'Em dot com," Ingrid announced proudly.

"What *is* Bee Cool Hold 'Em dot com?" I asked with extreme patience.

"Your website. I've been working on it all day. You're going to love it," she said decisively.

"Ingrid, why are you doing this?"

"Being your fashionista isn't keeping me busy enough, so I decided to become your imagista and of course you need a website. Everybody has websites these days. MySpace is the new info mall. You have a fan club. They deserve something. I gave it to them."

"Ingrid, I can't let you do this for free," I began. "Besides, I'm not sure I want you to do this at all."

"This is the deal," she said, opening the shopping bags and laying out her purchases. I tried not to look. One disaster at a time. "You give me ten percent of your winnings and endorsements starting today."

I felt relieved. At least she had a monetary motive; that I could understand. "Ingrid, ten percent of nothing is nothing. And nothing won't pay for the things you've already bought, not to mention for your time and trouble."

Ingrid waved one long tan arm in the air casually. "Don't worry about these things. You have an anonymous benefactor."

It was getting scary again. "You mean Ben?"

Ingrid laughed. "No way. He's too selfish to benefact anyone but himself."

Well, I had to like Ingrid a little better now. "Okay, who is it then?"

She shrugged. "That's what anonymous means. They are unidentifiable."

"You can't identify them or you won't?" I demanded.

Ingrid shrugged again, and pulled some white silk pants

out of the closet. Not me in white again. I stained things just thinking about them. I forced myself to tackle the argument first, fashion next.

"Who're you working for anyway?"

"I'm working for your image."

"My image won't pay you ten percent, my play at the table will."

"Wanna bet?" She raised her eyebrows, shooting me a cool look. I saw then how smart she really was. "This is the media age. The Internet is changing the game. Your image is everything. You can make more in endorsements than you can on the felt, if you play your cards right."

Unless she was lying, Ingrid had no reason to dump me into the Pacific, so I decided to trust her, just a bit. She talked me into the white silk pants (with the promise I would wear five napkins in my lap at dinner), a beaded, low-cut, loose-fitting emerald halter top and a wraparound gold chain laced with white beads that hung in five layers from my collarbone to my waist. Gold chain earrings hung from my ears. I was allowed my gold strappy Manolos. Grateful that only one chain and no zippers were involved, I acquiesced.

The hair caused some controversy. She wanted me to wear it down in my natural wavy curls. I thought I probably should wear it pulled back in a bun to hide the hunks the duct tape pulled out, which necessitated telling Ingrid sketchy details of my spa attack. Her face took on a protective anger, much like Marlboro Man's did. Of course, she had more cause since her potential 10 percent almost went out the ship window.

"Why and who would want to hurt you?" she asked as she watched me arrange my hair in the compromise—a sleeked-back ponytail.

"Maybe whoever hurt Rick and did something with Rawhide."

She raised her eyebrows again but didn't respond. She changed quickly into a pair of tangerine linen pants, a gorgeous, flowing, strapless organza top a slightly lighter shade of orange, ballerina slippers and a barrette holding her pale hair just off her face—an outfit that I couldn't make work if you paid me. Ingrid looked like she stepped off the catwalk in Milan. She wore her six feet well.

We decided to meet after Softer Secrets to go to drinks and dinner together. I did have to meet Ian and hopefully Jack too, at the bar first. Ingrid could help. I figured that I would orchestrate the conversation so she could talk to Ian while I quizzed Jack. As we made our way down the hallway to the elevator, Ingrid told me about my website, which she was going to work on while I did my workshop. I felt a tickly feeling at the back of my neck as I had lately whenever I walked down the hallway. I started to look over my shoulder but Ingrid dragged me forward to make the elevator. We squeezed in with a carful of people including the Santobellas, who'd been separated in the crush by a couple of people. Delia glared and a pale Rick threw me a meaningful look I unfortunately couldn't interpret.

When the elevator opened on the ninth floor, we got pushed out first and I angled myself off to the right where Rick would be disembarking. Delia was one step ahead of me, though, elbowing the two between them, grabbing his arm and guiding him off to the left past Ingrid, who'd gotten moved off along with the flow of bodies.

Ingrid waited for everyone to pass, then walked over to me, shaking her head. "That guy handed me something . . ."

"Which man?" I asked, stopping and turning around.

She pointed at Rick. *He'd seen us get in the elevator together.* I looked at her hand. "What does the paper say?"

Ingrid opened up the scrap of paper.

RG 4200 AT.

Ingrid looked at me as she handed it over. "What kind of code is this?"

I shrugged, taking the paper and tucking it in my clutch. "Maybe if I think about it for a while I'll understand."

"Good luck."

"She won't need to be wished that for the tournament. She had a bad enough day to be lucky tonight."

I paused as Richard came up on our left. "How do you know I had a bad day?"

He smiled. "I saw you in the Vegas pool. Stinky."

"I promise you, my day was lots worse than that."

"Super! I'll bet on you then," Richard chortled.

"Bet on me? Figure of speech or are you really betting?"

"I've got a good pool going. You are at twelve-to-one odds right now behind the Indian kid, and any amateur."

"Who thought of this idea?" I asked, laughing at the absurdity. "Gambling on gambling?"

"You did," Richard threw back cheerfully. I threw Ingrid a hard look that she met with an unapologetic shrug as he continued. "The advice on your website that says watching the game, knowing the players and betting on who will win will teach you to play better by showing you how to read the game. Of course, my own twisted version of that is: I'm checking out all the player's days to see if you've ridden the end of your lucky wave or whether you are due the next set. I think you're due the next set."

"So do I. Nice ocean analogy by the way." I observed, jostling him with my hip.

"I like to keep with the theme," Richard said as he walked on.

"See," Ingrid said. "People are already reading your website."

"Scary, since I've never seen it and don't know what I am supposedly saying on it."

"I'll meet you at the bar in an hour," Ingrid informed me as she turned and walked away.

I realized I didn't know where the seminar would be, so I sank into a chair next to the window and rifled through my purse for the itinerary Kinkaid had given me. I was speaking in a lobby area adjacent to the poker room, obviously in the hopes of filling up tables for the ship. Rising, I made my way to the stairs. I had just put my hand on the railing when the boat lurched, taking a hard bank left, which threw my body against the railing, then over it. I screamed, but I was so busy trying to hang onto the slippery wood that I don't think it came out very loud.

Seventeen

♦ ♣ ♥ ♠

My stiletto-clad feet scrambled for purchase along the curving staircase railing. My arms trembled with growing weakness. I foolishly looked down. If—no, *when*—I fell, I would be landing on the next curve in railing before I hit the deck. Ouch. This was going to hurt. People were running, confused and scared, up and down the stairs, either not seeing or ignoring me in favor of their own panic.

Two hysterical women stopped on the stairs, gripping each other.

"We're sinking."

"It's the Titanic all over again."

"I don't think so," I offered, hoping to get their attention. "Since there aren't usually any icebergs in the Gulf of Mexico in summer."

The women rolled their eyes at me and ran down the stairs. I guess I couldn't hope they would catch me when I lost my last vestige of strength. I closed my eyes and felt my fingers slipping the rest of the way off the slick wood. Then I was flying through the air. But I was going up . . . .

How did that happen?

I was dumped onto the pointy stairs, knocking the air out of me for a moment. My nose was buried in the carpet. I sucked in a breath, opened my eyes and blinked. By the time I looked up all I could see were a pair of black cowboy boots rounding the corner at the top of the stairs. I swear they were lizard. Their soles said Lucchese. At least my savior had taste.

"Are you alright, ma'am?" a cruise employee whose nametag read Rita stooped over me to ask.

I nodded and took a deep breath. "Did you see who helped me?"

She shrugged. "Some guy."

"What did he look like?"

"I didn't notice, I was more worried about you."

"Thanks." I said, rising gingerly. Ouch. I was going to have a mother of a bruise on my right shin. "What's going on? Is this still the turbulence from the storm?"

Rita shook her head. "I don't think so, I was told we left that a long time ago. I was just going to check with my boss when I saw you."

"Let's go."

I limped to the top of the stairs and we made it out on deck. The ship had done a 180-degree turn, which is why I'd been thrown head over tea kettle.

"I heard someone fell overboard and we're going back to get him," a man peering over the railing told us. The ship had slowed to almost a complete stop by now. We searched the sea alongside the ship as dozens more joined us, murmuring, concerned and excited—a bunch of sea-going rubberneckers. I heard a commotion from the stern. I left Rita chatting with a pair of passengers and made my way through the crowd. Cruise engineers had produced a large metal basket that they were lowering to the water from a pole off the side of the ship. They'd already dropped a rubber dingy. I worried for the poor guys who drew the short straws and had to be out on the treacherous-looking sea. They motored over the roiling waves in what looked like a grid pattern for about ten minutes.

"What are they looking for?" I asked a woman next to me.

"I heard they saw a treasure chest floating in the water."

Uh-huh, mister, and I have some oceanfront property in Amarillo for sale.

"No, it was a mermaid," a woman slurred.

Have another margarita, mama.

"I heard someone fell overboard," someone else reported.

Now we were getting somewhere.

"That's true," a third man said. "My girlfriend talked to the guy who saw something fly by his window."

Oops, hope it wasn't my pillow he saw. I'd feel bad for the rescue team getting soaked for a little goosedown.

"There it is!" A voice shouted to my right. A little girl pointed out at something bobbing in the water about five hundred yards off the ship. We all squinted as the rescue team motored toward it. I squinted at the blob. I couldn't tell what it was. We watched the pair review it and then pull it onto the dingy. It sure looked human to me. Two legs, two arms. It also looked dead to me. Limp, still. One of the guys started CPR.

The driver made it back to the side of the ship where the metal cage had been lowered to water level. The man doing CPR with no visible results stopped and, with the help of the other rescuer, flipped the body into the cage, where it wound up faceup. The cage began to rise. Too young and too much hair to be Rawhide.

The cage paused a few decks below us. I leaned over the

railing and watched as a door slid open on the side of the ship and the rig disappeared into the bowels of the boat.

"It was the insurance investigator."

Ben had oozed in next to me at some point. I looked at him in shock. "How do you know?"

"How many guys on the boat would be wearing a bow tie, handle bar mustache and green bowling shoes?"

Before I could answer we were all silenced by the sound of the PA system.

"Ladies and gentlemen, this is Captain Santiago. I apologize for keeping you uninformed as to the recent turn of events on board, but my attention has been focused on saving one of your fellow passengers. Unfortunately, it appears that he fell overboard. As many of you have seen, due to the heroic efforts of our trained crew, we did manage to rescue him. Resuscitation attempts are underway now, the ship's doctor is with him and an investigation will ensue. We encourage all of you to follow the cruise ship guidelines for safety and anyone with any information about this incident is asked to notify the ship security immediately. Now, please return to your activities and enjoy the rest of your day."

Sure. No problem.

Actually most passengers seemed more than willing to do just that, filtering back into the interior of the ship to dress for dinner or find an empty table in the casino. Drive by the wreck and onto the party. It wasn't that easy for me to let it go, but it never was. I'd long yearned for better emotional blocks. My fairy godmother had yet to grant my wish.

"I hope he makes it," I murmured, although he didn't look too good.

Ben shook his head. "It's pretty hard to survive a five to ten-story fall."

"But he fell into water."

"The surface of the water can be as hard as concrete unless you hit it just right. I wouldn't hold out much hope for the guy, Bee Bee."

"But why? Why would someone want to kill him?"

"I guess he asked the wrong question," Ben said as he walked away.

By the time I got to my appointed place to teach my workshop it was already scheduled to be over. A couple of holdouts who'd been oblivious to the man-overboard incident were still waiting. I promised them a wrap-up of the Softer Secrets on the website. That thing was really taking on a life of its own.

I traipsed to the top deck where Ingrid waited outside the bar. I could see Ian sitting at a table by the window, looking out at the sea. I found it interesting that a psychologist would study the water instead of the people, but maybe he was just tired of working. That instant, Jack, looking quite handsome in a charcoal suit, purple button-down and yellow and gray tie, entered the bar through the other doorway, so I tiptoed over and put my hand on his shoulder. That's when I noticed the button-down was streaked with sweat. This was a huge effort for him and I appreciated it. "Hi, Jack. How nice to see you. Won't you join me and my friends?"

Jack shot me a fleeting glance before going along with my formality. He cleared his throat. "What an honor, B-Belinda."

I led him to the table where Ian sat, supremely handsome in a sunflower open-necked button-down and indigo linen blazer. I introduced everyone around as Ian hid his vexation. He was definitely a man who didn't like not being in control.

The first ten minutes were monopolized, of course, by

the man overboard until I could guide Ingrid into a conversation with Ian about psychology. Jack stayed quiet for the most part, nodding at appropriate times. Ingrid caught my hint and captured Ian's attention with a lively story about her college professor. I leaned in to Jack. "How's it going? Any news?"

His eyes twinkled with excitement. "This and that."

Ian watched us carefully out of the corner of his eye. I smiled, leaning back in my chair as I laughed at Jack. "You'd better give, or I'm not telling you what happened with *my* day."

"Don't t-tell me, you were k-kidnapped," he joked in a quiet voice.

"Damn near," I answered just as quietly, smiling at Ian, who was listening to Ingrid.

Jack's eyes bugged out. "You have to t-tell me what happened. Who did it?"

"You're the investigative journalist. That's what you are supposed to find out for me."

Nearly bouncing up and down in the chair in excitement, Jack whispered: "I need all the details."

"After you tell me about Sam the Man Hyun."

Jack frowned, "What about him?"

"Whatever you know. All I know is he is an old Texas Hold 'Em legend and has a bad temper."

Shrugging, Jack threw out, "That could d-describe half the guys who s-started the game before it got to be a household word—including The Mouth and Poker Brat."

"Tell me more," I urged, watching as Ingrid began flirting with Ian. I could see the attention was fake, but Ian couldn't. His male ego, properly stroked, was responding appropriately. I'd have to owe Ingrid more than 10 percent if she was this good at her distraction techniques.

Jack had noticed the pair flirting too. He kept a close watch on Ingrid, and I had to touch his arm to bring his attention back to me. He cleared his throat, one eye still drifting to Ingrid every now and then. "Sam grew up in Salem, Oregon, and got caught at the age of fourteen running a Hold 'Em game in the toolshed behind his house. It made national news because it was a no-limit cash game with forty-five thousand dollars on the felt and the mayor, state representative and U.S. senator sitting at the table."

"Enterprising lad," I observed, noticing Jack hadn't stuttered once in his report.

"He grew up to be an enterprising adult too, winning God only knows how many millions in ring games all over the world. He is one of the smartest players I've ever seen, to tell you the truth—can calculate the outs before the card even hits the felt. But his two downfalls were the advent of the Internet and Hyun's own preference to fly below the radar. He refused to capitalize on his legend like Doyle Brunson did. Once TV became part of the game, he went the other way, playing in private ring games instead of the big tournaments. He tried to, in effect, kill his own legend."

And now maybe he was killing others as well? "So why is he on board the *Sea Gambler*?"

"He is?" Jack asked, open mouthed. After a thoughtful moment, he continued, "M-maybe he's made his peace with the part media plays in the game today and is trying to make a c-comeback. This wouldn't be a bad place to s-start. This ship's inaugural voyage is getting a lot of p-press. He doesn't have to do the poker star business but might win and still get the media attention from that after the fact. It certainly would be c-consistent with his personality."

"You don't think he might have a serious enough grudge against any of these players that he might want to hurt them, do you? When I talked to him today he seemed rather . . . resentful."

Jack sat up so high in his chair I wondered if he wasn't standing on it. Ian and Ingrid looked over, startled. Jack eased back down and smiled until they resumed their conversation. Then he leaned in to me. "You *t-talked* to him?"

"Yeah, why?"

"Because you are the k-kind of player he would most resent. First of all, he is a huge male chauvinist. Second, he despises the part luck plays in the game today and the fact that nobodies beat skilled players on a regular basis. Now, the same nobodies don't beat the skilled players over and over, but the same skilled player will get beat by different nobodies, most of whom learned to play on the Internet and think they know what they are doing, catch enough good cards and win every now and then.

"So a woman who didn't know how to play the game four days before a major tournament and wins would not be on Sam Hyun's hit parade."

"You've seen the website?" I blurted out.

"It's awesome, g-girl!" Jack gushed.

"What website?" Ian asked as their conversation waned.

"Ingrid surprised me by building it," I answered.

Jack looked at Ingrid and I saw the electricity zap between them. Feeling it must have been wild. What an odd couple; I smiled at the possibility.

"You are very talented," Jack purred, turning into male mush. "And b-beautiful."

"Not really," Ingrid murmured, uncharacteristically humble. "But thank you."

Ian looked at my outfit. "I see you found some clothes that fit. Fit in just the right places, by the way," he added, his voice turning to warm syrup.

I wasn't in the mood for pancakes so it didn't have much of an effect. I looked at his Timex. "It's nearly time for dinner."

"I need to see this website of yours," Ian said, getting up from the table and pulling out my chair. Jack had jumped up to pull out Ingrid's chair. She blushed.

"So do I," I admitted, rising.

"You haven't seen it? You don't know what's on your own website?"

I shook my head. "No."

"You are an incredibly trusting soul, Belinda," Ian observed in a way that sounded like he was pleased and, at the same time, disapproved. Huh.

"In this case, I didn't have much choice, because I didn't know about it beforehand."

"Then maybe it is more accurate to say you are an accepting soul." Ian clarified in a tone that made me think he was much more comfortable with me being accepting than trusting.

"With a twin like Ben, I had to learn quick to be accepting or choke myself to death with my pacifier."

Ian raised his eyebrows in a way that suggested I was a serious candidate for therapy. "Do you still resent your brother, Belinda?"

"Every day."

"It sounds like a sadomasochistic relationship," Ian observed seriously as we paused outside the glittering dining room. Ingrid and Jack were deep in conversation behind us. I could barely concentrate on Ian for watching them. I heard Jack apologize for hyperventilating. Ingrid patted Jack on the arm and told him he was cute. Go figure Cupid, but I had to like his master plan.

"Aren't all family relationships quirky and somewhat painful?" I finally responded to Ian's intense stare.

"Maybe we should talk."

"About what? Your family? Great idea. Where did you grow up?"

Ian blinked and I thought instantly he ought to rethink his affinity for older women. Perhaps he was better off sticking to coeds for company. We more mature females were a bit more headstrong, hard to control and tended to say what we think.

"I grew up in a normal household . . ."

As opposed to mine, I supposed, where infants contemplated suicide and fratricide.

". . . one of three children in Roswell."

Score one for Mom.

Before we could delve deeper into his normal childhood, a young woman came rushing out of the doors. She paused, flustered and wild-eyed, looking from side to side like she couldn't decide which way to go.

"What's wrong?" I asked. "Can I help you?"

"It's Mahdu. Something bad has happened."

Eighteen

♦ ♣ ♥ ♠

Eria was Mahdu's girlfriend. I could discern that much before she started babbling so fast I couldn't follow her.

Ian excused himself to go find security. Ingrid and Jack gathered around her. People filtering into dinner stared.

"Eria," I said calmly, even though my heart was racing too. "Start from the beginning. How do you know something is wrong with Mahdu? Where is he?"

She sucked in a breath and blew it out slowly. Good for her. Then she took another breath and blew it out. Then she took another breath. Okay, so much for deep breathing. I was ready to kick-start her by the time she finally spoke again. "We have walkie-talkies to keep track of each other on the ship, just like we did at Disney World. He was playing Hold 'Em in the poker room all afternoon and got back to the room after I'd already left for dinner. He radioed he was going to change clothes fast and meet me at the table. I'd just sat down and the radio beeped. As I got it out of my purse I heard him say, 'No, Ferris!' really loud and scared and then nothing. I can't get him to answer back."

Phil and another security man appeared at my elbow with Ian in their wake. "I'm with ship security, miss," the other man said, putting his arm on her shoulders, directing her away from the crowded dining room and toward the elevators. "Let's see if we can help you."

"Where's Hans?" I asked Phil. He just glared at me. I pressed, "Where are you taking her?"

"This is none of your concern, ma'am," the other security creep informed me. "Go enjoy your dinner."

"This might indeed be my concern if whoever is giving Mahdu trouble are the same guys who attacked me in the spa today. Certainly you've seen the report."

"There is no such report, ma'am," the security cretin threw over his shoulder as he ushered a frightened Eria into the elevator. "But I will certainly check into it for you."

Sure he would. The elevator doors shut on them. What was going on? Had Hans not filed a report? Seemed like there would be an APB out for my attackers.

"Why do I feel like I am in C-cold War Russia?" Jack asked in the stunned silence.

"Because I think that is where they learned to run this ship's security."

"You were attacked? Why didn't you tell me?" Ian asked, concern wrinkling his forehead. "What happened?"

I was more worried for Mahdu than for me at the moment, so I just waved my hand. "Someone tried to throw me out the spa window."

"What!" Ian shouted, shocked. "Why?"

"I don't know. I don't think it was Plan A but they went with it when I was too slippery to get a grip on."

"What was Plan A?" Ian asked quietly, suddenly so intense he was barely breathing.

"They didn't share that with me at the time," I answered before turning toward the elevators. I realized Ingrid had disappeared.

"Where's Ingrid?" I asked Ian.

"I looked around while that poor girl was talking and she was gone. Maybe she went to update your website?"

"I'll go look for her," Ian randomly offered.

Jack looked dismayed and started after him, but I held him back. "Ingrid can take care of herself. I need your help."

Jack didn't look convinced as he watched Ian head up the stairs. If the security department was going to try to cover this up, like they apparently were trying to do with Rawhide's, Rick's and my incidents, then someone else was going to have to take over. I looked at Jack, feeling the fury of injustice flowing through my veins. "Sure you still want to be an investigative journalist?"

He looked at me, nodding firmly and wiping a trail of sweat from his cheek.

"Okay, we need to do a survey of the dining room and find out where Ferris is. You take left of the chandelier and I'll go right. We'll meet up later."

Jack nodded and started off. I forced my stride to be re-laxed, my gaze to search curiously instead of intensely. I saw Delia, her back to me in the corner. I spotted four other poker stars by the time I got to the far wall. I'd sent Jack in the direction of my table so I could avoid my parents but then I remembered he didn't know to look for Paul Pennington. As I made it halfway through the other side, I tried to put three tables between me and my parents but Elva's radar was apparently on high. She spun around in her chair, spotted me and stood up, waving, nearly knocking our waiter into the next table. "We're over here, Belinda!"

Smiling apologetically at all the people now staring at

me, I wove my way to my seat. Across about fifteen tables I could see Jack looking at me questioningly. Extracting myself gracefully from Elva was going to take time. I nodded at him to grab a seat. He responded with a look of sheer panic.

"Where have you been?" she demanded.

Dad stood, kissed my cheek and shot a look at Ben, who was forced to remove his hand from Stella's lap to stand. Ben, being Ben, flourished a bow too. Stella giggled. Ingrid's chair was empty. Callie's torso was listing side to side.

"I've been talking to friends," I answered, smoothing my napkin in my lap and trying to figure a way out of eating, which would show how worried I was—I never missed a meal, especially not one this delicious.

"Friends? What friends?" Mom demanded, not waiting for the answer before she soldiered on. "Other than the delay when that poor man went for a swim off the side of the boat, Howard and I have been having the most *fab* time. I learned that word today, fab, you like it?"

"You're cool, Ma," Ben put in.

"Anyway, I swore I would never play shuffleboard because that was for old fogies, but some cute young kids were playing so we decided to give it a whirl and I won the tournament, can you believe it? Shuffleboard Queen of the *Sea Gambler*, free pizza the whole voyage."

"Ma, the pizza is free anyway." Ben clarified, looking down at our appetizer for the evening, cold pumpkin soup.

"Oh? Guess that was a joke. Ha ha, I fell for it. After we celebrated my big win, we went and played strip twister."

"You're kidding?" I murmured, flushing with embarrassment at the thought.

"Oh don't be such a prude, Belinda," Elva admonished, snagging a spoonful of soup. "We just stripped to our swimsuits anyway, and then played a game of Marco Polo in the pool and finished up with some bingo. Dad nailed a b-i-n-g-o and pocketed a hundred twelve dollars!"

Howard had been nodding proudly since the mention of the pool game, looking quite pleased with himself. I wondered who in a bikini he got to tag in Marco Polo and where he tagged them with his eyes closed. I let it go. "You're rich, Dad."

Stella asked where Ingrid was. "She was with me until a few minutes ago," I answered. "I guess she ducked out to the restroom."

A man with security written all over him ducked his head in the dining room door. I watched as he surveyed a couple of tables with empty seats. Then he shook his head and let the door close again. Jack caught my eye and nodded toward Ingrid's chair. I shrugged. Ian's chair across the room was still empty too. Maybe they'd all decided to go for the free pizza but I doubted it. I watched the group at the table, laughing and carefree, and envied them. I knew just enough of the trouble on the ship to make me crazy and not enough to do anything to stop it.

When my mother paused to take a breath with her story about the ice carving class she'd taken, I finally found the opportunity to excuse myself. "Going to rendezvous with that slimy shrink from alien country?" Mom asked.

I sighed, kept my mouth shut and smiled as I pushed my chair in. There was no winning with Elva. I hurried out. Jack was a step ahead of me, grateful to get out of chatting with strangers, no doubt. He'd beat me out the dining room door, and I saw him waiting at the staircase. "N-now what?" he asked, mopping his forehead with a handkerchief.

Good question.

"I'd like to go see what they found at Mahdu's room,

but of course the cruise staff won't give us his cabin number," I mused.

"Let's go deck to deck, then," Jack suggested.

"We can, but I'm sure we'll have to listen closely. They won't be keeping the door open for all the passengers to see. Besides, whoever is watching the video cameras will see us trolling the halls."

"They might not realize it's the same t-two people on each floor if we do things like let your hair down, then put it back up on the top of your head. I'll take off my jacket. You wear my jacket."

I cocked my head at him. "You're sneaky—destined to be a top network news star."

Jack grinned and started up the stairs. We were on the second deck, which along with the third deck was activity and community space. Decks nine through twelve were pool, bar, restaurant and sports decks. So that left decks four through eight to search. I could barely keep up with Jack, even taking stairs two at a time. Damn Manolos. I paused to shed my precious sandals, laced them through my fingers and ran up the stairs to catch up.

At deck four—the Turn Deck—we paused for a second to catch our breath. We were in the dead center of the ship, with the balcony entrance to the theater and the game arcade to the right and cabins to our left. I tilted my head right and we started off. We heard and saw nothing suspicious, so doubled back in the other direction. A door opening to our right startled us into each other, but it was only an older woman with a walker who apologized as her door slid shut.

I suggested we take the elevator to deck eight just to keep anyone monitoring our activities guessing as to our preferred mode of transport and our destination. I wound my hair at the top of my head and donned his suit jacket. Jack rolled up his sleeves and stuck his tie in his pocket.

We repeated our search method with no luck then headed down to the seventh deck and then the sixth. On the River Deck, where my cabin was, we passed by a cabin at the other end of the hallway where I could hear several voices—two low and one high—in a quiet conversation. We kept walking but suddenly something clicked and I backtracked. I knew at least one of the voices sounded familiar. Jack raised his eyebrows. I knocked.

The door opened a crack. "Bee!" Ingrid exclaimed.

"Ingrid," I answered, standing on tiptoe to see around her, suddenly wishing I were six three instead of five foot nine. "What are you doing in there?"

"What? I work for you now, and I get no privacy?"

"That's not it," I said, thrown off balance. "It's just, you missed dinner."

"So, maybe I have something better to do."

I was terribly confused. "Is this Mahdu's room?"

She looked genuinely surprised. "No!"

"Can we come in for a minute?"

Ingrid hadn't noticed Jack standing against the wall but the "we" made her look. She blushed and stammered. "I . . . I don't think you're invited, are they gorgeous?" She pulled a tanned, sinewy male arm across her midriff. It could have belonged to any man but I suspected I'd seen it before.

"I thought I heard three voices, are you having a ménage à trois?

"Maybe." She arched her left eyebrow, likely unaware of a guilty look she slid at Jack. "And that means three not five."

As she clicked the door shut I swear I saw the pointy toe of a black cowboy boot. Was that lizard or snakeskin?

Jack's face was scrunched up so tight I was afraid he was going to cry. Suddenly he blew out a couple of breaths and said: "Let's k-k-keep l-l-looking."

Poor Jack. My instincts had told me he and Ingrid had

chemistry. I didn't know what she was doing now. But since I couldn't solve the mystery of my own love life, I decided to leave theirs alone too and focus on the easier mystery—who was after the Texas Hold 'Em players on board.

I put my hand on his shoulder and we finished our rounds of the deck. Nothing outside of Ingrid's rendezvous, which I didn't trust was really sexual, was out of the ordinary. It had the air of put-on about it, but, if so, what was she hiding? Was she conspiring against me and the other poker stars? Was she conspiring with the security chief in a cover-up? Was she meeting with a master web designer to spiff up my website? Or was she really making whoopee with the Marlboro Man, whose arm and toe I thought I'd recognized, and if so, why hide it from me?

Maybe she was just hiding it from Jack, but there again, why? She could have shut the door without hurting him with the sexual innuendo. And, there was my answer. Unless she was doing our trick of hiding things in plain sight, then she was covering something up.

"Who'd you find m-missing at dinner?" Jack asked, breaking into my thoughts.

"I didn't see Rhonda, Sam or Paul," I answered distractedly. I hadn't expected Kinkaid to be there, since she was staff and finalizing details of tonight's tournament. "I haven't told you about Paul, but he's a college kid who's way deep in debt, according to Ian and one of his college friends, desperate enough to do something drastic to get out of it."

Jack nodded. "Motive enough. I also noticed that s-silly little college girl, Amber, missing. But, of course, we have to accept the possibility that any one of the suspects present could be c-conspiring with others."

"Like Ingrid" went unsaid in the air between us. I sighed. I still trusted Ingrid, Lord knows why.

"I want to try one more thing," I told Jack as I reached

for the house phone on the table next to the staircase. "Mahdu Singh's cabin."

"One moment please."

Jack glanced at his watch. "You'd b-better hustle if you want to make the tournament."

I nodded and waited. It seemed to take an interminable time to connect. Jack tapped his watch face. I nodded. Finally, I heard a ring and a small young voice answered. "Hello?"

"Eria, I'm Bee Cooley. My friends and I were there when you came out of the dining room tonight before security took you away."

"Yes."

"Is there anyone there with you now?"

"Yes."

"First, you can call my cabin 5456 when you need to talk or need help, okay?"

"Okay."

"Now I just want to ask you a couple of questions—"

A finger reached around me and broke the connection, and grabbed my arm in a light but firm hold. "Miss Cooley," nameless security guard number two announced. "You are late to the tournament. They are waiting on you to deal. We will be happy to escort you."

Suppressing the shiver that threatened under the gestapo tactic, I shook my arm loose decisively. "I don't need an escort, but thank you."

"We insist on showing you proper hospitality." He grabbed hold again.

I shook loose again. "And I insist on politely refusing it. Come on, Jack."

The two remained three feet behind us all the way down to the second deck where the ballroom was located. Kinkaid was pacing in a strapless pink flouncy organdy dress that made her look like a cupie doll. "There you are! Don't you know how to tell time, Bee Cooley? We have to go hunting you down so you don't miss your chance to make history and not to mention a little money."

Sure. That's exactly why you interrupted my conversation with Mahdu's girlfriend. "You could've tried to give me a call," I put in slyly. I made a show of looking at her waist. "Oops, where is your phone? I don't think I've ever seen you without a phone."

"This outfit really isn't phone friendly, now is it?" she answered testily.

Kinkaid was near impossible to read so I couldn't tell whether I'd made an impression or not. She could have her phone case back by now or not know it was missing. Or maybe it wasn't her jeweled case after all.

Argh.

"Have you had a massage or facial lately?" I blurted out. *What? Did I have a death wish?*

"I did, in fact, this morning. One of the perks of working on a cruise ship. Could you tell I was glowing?" Kinkaid asked, primping—touching her fuzzy hair, tracing her jaw and striking an alluring pose with her lumpy body.

"Of course." I smiled. I was absolutely no good at this Sherlock Holmes business.

"Who's this?" Kinkaid asked finally noticing Jack. "Your new amour I've been hearing about?"

"Of course," I answered to Jack's surprised face. He'd obviously had Ingrid on his mind but took my lie in stride, smiling and wrapping his arm around my waist. "Meet Jack Smack. Jack is a reporter for *Cadillac of Poker* magazine." I didn't tell her he was a freelancer working for them. That would have given him much less mojo.

"Really? Well, I have to treat you special then, don't I? For two reasons," she said, throwing me a bone, because I knew she was entertaining Jack for the publicity for the boat not for my sake.

Jack looked back at me, wide-eyed, as Kinkaid led him away. I threw him a thumbs-up for strength. I knew I was temporarily losing my Watson but it would be worth it if he could keep it together and we got an "in" with the cruise officials. There was a cover-up and I wanted to know if it was purely image oriented—which I could understand if not condone—or whether there was something more nefarious at work.

Nineteen

♦ ♣ ♥ ♠

Upon registering with the tournament for the second day, I was told positions were assigned by a computer. The girls consulted a laptop, and pointed at table four, seat nine. I saw a handful of empty seats besides mine. "Are we still waiting on others?"

"No, there are some no-shows from last night," one of the tournament hostesses, Claudia, informed me. "But we were given a heads-up so we know to start without them."

The gallery was packed. The boundary tape had been moved forward so more people could see more poker. I walked past to a couple of whoops and a "Bee Cool" called out here and there. Four women in "Poker Babes" T-shirts bounced up and down and waved. An arm stuck out and stopped me. I looked down at Ringo and smiled. "Hey, how's your cruise going?"

"Fun! Bee, where're your Gargoyles?"

My heart stopped a moment. My face flushed. "Oh no.

I'm an idiot. But you knew that. Things have been so wild this afternoon, I forgot them in my cabin. Again."

He reached into the inside pocket of his jacket and extracted a pair of Dolce & Gabbana women's sunglasses, black oversize square lenses, a big silver D&G on a slant on the sides.

"Why would you have these just hanging around?"

"Because I knew you would forget the others," he admitted shyly.

As I took the glasses from him, inspiration gave me a way to thank my Canadian pal for his endless tournament-saving sunglass supply. "Hey, Ringo, I have a website now."

He nodded. "It's totally cool. I just saw it this morning."

Apparently everyone on the boat but me had seen it. "I'd like to ask you a huge favor. Would you write a regular column for my site on how the sunglasses make the Hold 'Em player?"

I thought he might pass out with excitement. He blew breaths in/out, in/out, bounced on the balls of his feet and rubbed his hands together. "You're kidding, right?"

"I'm not kidding, Ringo."

"But I really don't have any authority, no real expertise."

"Who has poker-player sunglass expertise, anyway? Knowledge of what's out there, what kinds players prefer and why. You can interview players if you want, or I can hook you up with a psychologist for what the type of sunglasses you wear says about you and your game."

"Wow!"

"I can't pay much but—"

"P-pay? The honor of being asked is payment enough," Ringo stammered.

"Oh no, Ringo, I won't agree to that. What I was thinking was a small percentage of what I make playing Hold 'Em." I realized Bee Cool was becoming a sort of corporation, as

I sold shares of myself in return for services. Weird, but it just might work.

"Oh, that's too generous."

"Of which of us? If I don't win, you are working for free, remember." Out of the corner of my eye, I saw Kinkaid bearing down on us. I patted Ringo's shoulder. "We'll work out the details later. Before you leave tonight, leave me your cabin number."

He nodded bigger than a bobble head doll, jiggling loose his eyeglasses that he pushed back up his nose. "You got it."

I strode on quickly and made it to my seat before Kinkaid caught up with me. "I'm sorry to keep everyone waiting," I told the dealer as I extracted Frank's lucky marker from my purse. He waved off my apology and directed everyone to introduce themselves, skipping me. I broke in with, "Hi, I'm Belinda—"

"That won't be necessary," the dealer said, shuffling. "We all know you."

"But why?"

"Besides the fact that you started the tournament yesterday?"

Whoops. Forgot about that. Duh.

"Besides that, you're just the hottest woman pro playing right now, and you KO'd Steely Stan and we all loved to hate that guy." A couple of the men and one woman at the table murmured in agreement.

Okay then. I guess no one was mourning the loss of Stan at the felt tables.

"The only thing that would make you better would be a couple more big tournament wins and a movie star boyfriend," the dealer informed me. "Cuz today a lot of what's hot is image and you've got that in spades."

Having all that lavish praise only hexed me. I had to fold the first five hands with sorry pocket cards. A couple of the more aggressive players were eyeballing me like I was only image and no brain. It might have worked out for the best since I'd been afraid they'd be on their guard after what the dealer had said. I'd already decided to lose one early hand to further drop defenses around the table.

I got the chance in the next hand when I was dealt pocket jacks, both red. This hand seemed to be my nemesis. I could clean up with pocket nines and tank with pocket jacks. The table was loaded with five decent, thinking players, one jackal and two calling stations. Most of the table had something, if not much, all simply calling with one fold. I was to the right of the button and so in the best position to play a little looser. I raised before The Flop which earned three more folds and four calls. The Flop went five of clubs, Ace of hearts, Queen of hearts. I was already potentially beat by a building royal flush, or two higher pair. I should have folded. Instead I rode out the rest of the hand, calling through a Fourth Street eight of hearts and a Fifth Street five of spades. Ironically, I was beat, but by a full house fives and eights by one of the calling stations. I wouldn't have guessed that. But beat was beat, and I achieved my goal. The table certainly respected me less, which meant I could win more because my bet wouldn't chase others out of hands, thus building the pots.

I watched Kinkaid filtering through the room, outwardly relaxed, except for the frequent checking of her house phone in her hand, jeweled case nowhere to be seen. She got a call and disappeared.

The next hour I wondered if I wouldn't disprove Richard's theory. I'd almost been killed today, and I couldn't catch two decent pocket deals to save my Hold 'Em life. I won a couple of hands and was up five thousand but it wouldn't be enough to hang with the big boys later. It was like chipping away at Mount Rushmore. Finally, one of the calling stations, who'd been drawn down, was eliminated in the jackal's all in bluff on a face card board. Fortunately I'd folded on Fourth Street with pocket Aces. Sometimes, painful as it was, that had to be done. Good thing too, because the jackal hit a royal flush on The River. Lucky.

He'd be even more full of himself now, and easier to catch as long as I got some cards every now and then. I had an eight of hearts, ten of hearts in my pocket and had to go with my gut. I called the big blind and waited.

Kinkaid reappeared, looking a bit frazzled, sweat wetting the hair at the nape of her neck. She'd avoided my table so far tonight, but was so distracted, she walked right past me. I grabbed a wad of her skirt and brought her to a stop.

She smiled at the table and leaned in to me as the jackal raised two hundred on an Ace of clubs, nine of hearts, Jack of hearts Flop. "Where is Mahdu?"

"That's none of your concern, Miss Cooley. And I hope you haven't opened your big mouth," she whispered while flashing a counterfeit smile around the table.

The dealer reminded me it was my bet. It made me uncomfortable to try to draw to a straight, but instincts are what helped me win the Big Kahuna. I had to trust them now. Still gripping Kinkaid's skirt against the arm of my chair just below the table, I pushed out a conservative raise, scaring two players out of the hand.

Jack of hearts fell on The Turn. The first two bets were a raise and a reraise. We were headed for an all in.

Kinkaid tried to struggle unobtrusively against my skirt hold. "Are you okay, Miss Kinkaid?" the dealer asked, his head cocked.

"Fine," she smiled tightly. "My skirt just seems to be caught on Miss Cooley's chair."

Sneaky. I could out sneak her though. I learned from the best snake I knew, my twin. I faked a gasp, looking down in surprise. "Oh no, Miss Kinkaid, let me try to help you get it loose."

She tugged, and I tugged back, all the while keeping the telling action under the table. "Where is Eria?"

Kinkaid, her face growing red with her exertions, looked at me blankly. *Tug.*

"Mahdu's girlfriend? I imagine the poor young girl is easier to control than Delia Santobella. What have you done with her?"

The dealer forced my bet. I called, which was expensive enough.

Kinkaid's face darkened. *Tug. Tug.* "Miss Kharton is not feeling well. The ship's doctor is examining her now. I'm guessing she will have to be put ashore in Cozumel tomorrow for a flight home."

The jackal, chip leader, at the table, went all in. Six of the nine of us joined him, which left the six of us with no chips left in front of us. Scary.

"What about Mahdu?"

"He'll turn up like Rick did, I'm sure." *Tug. Tug, tug, tug.*

"Or like Rawhide didn't," I murmured as a Queen of hearts fell on The River. "Or floating, like the insurance dude did."

I let her skirt go to sweep up my chips before the jackal decided to eat them he was so mad. The five eliminated players rose in their chairs, one grumbling that I played like an Internet player. One shook my hand with congratulations, the others offered well wishes from a distance as they looked longingly at their decent, actually winnable, hands that had been beaten with instinct and lots of luck.

Once free, Kinkaid leaned in to me as she smoothed her skirt. "Thank you so much for your help, Miss Cooley," she said aloud, then dropped her voice to a whisper. "And if you try to help any more in places you aren't needed, I will see you get an airline schedule as well."

With a frilly wave and genuine smile that made me want to shiver worse than her false one, Kinkaid continued her rounds. I didn't know what to think except that I was on a floating prison with a Hold 'Em player–eating monster within.

"**You** *could* **leave, but then you'd have to tell Mom** and Dad. Mom would freak out, Dad would want to keep you under some kind of twenty-four hour guard for the rest of your life and they would have to leave the cruise too, of course. Then, Stella, Ingrid and Callie would have to go too. Me. Think of all the plane tickets you'd have to buy." We were on a ten-minute break and I'd found one of the two people on board the ship I could both trust and talk to about the situation. Jack was not around so I was left with Ben. It was almost scarier than the homicidal maniac on board. Ben leaned over the railing and flipped the toothpick out of his mouth and into the sea. "Wouldn't it be cool if that speared a fish down there?"

"Ben, please try to focus. How come I can't wedge you off a subject you choose but when *I* want to talk about something, you can't stay on topic for two consecutive sentences?" I demanded impatiently.

He turned to me, leaning one elbow on the railing, looking very miffed. "Well, it went in at the right angle to nail a fish if it was going by just then."

"Impressive." I pushed off the railing. "I'm going to find Jack." And by the way, where was Frank when I needed him, yet again?

"I thought the slimy dude you were hanging with is named Ian? Who's Jack? A new boy toy?" He winked.

I fixed him with a dead-eyed stare.

Undaunted as usual, Ben smacked himself on the forehead. "Oh, Jack. Is that the nervous dweeb?"

"Jack is a journalist."

"For the *Freaks-R-Us Times*?" Ben chuckled, amusing

himself as usual. I made a mental note to keep him away from Jack. Ben would totally destroy his newfound confidence.

"Jack is a friend, get off his case," I warned, blowing out a sigh. I turned and strode toward the glass doors leading back into the interior of the ship. Ben grabbed my ponytail. "Ouch!"

"Wimp."

"Jerk."

"Look, Bee Bee, you've got to understand that the cruise ship wants to keep a lid on the disappearances to avoid a mass panic on board, hence the quiet investigation."

"If they're investigating at all!" I interrupted.

"I'm sure they are, and I'm sure they'll step it up once we dock. I wouldn't get too paranoid about that. Now I do agree you ought to protect yourself, so make sure you're never alone. If you aren't going to be with Slimeball, or Freakafellow, or Ingrid who could whip anybody's butt, then call me and I will sacrifice and hang with you a bit."

"Speaking of Ingrid, what *is* your relationship? I'm confused."

"Me too. We're friends," he shrugged and looked off at the barely waning moon rising over the horizon.

"Come on, Ben," I said. "No woman is your friend."

He shrugged. "What can I say, she didn't want to play hide and seek with Utopia."

I rolled my eyes at his favorite moniker for his manhood. Ben winked. "I told her she needed her head examined because no one with ovaries had ever refused that offer."

"How did you meet her?"

"Actually, she's a friend of Frank's."

"My Frank?" I blurted out, then corrected myself. "I mean, Frank Gilbert?"

"The very same." Ben nodded. "I looked Frank up about

a month ago when I was in L.A. for a pharmaceutical conference. We met then."

"You looked Frank up? How do you know where to look? Where does he live? What does his house look like?"

"Oh, get your panties out of a wad, Bee Bee, don't be so literal. I called him and we met for drinks at a bar."

"He's drinking again?" I could feel my knuckles whitening as I gripped my clutch tighter.

Ben shrugged. "He had a Corona. No big deal."

"All alcohol is a big deal for an alcoholic," I preached to Ben. "Next time take him to Starbucks, you fool."

"Come on, Bee Bee, a beer's cheaper than Starbucks. I was treating."

I wanted to strangle him but it would do no good. His four and a half brain cells could live without air for longer than I could squeeze.

"So how are he and Ingrid friends?" I said, evenly, considering my heart was thundering, my palms were sweating and I couldn't swallow. Ingrid was gorgeous, young, and smarter than I'd given her credit for being even yesterday. I couldn't blame Frank if they were very, very close friends.

"I don't know," Ben frowned impatiently. "Men don't ask questions like that."

"Okay, what kind of questions do you ask?"

"How about: 'Can I pork her without pissing you off?'"

"Charming. What did he answer?"

"That a woman isn't a side of bacon, but if I found some manners I could ask her out on a date because Ingrid could take care of herself better than any woman he'd ever seen."

Why did that particular compliment make me see red worse than knowing they were lovers? I guess because I could blow a dalliance off, but admiration usually makes a longer-lasting impression.

Why did I care? *Frank stood you up on the cruise,*

remember, you idiot. Let he and Ingrid have a mutual admiration society. So what.

"You are so jealous," Ben hooted, doing a little dance. "Your face is all scrunched up and you look a thousand years old."

The bells started ringing over the PA system, calling the players back from the break. I forced myself to focus. "So how did Ingrid and her friends end up on the cruise?"

"Frank started talking about it while she was there. I was still trying to get in her pants and so I said I could fix it so they could have a cabin. The Bee Cool agent thing was a flash of inspiration. Kill two birds with one stone."

I shot him a loaded look. "Considering the direction this cruise is going, you might actually accomplish that."

Twenty

When the tournament resumed, a tournament host-
ess spread the remaining four players at our table in empty
seats around the room. It was advantageous for me, since
the jackal guy was out for blood. He looked seriously dis-
enchanted with Bridget and tried to convince her to move
one of the players at my new table to another so he could
sit with me.

"Sir, you can get together with her later."

I laughed because that was the last thing on his mind.
"The only thing he'd like to get together are his fingers
around my throat," I told Bridget.

She grinned.

He glared and stalked off to his assigned table. Introductions went around. This dealer wasn't into idle chitchat
and spread the cards quickly. A King of diamonds, Queen
of spades stared back at me from the hole. I hated it when
this happened. It seemed like such a good hand but it rarely
won for me. I might be able to play it smarter if I knew the

table but I was coming in completely blind to the players'
tendencies. So far I pegged one woman with a dwindling
chip stack for a lucky neophyte (it takes one to know one)
already giving in to nerves as she bounced one leg vio-
lently under the table, one grandma who by the comfortable look of her cleaned up on the felt every day at her
retirement community, three men of varying degrees of middle age who probably frequented Internet games, a young
punk kid whose face was hidden under a black ball cap and
behind huge, mirrored Hell Cats who was chanting verses
from the Koran under his breath, and the two sitting at the
blinds—a nerdy twentysomething man who had a violent
twitch in his left cheek and a man about my age with a five
o'clock shadow who kept picking at his incisors with a silver
toothpick. The man wearing an old-style Humphrey Bogart
hat and a white shirt sitting at the dealer button had been fid-
dling with his stack since I'd sat down. Now he looked up at
me and smiled. Uh-oh. Ian Reno. Damn. This was going to
be awkward. I forced myself to ignore him. If I didn't, I was
sure I'd lose.

The dealer urged me to bet. I was just ahead of the blinds,
unfortunately, so had to either fold or jump into the pot.
I jumped with a small raise just to gauge the others behind
me. Four of the six folded, including Ian and the two
women. A check round cleared the way for The Flop.

It came three of clubs, eight of diamonds, Queen of
hearts. One was good for me, the rest muck for everyone remaining, apparently, because no one bet the round. Ian was
watching me intently through his mirrored lenses.

I saw Kinkaid walk into the room, spy me immediately
and roam the other side. I wondered if she'd fulfill her threat
if I pushed her. I thought of the note . . . stop investigating or
I'd be gone too. I assumed gone meant dead, or pitched into
the Gulf, but maybe gone just meant off the ship. Hmm.
I thought I needed to see Miss Kinkaid's handwriting.

Jack of hearts landed on Fourth Street. The small blind raised a thousand which made all of us think he was working a royal flush. I called along with the rest of those remaining at the table. Ian stared.

And then came my scare card, an Ace of hearts. It might complete his royal flush or more likely gave someone hanging in with an Ace-high kicker enough to beat my pair of Queens. The tepid raise of five hundred by the big blind—twitch, twitch—could mean he was the one with the Ace. Still, it wasn't strong enough, I thought, or maybe he was scared of the guy with the royal flush who was next to bet. Peeking at my cleavage as he pushed his chips forward, the small blind went in for another five hundred, which to me didn't say much. If I had a royal flush, I'd be going all in. But a raise could be the equivalent for this guy, who might be a calling station. I held my breath and tried to hear Frank's advice in my head. "Go with your instincts" is all I could hear. So I did. Ian shook his head as I raised another thousand, knocking everyone into a fold except the big blind. We raised and reraised for another five thousand until it was time to show our cards.

Big Blind, whose twitch had escalated to painful-looking proportions, had a pair of Jacks.

Small Blind groaned and frantically picked his front teeth which made me wonder what he'd had. He didn't show us, though. He was the one I'd have to beat in the end, I guessed. Conservative players were always tough. Ian had removed his Ray-Ban aviators and looked at me like I was someone he'd never met before, but someone he definitely wanted to meet.

At the next break, which Kinkaid announced would be a half hour, we were invited to an apertif and cappuccino reception in an adjoining room. Our table was down to six, the neophyte, punk and silver toothpicker eliminated. Rhonda the Ruler had just been placed across from me when the bell rang.

Ian left his hat and sunglasses at the table and came around to my chair, pulling it out for me. I introduced Ian and Rhonda and felt an undercurrent of—what?—perhaps dislike between them as Rhonda's lips drew in a line and Ian only nodded once, not his normal effusive self. Shrugging, I blew it off, as Rhonda was more uptight every time I saw her and Ian probably was a little torqued that I had beaten him at every hand but one.

"Would you like to join us?" I asked Rhonda.

She shook her head sharply. "I hate coffee and don't drink. I'm going to the ladies' room."

"You're a conservative player," I observed as Ian took my arm. "Which is often smart."

"You are an enigma who always wins," he said with a smile.

"Oh not always, just when I'm lucky."

"I am fascinated at how you use your mind, your heart, your gut in varying degrees with seemingly each bet. How do you decide which to listen to?"

"I couldn't tell you I have a formula. You'd have to get inside me to figure it out and let me know."

"Maybe I'll just do that," Ian said, with a small smile and an introspective look in his eyes as we entered the reception. He paused at a waiter to order me a crème de menthe. Good thing I liked them. He chose a Baileys Irish Cream for himself.

Suddenly I felt like I did when I was walking down our hallway from our cabin—as if attention was focused on me from out of my line of sight. The sensation seemed misplaced here in a room full of people. I looked around and saw Ringo standing in line for a cappuccino. He waved. I didn't think it had been my sunglass pal giving me the heebie-geebies but I shrugged and walked toward him. A cruise employee, standing near Ringo, ducked his head and walked toward the door. Something about his walk seemed familiar. Was he the same employee I'd seen talking to the Marlboro Man earlier? I picked up my pace, Ian jogged to keep up. "What's the hurry?"

"I want to introduce you to my friend, Ringo." The cruise employee was almost to the door.

"Is Ringo going to run away if you don't catch him?" Ian asked.

"Wait!" I called to the employee, who didn't hear, or didn't want to wait. He disappeared out the door.

"Are you okay? Who were you calling to?" Ringo asked, putting a concerned hand on my arm as we made it to him.

"Long story," I answered.

Ian and Ringo both gave me raised eyebrow looks. I introduced them. "This is the psychologist I told you about, Ringo. Maybe he'll agree to consult on the column."

"What column?"

"Bee's asked me to do a column about sunglasses and poker on her website. It's a really hot topic right now, the old-timers against wearing them versus the moderns who wouldn't be caught dead at the table without them, so it should be interesting. Annie Duke says to ban sunglasses from all casinos. Phil Ivey claims to have lost a $100,000 pot because he wore sunglasses and consequently misread his hand. There's a new faction claiming that sunglasses dehumanize the game—make it more like an Internet game and less like an old brick-and-mortar game."

"That could be true," Ian said, well warm to the subject. I glanced out the door to see if my employee had reappeared. Nope.

Ian continued, "Eighty percent of human emotion is

translated through the eyes. But that's why liars often make great poker players." He smiled wryly.

Ringo put in, "Some players think headphones work better than sunglasses, but you have to ask, what's the purpose, to filter outside stimuli or block your own tells?"

"You're right, headphones would work for personal focus. Sunglasses are worn to hide tells and perhaps see more tells as you can stare at someone without them knowing. Sunglasses do block some tells—the classic worry that your pupils will dilate with a good pocket. But I have a theory that often when they are worn as a 'shield' they make the wearer complacent, which leaves them open to other tells if he's not careful."

"Like what?"

"A perfect example is tonight at our table," I broke in. "Everyone but a grandma wore sunglasses and she might as well have since she looked at everyone like they were Johnny being bad. Anyhow, we had a guy who sweat only on his upper lip when he bluffed, a man with a twitch in his cheek that escalated when he realized he'd overbet and a woman whose leg bounced so hard from fish nerves I wondered if she'd be able to walk away from the table. Sunglasses didn't help them."

"They might have helped someone else at the table, though," Ian offered.

I shook my head. "No. I knew you were staring at me and not those chips. I felt it the whole time."

Ian looked impressed instead of caught. "The ability to intuit—that may be the new advantage in the modern sunglass-wearing poker culture. Belinda's ability to feel to believe instead of see to believe makes her hard to beat. I'd like to be able to prove that theory."

I shook my head. "Women are better at it than men, they should win every time they catch cards."

Ian shook his head. "Women need to get over being intimidated. They might use their sex to manipulate a man at the table, but not all use their intuition to outfox them at their game."

Out of the corner of my eye I saw a man in Wranglers carrying a cup of coffee stride through the crowd sipping their after-dinner cocktails. Ack! I spun around. The Marlboro Man was headed out the far door on the other side of the room.

"Gotta go," I threw over my shoulder as I shoved my crème de menthe into Ian's hand and took off through the crowded room.

"Belinda!" Ian demanded.

"Bee?" Ringo called.

I made it out the door, too many seconds after my quarry, but I saw him head down the hallway then into the casino. My silly Manolos were not helping me gain ground. I paused just inside the casino doorway, leaning against the wall as I slipped them off my feet, opened my clutch, drew its strap out and slipped it over my shoulder. This was inconvenient during an important chase. If I was going to keep getting caught up in this Nancy Drew business, I was going to have to rethink my shoes. I stared at the shiny stilettos in my hand as I ran on bare feet. They were so pretty. I don't think I could do ugly sensible shoes even for a good cause. I didn't mind going barefoot every now and then.

The casino was as raucous as the Hold 'Em room was focused. I passed a man who hit three oranges on a slot and grabbed me for a dosey-do. Marlboro Man was passing the craps tables and almost to the exit. I broke loose and ran. Why hadn't I asked his name? At least I could try to scream over the din. As I passed a roulette table, a woman saw the ball hit her number, and she screamed. I covered my ears and ran faster.

A security dweeb grabbed my arm just as I was about to make it out the doorway. "Excuse me, ma'am. Slow down."

"Yes, sir." I tried to shake my arm loose. He held fast. I could just barely see Marlboro Man disappearing out the glass doors to the outside deck. "Please let me go."

"Can I ask you why you are in such a big hurry?" He was scrutinizing me, for possible drunkenness, theft, who knew what. I tried not to imagine that Kinkaid had me on some sort of cruise ship OnStar and had radioed for me to be stopped. "Can I help you?" he asked, meaning, "Can I help you get out of the view of all these content passengers, you freak?"

I remembered what Frank had told me about all fake cops being allergic to domestic arguments. "Yes, you can! My husband is such a jerk. I just can't believe he would do this to me. It's so unfair. Let me tell you what he did—"

He'd directed me out the casino and into the quiet hallway the moment I said "husband." "That's okay, ma'am. You go find your husband and work it out."

"Humph. Big help you are!" I fussed.

He disappeared quickly back into the casino. I ran out the double glass doors and was assaulted by the strong sea wind and nearly ran into Sam Hyun, who was apparently trying to come back into the ship. Muttering an apology, I noticed the ship was moving a lot faster than it had during the day and wondered if that was by design—cruise along slowly during the day so everyone has a nice leisurely voyage and haul ass at night to get where we needed to go. Sounded like the way I worked on ad campaigns. As Sam pushed his way through the doors behind me, I looked right and left and could only discern in the half light from the ship's interior two figures to the left and a single figure to the right. I went right and found the figure to be a woman, crying and looking off at the moon. She ignored me, which was convenient because I could turn and run back the way

I'd come without being polite. I ran to the end of the promenade and encountered no one. I'd missed him again! I was about to turn around when a thump on my head hurt for a second before everything went dark.

Twenty-one

♦ ♣ ♥ ♠

"Who are you?" I breathed as I looked up into the face of the Marlboro Man who, as far as I could tell, was carrying me in the dark.

He smiled and took a moment to answer. "Just think of me as your guardian angel."

"Angels don't hit people on the head." I winced as my hand went instinctively to my throbbing noggin that had been assaulted twice in twelve hours. First tortured by duct tape and second by . . .

"What did you hit me with anyway?"

He chuckled now and shook his head, muttering under his breath, "He warned me she was a pistol." Then, louder he said, "I didn't hit you."

"Who's he?"

"You're not making any sense," he said. "Who's *he*?"

"That's what I asked you!" I insisted, squirming a bit in his arms. Ooo, he had nice, firm abs.

He cleared his throat. "You have a concussion, just take it easy. Everything is going to be a bit hazy for a while." He kicked open a door and we were in some kind of bland utility staircase.

"If you didn't conk me on the head for chasing you, then what happened?"

"Why are you chasing me?" he asked, descending the stairs.

"Because you're always there when something is going on and it's a little fishy. You were there in line when I was checking in and when my mom accused me of having saggy pants."

"Your pants looked fine," he assured me.

"You say that now, not in front of my mother, making you a coward." I paused; he grinned. "Then, you were there at lunch when I got some weird threatening note."

"What note?"

"Like you don't know. Anyway, it said stop snooping or I'm gone."

His face got hard. If Tom Cruise could act, anyone could. I continued, unaffected. "And then you were there when I barely escaped death."

"You mean when you were running around naked with seaweed and mud all over you?"

"It was a life and death situation. And, I need to return your shirt."

"Don't worry about the shirt."

He wasn't even huffing and we'd traveled several floors. Or rather, he'd carried me several floors. I was impressed.

"Where are we going—to the ship doctor?"

"I don't think so, you're better off on your own. I leave you there you might end up in a Cozumel hospital tomorrow."

"Smart man," I said, but his words gave me a chill.

He opened a door and we were in a familiar hallway. He

stopped and produced my purse. "Do you want to find your key?"

I reached for the clutch and felt the strap was broken. I dangled it in front of him. "What happened?"

"Broken during your altercation, I guess."

"With whom?"

"Wish I knew."

I handed over the keycard and he let us into my cabin, pulling back the covers and easing me down.

"I think your roommate can help you off with your clothes later."

"You'd know if she could, because you spent the afternoon with her."

His mouth twisted in a wry smile. "You are very sure of yourself. But you're wrong about that."

Dammit, I believed him, but how many pairs of black something-skin cowboy boots could there be on board a summer Caribbean cruise ship? He busied himself with putting ice into a towel and pressing it to my head.

I shook my head in confusion as I took over the compress. I was beginning to feel hazy. "I don't understand why you want to help me."

"That's the way it's gotta stay. Some things in life you just have to accept. I know the cell phone service doesn't work out here well, but call this cabin number if you get in a bind and can leave a message. With two passengers missing and one overboard dead don't go around the ship alone anymore. Buddy system. Promise?" He handed me a card with a different cabin number from the one I'd discovered Ingrid in earlier today. Darn. So I still didn't know who he really was. The guy who went off the side drowned, huh? Uh-oh, things were getting very fuzzy.

"Wh-what's your name?" I slurred as I drifted off.

* * *

"*H*ello, passengers."

I woke to the sound of the intercom. I pulled the covers over my head and listened. "This is Captain Santiago at the bridge this morning. I hope everyone is enjoying the Hold 'Em tournament and side cash games as well as our casino. We promise gambling second to none on this the world's first poker ship. It's been quite exciting, with a lot of big money winners. Remember you can get credit on your winnings at the cashier, just not the cash until we dock back in Galveston. We try to make it easier for you. Now, we will be docking in Cozumel in a few hours. Many of you early risers can see the shore already. We have to issue a warning to you as per United States and Mexican authorities this morning. Unfortunately, they have asked everyone to remain on board the ship if at all possible. As many of you know, political unrest and drug violence have made the country quite unstable. Over the past two days, political protestors have targeted tourist destinations to make their cause known to the government. Hence the places you would normally go when at port will be mobbed with protestors who can get out of hand. We want every-one to enjoy this vacation and we have lots to do on board. However, if you have signed up for a ship-sponsored ex-cursion, we will still take you ashore if you wish—under guard. Let the tour director know as soon as possible only if you wish to participate in your excursion. All others will be assumed to be cancelled. Have a terrific day, and good luck on the felt!"

Nice. I was a prisoner on the ship where I wasn't some-one's favorite person. For a moment I felt sorry for myself. Most people had pleasant, relaxing vacations. I had vaca-tions where I ended up in jail, at the morgue, finding body parts in a Dumpster, looking down the barrel of a 9mm Glock, blindfolded and nearly thrown out the window, conked on the head in the dark, diverted for a hurricane and hindered by political unrest. I couldn't blame it all on poker, because the jail thing had been years ago with Ben in Bermuda. Hmm. It was Ben, not poker, that was the common denominator. Note to self: don't go on any more vacations with brother.

Elva would be ticked. She'd been looking forward to hiking the Mayan ruins for months. Too bad. She'd have to win another shuffleboard tournament or carve an ice goose instead.

The phone rang. I reached out of the covers, picked up the receiver and brought it under the comforter with me. "Yes?"

"We're going to hike Chicken Iza."

"It's *Chichén* Itzá, Mom."

"Whatever. I'm scaling that puppy."

"No you're not, Mom."

"Yes. I am, dear. I am not calling for my daughter's permission. I am calling to see if you're still coming. The tour director needs a head count."

I shivered. Terrible visual with that one. "Why? So they know how many stakes to bring so the insurgents can walk around with your tourist heads instead of signs in protest?"

"Very funny, dear. We're going to have armed guards. I promise to carry my secret weapon—the pepper spray you gave me. I swear this will be safer than walking through downtown Houston at night."

Well, she might have me on that one. "Mom, why don't you just stay on board and climb the rock wall or ride the zip line?"

"Been there, done that, Belinda, on day one. Now are you going or not?"

I sighed. I really needed to do a thousand other things, including getting Hans to show me the video from the deck where I was conked last night, pressuring Kinkaid into stepping up the investigation and finding Eria to get her story about Mahdu's disappearance, but I couldn't let Mom and Dad go to their deaths alone. "Is Ben going?"

"Of course not! He's afraid he'll be kidnapped and held for ransom. He and Stella are playing pool poker all day instead."

Anything was better than that.

"Okay, Mom. I'll go," I mumbled, thinking I could find a way while ashore to get a hold of U.S. authorities in Mexico and notify them of the disappearances and the dead man overboard.

"Great! We're meeting the tour guide and armed guards on the dock as soon as we can get off the ship. See you there in a couple of hours!"

Wow. Sounded like a blast. The right side of my head was throbbing from the mystery wallop, and the left side was burning from the duct tape torture. I needed drugs. I pulled the whole phone in with me and called Ben.

"I need drugs," I moaned when he answered.

"I'll be right there," he answered.

I threw back the covers and saw Amazonian Ingrid standing in the middle of the room, arms crossed over her chest, tapping her toe, glaring. "I can't work for someone who uses drugs."

I raised my eyebrows, slid my legs over the side of the bed and sat up. Ouch. My neck was killing me. Cradling the phone in my lap, I dialed again. "Bring the hard stuff," I croaked before hanging up.

"What is it?" Ingrid demanded, infuriated. "Ice? Cocaine?"

I shook my head, rose stiffly and shuffled to the bathroom with Ingrid breathing down my neck. I grabbed the door knob and tried to pull it closed, but she was in the way. "Crack?"

"Ingrid, I'll tell you what I'll crack if you don't let me close the door."

Stunned, she stepped back. I splashed my face with water and heard the knock at the door. I opened the bathroom door to see Ingrid opening the cabin door to Ben, who held up an array of small packages. Ingrid grabbed his arm and pulled him in.

"Happy to see me, are you, Ingrid? I knew you'd come to your senses. Let's get rid of my sister and get down to it."

Ingrid was looking at the little packages of painkillers in Ben's hand. "These are pharmaceutical samples," she said, stating the obvious, yet leaning against the wall in shock.

"Very good, Ingrid," Ben said, throwing me a look that said "psycho!"

"Ingrid thought I was a meth freak," I explained, fingering the boxes. "Which one is best for torturous neck pain, searing scalp pain and large-lump-on-head pain?"

Ben plucked out one and handed it to me. I retrieved a water glass from the bar and filled it in the sink, gratefully sucking down the capsule.

"So why are you so banged up?" Ben asked. "Kinky sex with that slimeball you're hanging with?"

"Ian and I are just friends."

"So are Ingrid and I, but wild animal lovemaking is only a word away. I'm guessing Ian is about at that place too."

Ingrid and I shared a grimace. "*All* men are at that place," Ingrid murmured.

"Listen," I said, "Ian doesn't have anything to do with my feeling like I've been pulled through a knothole backwards. I was attacked twice yesterday—in the spa and then out on deck during the aperitif reception."

"I wondered why they suspended the tournament for the night," Ben observed, gingerly investigating the bump on my head. He actually looked concerned. Amazing. "You think it's because you are a poker star or are you sticking your nose where it doesn't belong again?"

"What do you mean, *again*? If I hadn't stuck it there last time you'd be a goner—might I remind you, in an especially painful and sick way."

Ingrid raised her eyebrows at that. Ben shrugged.

"It's a good thing you're getting off the ship with Mom and Dad today, Bee Bee. Maybe the ship security will get to the bottom of this weirdness by the time you're back on board."

"We can hope, but I doubt it. They seem more enthused about covering up the disappearances than finding out who's behind them. As for the poor investigator, no telling what excuse they will come up with for his demise."

"Hey, another reason it's good you're outta here for the day is that maybe Slimeball will find someone else to play with."

"Why does everyone think Ian is slimy?"

"Because compared to Frank-Mr.-Rough-Around-the-Edges, he is," Ben stated.

Ingrid turned away but I saw her small smile. Gut twist. That reminded me. "By the way, Ingrid, how come you didn't tell me you are Frank's friend?"

"Is that important?" she asked innocently, face in closet, reviewing my fashion options for the day. I hated to tell her but I thought the saggy butt capris were going to be the only way to go if I were scaling crumbling rock structures in a hundred humid degrees.

"It's that important to me," I said defiantly.

"Okay," she said, turning from the closet with an impossibly short strapless sundress and tie-up-the-calf sandals that were at least flat, her one nod to practicality. She elaborated as she searched the top drawer for jewelry, "Frank and I are really more business associates than friends."

"Business associates?" I demanded. "I thought you were a student?"

"I *am* a student, getting my PhD in psychology."

Oh geez, she was probably my age and just *looked* eighteen. That would really depress me.

"But when you aren't in class, you work in 'security' with Frank?" I prodded.

"No, I'm really more in public relations. Sometimes our work overlaps, then we work together. Simple as that."

Simple as the Pythagorean theorem.

Ben looked from Ingrid to me and back, then shrugged. Mysteries and unanswered questions never bothered him much, which I'm certain is why he looked like a movie star and I looked like our great uncle Wilbur. "If you're on the road to semirecovery, I'm off. Stella and I have to hit the Astroturf," Ben said, laughing at his own poor joke.

Ingrid cocked her head at me as he let himself out the door. "Football?"

"No, the Vegas pool has poker tables in the water with Astroturf instead of felt."

She nodded. "Weird boat."

"Smart boat, if you think about it, offering gambling to everyone at every opportunity. I hear there are even slot machines next to every chair in the burger and pizza bar."

Ingrid picked out a twenty-six-inch silver and colored sea glass necklace and matching dangle earrings and put them with the sundress.

I shook my head at the ensemble, pulling out the practical outfit I'd already figured on wearing. "Ingrid, I'm going hiking in a third world country not cruising Rodeo Drive."

"Image is everything. You never know who you'll see. What if the ESPN crew decides to follow an excursion and it's yours?" She waved at the crinkled up pair of capris, T-shirt and Pumas I'd chosen. "You don't want *that* on national TV, do you?"

"I just want to get my parents back to the boat in one piece," I said. "Now back to Frank. How often do you work together?"

She shrugged. "Sometimes for a month straight, sometimes only a day every six months."

"So could you find out what work kept him from taking the cruise?"

"I don't think so," she said, looking out the glass at the balcony.

"Okay, how about you tell me all you know about him."

"He's extremely private, super focused, good hearted, tough skinned. An ultra type-A workaholic with baggage he tries to hide."

I think I knew about the baggage but I thought I'd better ask in case there was more. "Like what?"

"Alcoholism and personal relationships that don't always go his way."

Control, Bee. I let out the breath I'd been holding. I picked up the dress and hung it back in the closet. I could ask about girlfriends, but decided I didn't want to know. "Have you met his ex?"

"Nooo," she answered but still didn't meet my gaze. "I didn't know he had one."

"Still, you seem to know him pretty well." I tried to keep my voice neutral but my alto cracked a bit on the last word. Don't think I fooled her.

"Not really," Ingrid smiled casually. "I'm a psych major, I analyze everyone."

"So why would a flack need a psych degree?" I asked, still bothered that it all wasn't jibing.

"You don't think knowing how and why people act they way they do would help you in advertising?"

"Of course it would."

"PR is nothing but advertising image. Speaking of which, we need to talk about your website."

I started to tell her about Ringo's column when a knock sounded at the door. I opened it, assuming Ben had forgotten to tell me something but instead Jack stood in the hallway. I stepped back to let him in and he paused, blushing madly, when he saw Ingrid, who'd suddenly struck a coy pose, batting her eyelashes.

After an awkward few seconds, Jack turned to me. "We've got to t-talk."

Twenty-two

♦ ♣ ♥ ♠

"**D-d-don't ever d-do that to me again.**"

"What did I do?"

"I've been worried sick," Jack told me as he paced the cabin, his words coming out in such a rush, he didn't have time to stutter. "You never came back into the ballroom from the cappuccino break. Kinkaid came into the tournament and called it off for the night, saying another weather system had forced us out of international waters, which was crap. You wouldn't answer your cabin phone so I came down here and saw some big cowboy coming out of your cabin. He didn't stop when I called out. I thought he'd flung you off your balcony.

"So I got my video camera, bribed the people in the cabin directly below yours to let me in and taped my camera to their shower curtain rod and lifted it up to your balcony. I could see you on the bed and panicked. But then you started snoring so I felt better."

"You have that on video?" I asked.

He nodded proudly.

"Let's put it on the website," Ingrid offered.

He grinned at Ingrid, and she grinned back. I guess he'd forgiven her for yesterday's dalliance. They would've probably spent hours grinning at each other except I broke it up with the story of what happened to me on the promenade.

"Awful," Ingrid murmured at one point when I paused to catch my breath. She turned away and began reviewing my jewelry.

"So who is this g-guy?" Jack mused when I'd finished, throwing a secret look Ingrid's way.

"I still don't know."

Ingrid shrugged, still avoiding eye contact. She was hiding something for sure. But what? And why?

Jack had been busy since he'd left me snoring. He'd found Eria's cabin on the fourth deck pretty easily later that night as he stalked the hallways and finally found a mute security cretin who sounded like Phil stationed outside a cabin door. Showing great potential to be a real investigative journalist or a career criminal, Jack got some fishing line from his cabin, tied it around the vase of flowers on the glass table at the elevator, pulled the line up from the bottom of his pants, through the waistband, under his suit jacket and held it on his finger. As he walked six feet past Phil, he yanked it. The huge crash at the end of the hall sent Phil racing to check it out. Jack knocked on Eria's door and she opened it.

Once inside he got the scoop. She'd found their cabin in slight disarray, clothes here and there, bedcover askew, but it just as easily could have been attributed to Mahdu rushing to get ready for dinner as it could have been an attacker. The walkie talkie was nowhere to be found. His wallet was missing. Ferris was nowhere to be found, his cabin undisturbed. Kinkaid and her cruise cronies had scared Eria into leaving the ship in Cozumel with the promise they would continue to look into Mahdu's disappearance, although they filled her with propaganda that made her believe he was just taking a hiatus from her or from life. In other words, his disappearance was his fault. They fed her statistics about people (like Rick) who went mysteriously MIA for hours just to reappear and people (possibly like Rawhide Jones, they told her) who got so depressed they jumped or so drunk they fell off the side. Sometimes people had medical conditions they were unaware of, like epilepsy, that left them in potential danger of falling over the railing accidentally. Even though Mahdu had no history of depression, binge drinking or mysterious neurological disorders, and had been heard yelling at another man who was currently missing, Eria was young and scared and intimidated by authorities. I couldn't blame her for leaving.

If I were smart, I probably would too.

"So that was pretty much a dead end," I told Jack. "Even though you were ingenious."

"How did you get out without the security guy seeing you?" Ingrid asked.

"Eria went on the b-balcony and called out for him to help. He ran past where I hid behind the door and I s-slipped out. Then, I got lucky."

"Sounded like you were already lucky," I observed.

"I went to the Marker Bar and some off-duty employees were having a late night drink. After eavesdropping a while, I t-talked myself into the group. Two beers later I found out Valka and Alyce Kinkaid are l-lovers."

"What!?" Ingrid and I asked simultaneously.

Jack smiled proudly. "Yep. They don't think anyone knows but another girl who works at the s-spa says she walked in on them together and backed out before they saw her."

"Wow," I said, "So they could be conspiring—in the disappearances or simply in the cover-up. Or maybe Kinkaid's phone case was left there during a romantic encounter she wants kept secret."

"Or all of the above," Ingrid pointed out.

"The plot thickens, because once I made it to my c-cabin, Kinkaid appeared and told me that they had a t-tape of me slipping into Eria's room and, if we were running s-some kind of life insurance scam, they could help prove it."

"Intimidation tactic," I said. "She just wanted you to know they were watching you, because you were hanging with me yesterday."

"What amazes me about this whole thing is how well their c-cover-up is working. Even the few cruise employees who know about the d-disappearances, or will admit to knowing, t-tow the party line."

"Lemmings," I said.

Ingrid and Jack cocked their heads at me.

I explained, "Most people are lemmings, following the guy in front of them, doing what they're told without question. It's a theory I consider every time I do an ad campaign."

"Except us, Bee, we're antilemmings," Jack said excitedly, bouncing on the balls of his deck shoes.

"Right you are. Okay, antilemming league, how would you like a project for the day?"

I left the ship, having my cruise ID card scanned and a piece of paper pushed into my hand, giving me instructions on how to stay safe while visiting Mexico. Of course the best way to stay safe in Mexico was to stay out of Mexico which is why at the bottom of the paper it said: "Following these is no guarantee against injury or death."

Jack had told me before I left that he'd just read on the Internet that human heads were washing up on the beaches of Acapulco—apparently messages from the insurgents that they were serious about killing the tourism trade, literally.

"You don't have much cash on you, do you?" the cruise employee asked me as he handed back my card.

"Five dollars in my right shoe, five in my left, ten in my bra," I answered. "My cell phone is in my pocket."

"You're rich here, even without money. You're American. You can be ransomed. Be careful," he warned. "And good luck getting cell service."

I had to elbow my way through a ragtag group of protestors holding signs proclaiming the government a fraud, the president a cheat, tourists stupid for spending money to promote corruption, not quite that eloquently, but that was the general gist.

Elva and Howard were waiting on the corner of the filthy dock with two other cruisers, obvious in their matching Absolute Hold 'Em golf shirts and plaid Bermuda shorts. The quartet was surrounded by a bunch of skinny, ragged hoodlums brandishing knives at each other. It was only when I was running up to the mob to save my parents that I realized the gangsta wannabes were our official armed guards giving a display of their bodyguard skills. Scary.

"This is our daughter," Elva announced, pointing me out to the assembled group.

The gangstas all settled down, sheathing their knives, mostly in ankle scabbards or waist scabbards under their loose T-shirts.

"Oh, my dear," Elva exclaimed to one of the boys. "Aren't you afraid the knife will come loose and, uh, scar your manhood?"

One who apparently knew English translated for the others and they elbowed each other, hooting with laughter, the boy in question slapping Mom on the back. "*Gracias, por su cuidado con mi cojones, vieja,*" he said.

Well, and wasn't this going to be fun?

"What did he say?" Elva asked me.

"He told you thanks for caring." I left out the mention of his testicles and, especially, the "old woman" part. Knife or no knife, Mom would take him on about the latter.

"You. Are. Welcome," Elva mouthed slowly.

"*De nada.*" I told her under my breath.

"De. Nada." She enunciated again like the boy was mentally challenged. Ack.

The boy bowed his head and snickered. His friends jostled him. Dad had struck up a conversation with one of the protestors, a guy with an ugly scar that spanned his face from his left ear to above his right eye. Dad took out his wallet and handed him a five. I rushed over there, leaving Mom with her new buddies. "Dad, don't pull your wallet out like that," I whispered harshly, smiling at Scarface as I guided Dad away. "In fact you shouldn't have it at all away from the ship."

"Girlie, you should be more trusting of human nature. People are good."

Unless they are desperate. Unless they are offered an opportunity to be bad and get away with it. Unless they decide to advertise their cause by surfing disembodied heads onto the steps of resorts. How had I been raised a cynic by such Pollyanna parents?

The tour guide had arrived by the time Dad and I returned to our cozy group. He gave us a rundown on safety precautions, pretty much a candy-coated version of the cruise handout, and then we were on our way to our little bus. I couldn't help looking down at the water off the side of the dock to see if I could locate any floating heads.

We paused at some street vendors who displayed handmade silver jewelry in their hands. A mariachi band was weaving its way through the crowded dock. When the other cruise passengers on our tour stopped to shop, I pulled my cell phone out and dialed Frank.

I got a signal for a second, then lost it. I moved a couple of feet to the right and tried again. This time it went through. I was so prepared for the voice mail that when Frank answered, I almost dropped the phone. And when I didn't do that, I walked three steps to the left and lost him anyway.

Damn.

I returned to my good spot and dialed again. Frank answered on the first ring. "Honey Bee."

"Frank!" I said, pressing the phone to my ear. There was a lot of background noise, from my end certainly, and I couldn't tell how much from his end. I was so relieved to hear his voice that I spoke what I felt when I heard it. "I miss you."

"I miss you too. I'm so sorry I've wrecked our vacation."

"It's okay." Even though it wasn't. I didn't know what to tell him. I didn't want him to worry, but I needed advice. "I just wish you were here."

"I wish I were touching you right now, Honey Bee," his deep, reassuring baritone rode smoothly through the phone, spilling right into every erogenous zone I owned.

"I think I'm desperate," I purred back.

"Desperate for what?"

"Generally desperate—desperate for your counsel, desperate for your voice, desperate for . . . lots of things you could do for me."

"Hmm . . ."

"Don't do that." I moved too far left again as I squirmed. I moved back. "Are you there?"

"I'm here, unfortunately, and want to be there," he said. "So, because I'm not, you need to tell me what's going on."

"You didn't get my e-mail?"

"No."

"Oh, damn, I don't know where to begin then," I said, sticking my finger farther into my ear to drown out the mariachis. It sounded like they were in stereo.

"Start anywhere," Frank urged. "I'll catch up. How's the tournament?"

"I'm still in it."

"Of course, you had the best teacher in the world."

"Complimenting both you and me in one sentence. Talented. I haven't been catching the best of cards, though, which disproves Richard's theory of gambling and love."

"Who's Richard? Should I be jealous? And what's his theory?"

"A nerdy but nice mathematician on board. No. And his theory is if you are unlucky in love, you will win at cards."

"So you think you aren't lucky in love and therefore should be winning? I'm offended."

"Well, I'm the one who got stood up."

Frank was quiet.

"Frank?"

"I'm with you in more ways than you can imagine," he finally said, quietly.

Humph. He didn't know I was imagining warmed Dove soap scent around every corner of the ship. Good thing too or he'd get a big head.

"Sure I shouldn't be jealous?" he prodded. "There's no one on board you've met who you want to tell me about, is there?"

Did he have a sixth sense about Ian?

"I met Ingrid," I said in a challenging nonanswer.

"Bee!"

His tone was suddenly urgent in warning. It caught my attention so sharply, I looked around. I saw an object sailing through the air at the other end of the dock and ducked behind one of the street vendors just as it exploded. The force knocked the rickety vendor stand onto me, the vendor and a dozen other people who'd piled behind it with us. We held ourselves still, waiting in the sudden silence. As the smoke and dust began to clear, we began to move along with other huddled groups. Unconsciously I'd used my body to shield a small boy, whose mother, carrying an infant, grabbed his hand, thanking me profusely. She dragged him off, running. Others ran, others stood stunned. Sirens whined in the distance and a half dozen people closest to the blast lay alive but bleeding.

I looked frantically for my parents and finally saw them safe in the bus two hundred yards away. My phone had been knocked out of my hand in the scramble for cover, and I'd be lucky to find it again. Then I heard the ring under a pile of woven blankets. I dug toward the sound and picked it up. "Hello?"

"Are you okay?"

"I'm fine. It wasn't a big bomb. How did you know something bad was going to happen?"

"I'm in security. We have an instinct about these things."

The sirens were getting closer. "The cops are almost here. I guess I should go help the injured."

"Bee, listen to me, go ahead on your tour. You don't want to talk to police in Mexico. You don't want to go to jail in Mexico."

"Why would I go to jail?"

"Because that is where most people end up when the Mexican police are involved. Unless you have a lot of money on you."

I doubted the twenty dollars I had on me would do. "But I actually wanted to tell them about all these disappearances we have on board the ship—"

"Bee, a bomb just went off and you think they want to hear your story about missing Americans? Get out of there and watch your b—"

Static roared in my ear. Damn.

My mom had spotted me and waved out the bus window. A pair of our gangsta guards came walking my way, also waving at me to hurry. One of them had a gun. Where did that come from? The sirens were getting louder. I ran, still trying to dial Frank. The phone reported no service.

As I stepped up into the bus, the driver gunned the accelerator. The boys jumped in behind me and shoved me up the stairs. I crawled into the first seat and saw the police cars wheeling around the corner. And down an alley I saw the sun glint off blond hair. It was only after we'd sped past, that what I'd seen registered. I'd swear it was Ian Reno, a tall blond young man wearing shorts with toucans on them and a small dark-haired woman in khakis in an intense conversation with two men.

Twenty-three

♦ ♣ ♥ ♠

Undaunted by the explosion (in fact, thrilled by it since it would make her the talk of bridge club for generations), Elva was bound and determined to see the Chichén Itzá ruins. We really didn't have a choice, as the police were in the process of blocking off the entire pier, the *Gambler* was pulling away from the dock and the tour director admitted we wouldn't be able to get to the ship until later that afternoon, once they sent the dinghies for us. So it was spend the day with the Mexican cops or go climb around on ruins where people now long dead had lived.

What a vacation.

The day actually went smoothly after the big bang with which it began. I never could get a cell signal again, so was left replaying the conversation with Frank over and over in my mind. I hadn't told him I was in Cozumel—how did he know I was in Mexico? Of course, he had the cruise itinerary so he could have guessed, but how did he know I was taking a tour? But the biggest question of all was how did

he know I'd been in danger? Maybe he heard the zing of
the bomb over his fancy high-tech security-expert phone.
Maybe he didn't know but was getting ready to yell at me
about something and hollered my name that I interpreted
as a warning. Maybe we were so psychically intercon-
nected he could feel what I felt no matter where we were.

Okay, I didn't believe that one, but it sounded cool.

Every time I gave up trying to solve that puzzle I returned to Ian in the alley. Had it really been him? Who'd
been the American woman with him? And why were they
in a dark alley in Cozumel?

The bomb at the pier had probably increased our safety
the rest of the day because police had gone to all the tourist
venues, gathered up the protestors and hauled them off to
jail. So much for free speech. The paddy wagon was just
speeding off as we arrived. The ruins were empty, so it was
a quiet day except for the time when Mom talked one of
our bodyguards into showing her how to rappel.

I'd had to put a stop to that before Elva killed herself.

By the time we headed back to the ship, my mind was in
so many pretzels I wasn't sure if I'd ever think straight
again.

Jack was waiting for me when we got on deck after
bribing our way through the police barricade. Good thing
Dad brought his wallet after all. Because while they seemed
titillated by where my remaining ten dollars had been located, I don't think it would have kept them from detaining
us. Dad's couple hundred did.

"Guess I have to win the tournament to pay you back,
huh, Dad?" I asked, giving him a squeeze.

"Aw, you're worth it—most of the time—when you
aren't ruining my fantasies."

"What are you talking about, Dad?"

"I always wanted to go out with a rock climber." He reached over and pinched Mom on the rear then chased her up the stairs. Oh dear.

Jack watched them go, looking a little soft around the edges himself. "C-cute c-couple," he murmured. "For a pair of geriatrics."

"Who are you?" I asked. "I thought you were Jack Smack, tough investigative journalist?"

"So? I c-can appreciate a healthy human relationship, can't I?" Jack demanded defensively.

I peered at him. He looked a little high. I wished I could blame it on something other than the obvious. "What have you been up to today, Jack? Did you get your project done?"

"Of course, that only took us a c-couple of hours, then we had t-time to k-kill before you got b-back, so Ingrid and I h-hung out." Jack blushed and avoided eye contact.

His exaggerated stutter was a dead giveaway but since I didn't want to know what they hung out or where they hung it, I changed the subject. "What did you find out?"

"First, no one c-came in or out of the c-cabin number the Marlboro Man gave you to call. No one answered, either. Some big dude named Hans from security ran us off for loitering after about an hour d-down there. I did cajole a member of the staff into telling me the c-cabin was paid for by a FBG Enterprises with a sole occupant named John Smith."

I snorted. "His name isn't John Smith."

"I was skeptical too, but maybe it is. S-someone out there has to be named John Smith. Call him John next time he s-saves your life and see if he responds."

"Thanks for the advice. What's FBG Enterprises?"

"I don't know. The Internet is d-down."

"What do you mean, the Internet is down?"

"There is some kind of mechanical d-difficulty. The

captain announced after you'd left that they were working on it but we might not have a c-connection for the rest of the cruise."

I frowned. "That's by design, I'm sure, so we can't contact anyone. We really are isolated from the outside world, aren't we?" I staved off a shudder and tried not to miss Frank again.

"What happened on board when the bomb went off?" I asked as we began climbing the steps to the third deck.

"The c-captain told us to remain calm, that Mexican authorities had everything under control, that they were s-sealing off the pier. No one else was allowed to leave the ship and we would be waiting for those who had gone on excursions to return before we shoved off. The rest of the d-day was pretty routine. I think everyone on board felt smart that they had been weenies and stayed home for the day."

"Did you see Ian?"

Jack nodded. "Sure did. He got back on board right before you did. I guess he went on an excursion t-too?"

I raised my eyebrows. I guess it was possible. Maybe he and the woman were meeting the tour guide when I saw him. "Anyone else reboard the ship that you recognized?"

"No," Jack shook his head then stopped. "Oh, yes. One person, but I don't remember her name. I j-just recognized her from the opening night of the tournament when all the poker stars were introduced. She was the c-cute young Hispanic woman."

Rhonda the Ruler.

We found Ingrid with Ringo, their heads together over a piece of paper in the Internet lobby where all the computers were powered down.

"The column design is all planned out," Ringo announced excitedly, waving the paper with drawings on it.

"And we have the first couple of topics all lined up," Ingrid put in. "This is going to be the hottest Hold 'Em blog on the web."

"I don't doubt it," I said, trying to sound encouraging. I could advertise any product but had absolutely no interest in advertising myself. It was beyond me why someone would want to read about me muddling my way through a game millions had played for a lot longer and better than I had. It made me slightly uncomfortable. "Hey, maybe we can go with a Hold 'Em for dingbats type theme?"

Everyone stopped talking and turned to me. Oops. Ingrid cocked her hip and planted a fist on it. "Bee, your image is one of a cool, sophisticated-with-an-edge, ultrasmart, supersexy woman who wins at the biggest poker game in the world. Please refrain from this kind of talk."

"Sorry," I muttered.

The trio shook their heads at the dunce and finished their conversation. Ingrid had talked Jack into doing a "Hold 'Em Hearsay" column with tidbits from his poker reporting travels. "Champions' Tips with the Chips" would be written by invited guests, recent winners of tournaments around the world. That was the best idea yet, at least I wouldn't have to write them.

I wandered away for a moment to the interior railing that looked down on the lobby below. I saw Delia walking along the shops to the right side of the lobby. She slipped into the liquor store. I looked back at my team and decided they could do without me for a few minutes while I slipped away to chat with Rick.

At the first house phone I could find, I dialed his room and held my breath until he answered. "Rick, it's Bee. Can you meet me on the Sky Deck in a few minutes?"

"It's supposed to be dangerous for me to leave the cabin alone."

"Says who?" I demanded.

"Says my wife."

"She just doesn't want you messing around on her."

"To tell you the truth, I haven't been feeling great since you found me in the chapel. I get little flashes of clear thinking but mostly, everything's fuzzy. The ship doctor has been sending over some medication for me to take twice a day—before breakfast and before dinner—but it doesn't seem to be helping."

Hmm. Besides not remembering everything about his attack, he'd seemed okay when I'd left him that night. Something was wrong. "What do the pills you're taking look like?"

Rick said they were white oblong pills. I'd have to ask Ben to know for sure, but I'd bet he was being given something that affected his memory. Someone didn't want Rick talking or remembering anything that happened to him and I bet it wasn't the ship doctor. If it was, there was proof the cruise line was involved.

"Rick, do me a favor, would you hide tonight's pill and I'll find a way to get it?"

"I guess, but why, Bee?"

"Because I need you to help me find Rawhide and Mahdu and keep me from disappearing. You are the only witness. Can you remember what the woman looked like any better than you did last time?"

"What woman?"

Oh dear.

"Can you remember what the note meant that you passed to my roommate outside the elevator yesterday?"

"What note?"

Rick did know enough to tell me that while he ate room service, Delia went to dinner every night. I agreed to swing by his room during dinner and pick up the pill. At this point I didn't really care if the cruise cameras caught me in the act or not. Something creepy was going on, and my anger had far surpassed any fear.

As I walked back to the Internet nook, I heard a commotion. "Th-there she is!" Jack shouted.

Ingrid reached me first. "Where did you go?"

"To call Rick."

She bored me with a look, deadly serious. "Look, Bee, you can't do this anymore, this wandering off alone. Something bad is going down here on this ship and you are in the middle of it. Promise you won't go off by yourself again?" I stood dumbstruck. "Tell me you won't do this again," she demanded.

I nodded.

Whoa. Was this the same woman who argued over thong versus boy-short undies and was more concerned about what color background to put on the website than a bomb going off on the pier?

Just as soon as serious-as-a-heart-attack Ingrid appeared in my face, she was gone, flitting back to the group, dismissing the security stiff. I recognized him from patrolling the tournament—Rico walked past me and whispered, "Watch yourself."

What?

"What?" I finally asked when I found my tongue, but he was already out of earshot. I could be wrong, but I think Kinkaid was mad at me again. I'd been off the ship, behaving myself all day long, so this disapproval made me wonder if the phone in Rick's room wasn't tapped.

Twenty-four

♦ ♣ ♥ ♠

When Ingrid and I returned to the cabin, Ian had left a message on our cabin phone that he'd seen me chasing after "that cowboy" again, and we needed to talk.

His voice sounded extremely patient and brilliantly reasonable but I wondered fleetingly whether he was jealous enough to have whacked me on the head for ditching him for Marlboro Man. No, I dismissed the thought the instant after it formed. For him to commit such an act would be very ridiculous and slightly psychotic. I'm sure a professional-minded man wouldn't even consider such a thing, or if he did, he would know how to talk himself out of it.

I rang his cabin and left a message that we'd be at the In the Chips bar on the top deck before dinner if he wanted to look me up there. If not, then I'd see him at the tournament, since we'd be sitting at the same table. Along with Rhonda, I suddenly realized. It was going to be an interesting evening.

Made more so by the outfit Ingrid had laid out for me on

the bed when I emerged from the shower—a form-fitting teal sheath minidress trimmed in peacock feathers, teal iridescent pumps and some breathtaking blue topaz jewelry.

"I'll wear the earrings, ring and necklace."

"That ought to make things exciting. A naked woman dressed only in topaz, playing poker on the seas. Can I put it on the website?"

I glared at her grin. "I'm not joking. I can't wear that cha-cha dress to play a down and dirty card game."

"Why not?"

"I always feel so overdressed anyway. No one dresses to play this game, even in Vegas. As hodgepodge as my dress was at the Big Kahuna, I was loads fancier than most of the players who favor sports jerseys and shorts. Here, most of the passengers go to the effort to change *out* of their nice dinner clothes to play. I feel like Audrey Hepburn in the middle of a Midwestern wienie roast."

Ingrid laughed. "Different is good. It makes image building easier."

"I'm so glad someone's job is easier."

"Well, wearing this will make yours easier, because the distraction factor will be higher. If you can withstand all the stares, you can use this to win. And if I'm wrong, when is being overdressed ever bad?" Spoken like a true fashionista. "Besides, you aren't going to wear a sport jersey anyway."

I had to agree with her about that, so we dressed and headed to the elevator. "I talked to Frank," I said.

Ingrid halted. "You saw Frank?"

"I went to Cozumel, not L.A. I talked to him when I got a cell connection, briefly. How would I have seen Frank?" I watched her closely.

Giving a little laugh, she shook her head. "I guess I thought you'd gotten ahold of one of those video phones. I'm so used to traveling in Europe; I forgot we were in Mexico. They'd probably be hard to find there."

Hmm. She was covering again. I liked Ingrid, Heck, I trusted her, but she was lying about something and it wasn't about where she'd traveled.

I an asked to speak to me outside. Ben and my friends shared a weighty glance. "Actually Bee Bee is not allowed to be alone," Ben explained. "We have a pact."

"If she's with me, she isn't alone," Ian said, impatience only slightly veiled.

Everyone at the table looked around at each other and finally shared a mental shrug. Ian rose, pulled out my chair and guided me out the door of the bar, around the corner from the floor-to-ceiling windows, behind the thousand times lifesize concrete die that decorated the deck and to the railing. The breeze was so salt laden I could taste it on my tongue.

"I feel like I've been called to the principal's office," I said lightly. I was facing the direction we'd come to keep the wind from blowing my hair in my face and now I saw Jack peek around the corner. I bit back a grin.

Ian nailed me with his best professorial look. "Belinda, let's be serious."

"Oh, let's," I said, "I wanted to ask you what you were doing in Cozumel this morning with Paul."

"I don't know what you're talking about." Ian was a master of the poker face, but he couldn't stop the small involuntary twitch just above his left ear. He probably shouldn't try to lie around a poker player. If I won on any skill at all, it was on people's tells. He'd showed this same tick when he'd bluffed a big hand at poker.

"Don't lie to me, Ian. I saw you two in an alley."

His face softened in defeat. "I'm sorry, but I agreed to keep this in confidence. Paul asked that of me."

I continued to look at him expectantly.

Finally he sighed, looking off into the sea. "I suppose since you saw us, I will tell you this much: I agreed to help Paul find some way out of his financial dilemma. What you saw was part of it."

His twitch was gone.

"That's awfully nice of you," I offered, remembering what Paul had said about being offered a way out, but I'd gotten the impression the option seemed repulsive to him. Was this the same deal? How was Ian helping? I really wanted to ask details but Ian had made it clear he wouldn't give any.

"Now it's my turn for twenty questions," Ian interrupted my reverie. "Who is this cowboy?"

"I don't know."

"So you never caught up with him last night?" Ian tapped his hand against the railing. This tell wasn't as obvious. Was he nervous or angry? "Did you catch him?" he asked again.

Technically . . . ? "No. I didn't catch up with him."

Ian stopped tapping, seeming so relieved that I almost told him Marlboro Man and I got naked on the promenade. I'm perverse that way. Instead, I continued reasonably, "He's just always there at the wrong place at the right time, and I want to know why."

"Do you always tend to be this obsessive-compulsive?"

"I don't think I ever am, actually." Although I had thought about Frank incessantly since I'd talked to him, I doubted Ian would appreciate that example. "I just think knowing *who* he is could be the easiest piece to fit in this crazy puzzle."

"Here's what I think," Ian began. "You need to employ some thought-stopping techniques to get over this and on with the tournament. You aren't playing your best cards right now."

Thought stopping? What the heck was that? "It's hard to

thought-stop two acquaintances vanishing from a ship and an investigator tumbling off the same ship to his death."

"I could teach you how," he offered smoothly. "You could use it during your poker games when someone is intentionally trying to distract you, during your ad campaigns when personal issues might creep into the work day, even during sex, if you are thinking about an old flame when trying to make sparks with a new one."

"Whoa, uh, thanks, I think I'll take a rain check on that," I said carefully, deciding I'd better change the subject quickly. "Besides, as considerate as it is, why would you care if I were playing my best right now? Let's be realistic, it gives you an advantage to beat me. Use it. I don't blame you. I'd do the same to you."

"You don't get it, Belinda. I'm at the table to watch you play, not play myself. It's worth more to me to watch you win than to win myself."

While intellectually I considered his attention somewhat inappropriate, considering we barely knew each other, emotionally or maybe pheromonally, I was flattered such a young stud brain would be so focused on me. The physical attraction still zinged between us, even though there was something about Ian that made me slightly uncomfortable. Maybe I was afraid he would see too far into a mind I didn't necessarily understand all that well myself.

Our table that night at dinner was subdued, which made it difficult for me to slip away unnoticed for longer than a bathroom trip might take. I certainly didn't want anyone panicking and sending out a search party when I went to get the pill from Rick. I made sure I kept Delia in my sights. She had spotted me when she sat down across the room and glared, a random pissed-off look, though, not one that showed me she knew what I was up to.

At least, I hoped not.

I figured that if I got Ben wound up enough about some topic, he would distract not only our table but probably the surrounding ones as well, with his impassioned discussion. Anything having to do with Texas Hold 'Em would probably do, but I had to find something he wouldn't expect me to chime in on at the same time. And something Mom and Dad would get worked up about.

"How about all this naked poker on the Internet?" I threw out, sneaking a hand down to pick up my clutch.

"It's awesome," Ben enthused. "What a marketing plan— get the porn freaks hooked on poker and then we can all beat the pants off them."

Stella giggled at his play on words. Elva's face was going red. I hadn't seen her mad at Ben but maybe a half-dozen times in his life, I might have started the seventh. "Benjamin, bite your tongue."

I rose and excused myself to Ingrid.

"I'll go with you." Ingrid said.

Damn, I'd forgotten the buddy system pact. I'd have to lose her while she was in a stall. We exited the dining room.

"What did Ian want to talk to you about?"

"I think he's a bit jealous of your boyfriend."

"Who, Frank?"

Ah ha! "Frank's your boyfriend?!"

"No! I just thought that is who you meant. Bee, your sarcasm is so dry sometimes it is difficult for me to understand."

"I was talking about the Marlboro Man. I know he was with you in that cabin yesterday."

Ingrid shrugged as we both entered stalls. "Well, he wasn't."

"Yuck!" I said loudly as I backed out of the stall next to Ingrid and walked down like I was getting into another. I shut the door with a bang and removed my shoes and tiptoed out the bathroom door. I ran on bare feet around the corner. I saw Kinkaid and Valka chatting on the stairs I'd planned to alight, so I stole a trick from Jack and paused just behind a potted palm to listen for a moment.

"That Bee, she's a loose cannon," Kinkaid said.

"We'll just have to take care of her, then." Valka put in ominously.

Ack. They were going to kill me. I changed direction and headed out on the promenade.

I felt someone grab my arm and immediately thought Valka or Ingrid had caught me. I spun, hoping to see Ingrid, and saw a large Korean man looming over me instead. Ack. He was taller than he looked sitting down.

"Bee Cool, long time no see," Sam Hyun intoned in a low, tight voice as he squeezed my upper arm a little harder than he needed to for a friendly chat.

I nodded, opening my mouth and moving my tongue. I couldn't get a sound to come out of my larynx—not even a squeak. This wouldn't help my survival odds when he tried to pitch me over the side of the *Gambler*.

"You know I really want to kill you," he said.

Not Sam too!?

Why had I ditched Ingrid? She could have come with me to get the pill from Rick. I could've figured out a way to explain it. Now I would never know who was trying to keep him drugged up and why. I would never win the *Gambler* tournament. I would never see my pet snake Grog again. I would never have children with Frank.

"You're still in the tournament." It was an accusation.

I moved my mouth. Still no sound. I nodded.

"I told you I hate players like you. You just throw shit up against the wall and see what sticks. You beat out conservative, smart players with no skill. You wear fancy, tit-showing getups and hope it distracts people. You have a fricking *website*. And, you're a woman."

"That," I peeped, surprised to hear my voice, *finally*. "That's not my fault."

"Everything else is, though."

"Well, the website really isn't—"

"Shut up!"

I looked up and down the promenade. Remember the karma thing? It still stank. Thousands of people on board and no one on this deck at this moment. What about the video camera? There wasn't even one around us to be covered. That's double bad luck.

"What will killing me accomplish? There are millions of women playing the game now. You can't kill us all."

He barked a single laugh. "I'm not going to kill you. I'm just going to kill your game."

Twenty-five

♦ ♣ ♥ ♠

"**I** thought you'd never show," Rick said as he opened the door and ushered me in hurriedly.

"It's a long story. It has to do with Sam Hyun," I began.

An old ex-wrestler is an imposing sight. An old ex-wrestler in his bathrobe, fuzzy slippers and a mildly vacant look is a frightening sight. He frowned, his eyes growing more focused as he looked inward. "Steer clear of Sam. He has a bad temper and doesn't like women."

"I noticed," I said. "Do you think he's angry enough to kill?"

Rick shrugged. "I haven't talked to The Man in probably a couple of years. He was hating the way he saw Texas Hold 'Em changing with the Internet back then, and I can't see him reconciling himself to it now that it's a hundred times worse."

"That doesn't really answer my question."

"I don't like to think one of my old friends would be homicidal, but Stan was," Rick admitted. "Of course, I don't like to think I'm losing my mind, but that seems to be happening too."

Rick pulled an oblong white pill out of his pocket and handed it to me. "At first I couldn't remember why I was supposed to save this. Then I realized as the one I took this morning started to wear off as I sat here for the last hour or so that I can't remember much that's happened over the last couple of days. I think that, more than anything, made me not take the pill. Then I reached for a glass of water and saw this." He pulled up the sleeve of his bathrobe and saw where he'd written *Pill 4 B, 6:00.*

"Did you remember talking to me then?"

Rick shook his head, his brow furrowed. "Not really. I wasn't sure then whether I'd decided to save it for you to check on or whether at some point I saw you and you told me." Rick paused, his eyes filling with tears. "What's happening to me? Was it the knock on the head?"

I shook mine. "I think it's the pill. I think someone has been drugging you. I'll show Ben and see if he can identify what it is. I hope the effect is only temporary."

"Me too."

"Do you remember what the person looked like who brought you the pill?"

Rick pondered that a moment, hard, then shook his head sadly, "Bee, I can't remember anything from the time the cruise security brought me back to the room. I mean, I have flashes, like a strobe light showing certain things, Delia standing over me. Watching a dolphin off the balcony. How long have I been this way?"

"Two days." I answered, reaching into my clutch and pulling out the piece of paper he'd handed Ingrid. "Do you remember this?"

He looked at it and frowned. "This is my handwriting. I gave you this?"

I nodded. "You gave to my friend to give to me."

"I don't remember." He paused. I sighed in disappoint-
ment. I knew it was important but it might remain a mystery locked in Rick's brain.

"But I can figure out what it means," he added.

"You can!"

"Tonight is August thirty-first. Cabin 4600 is where we
were going to play that secret ring game—with Rawhide,
Mahdu, Ferris, and three other players we didn't know. AT
would be after tournament, I'm guessing."

Duh. I felt stupid. I'd heard about the ring game and
completely forgot about it. "Considering most of their guest
list has disappeared, I guess they'll be looking for extra
players. Are you going to play?" I asked.

"Oh, sure, I think that would be great for someone with
serious short-term memory loss, who can't remember from
one moment to the next. I'd forget my pocket cards before
I pushed in my bet."

"Can I play in your place?" I asked.

"You can try."

"No-limit 10/20?" I asked.

"Thousand," he answered.

Ouch. I stood and looked at the bedside clock. I'd been
there way too long. Ingrid would have reinforcements out
searching the *Gambler* for me. I headed for the door.
"Okay, start flushing your pills. Call me in the morning as
soon as the guy brings your pill and describe him to me. Or
better yet, call me and keep him talking so I can see him."

"I'll do my best," Rick said, making a note on his wrist.
"I'm already feeling better. I can still remember you walking into the cabin. That's a good sign."

I nodded and opened the door.

"Are you going to play the ring game?"

"I'm going to try to get in."

"Knock 'em dead."

I hoped I wouldn't have to.

* * *

I decided to go up the stairs on the opposite end of the ship from the dining room in case Delia decided to head back to her cabin. I was looking behind me as I rounded the corner by the big tournament billboard when I ran smack into a wide chest. Hands clamped down on my shoulders.

"You are in such big trouble," Marlboro Man said, maneuvering me around, propelling me forward.

"What are you talking about?"

"I might be able to talk you out of most of the trouble if you go jump in the pool."

"You're crazy."

"See, if you're wet, we can say I pulled you out of the sea and she won't be mad at you since you'd been off getting yourself drowned. It will soften the helluva lecture you are sure to get."

"Who is she?"

"Ingrid."

"I knew it. I knew you two had something going on. She lied to me."

"We have something going on but it's nothing what you think, so she didn't really lie. Except perhaps by omission."

"What did she omit?"

"What we've got going on."

"Which is?"

"What she is omitting."

Argh. "And that is?"

"I'm not at liberty to say."

"Cops say that."

"I just hate those guys." Marlboro Man winked.

"Where are we going?" I asked.

"Someplace safe. You can't be trusted. Say you are going to the restroom and end up two decks away on the other end of the ship. An extremely renegade move."

It suddenly occurred to me that Marlboro Man and Ingrid could work for the cruise line—plainclothes plants who were paid to keep order on the seas. It wasn't completely logical, but I had to find out, especially since the alternative was spending the rest of the cruise locked away in a cabin somewhere being fed pills. I stopped in my tracks and screamed.

People stopped. Some stared. A few scurried away. A brave middle-aged man approached with a worried look on his face.

I had to hand it to my companion. He remained relatively unruffled, smiling at the other passengers staring, waving off the man approaching. "What are you doing?" Marlboro Man leaned down and asked quite reasonably, which made a good case for him being with the cruise line. Except wouldn't they want to make my capture as unobtrusive as possible? Hmm.

"I think we need to go now, Bee."

I screamed again. Marlboro Man put his watch to his ear, nodded, patted me on the head and hurried off.

Valka, Kinkaid and Hans wheeled around the corner just as Marlboro Man reached the stairs, loping up them four at a time. Hans reached me first.

"Was that man the one who attacked you at the spa?" Hans said, speaking into his lapel as he waited for my answer, looking somehow vindicated that I finally might have proof of an attack at all.

"No," I answered, although I couldn't be sure and hated to disappoint Hans for some odd reason. He was ineffectual, but I liked him. After all, he wanted to be giving tours not packing heat. It was hard to do well in a job you hate.

"Why were you screaming then?" Valka asked, crossing her arms over her chest.

"I was just reenacting what happened when the bomb exploded out on the pier this morning. I must have scared him away." I shrugged.

Kinkaid and Valka both rolled their eyes and threw Hans looks that told him I was a head case. I was halfway to believing that as well.

"It's almost time for the tournament, Miss Cooley," Kinkaid informed me frostily. "Try to avoid any more reenactments before then so we can get the deal off on time."

By the time I returned to the table, everyone was angry with me. Most of the dining room had cleared out, with only about a half-dozen tables still semioccupied except for ours, which only had two empty seats. Ingrid hadn't returned.

"Really, Belinda, try to think about someone other than yourself for a change," Elva admonished. "We wanted to get front row seats for the tournament but since it took you forever to return from powdering your nose, that's out of the question!"

Dad threw me a forgiving look with just a dash of guilt thrown in for good measure.

"Where's Ingrid?" I asked.

Ben frowned which was more shocking to me than Mom's verbal spank. Ben never frowned because a) he rarely worried enough for his face to even consider the action and b) when he did have that rare moment, he resisted because frowning causes wrinkles which would ruin his natural beauty.

"Ingrid came back to the table a while ago, said you'd gotten separated and went back to look for you." He narrowed his eyes at me. Two beauty-marring actions in less than a minute. Ooo, he *was* mad. "What I don't get is how do two women get separated in the bathroom? It's not like you went into battle. Anyone who can negotiate the Galleria at Christmas shopping season can keep track of another person in a cruise loo. Unless one of you *meant* to get lost." What do you know, Ben's one forage into murder and mayhem had left him suspicious of others' actions. Those four brain cells were working overtime.

"You think Ingrid is getting tired of my company?" I asked lightly.

Mom was gathering her purse, chatting with Stella about tomorrow's agenda. Dad rose to pull out her chair as Ben walked around to me. "Ingrid wasn't the one I was talking about," he said, his tenor low. "Why did *you* get lost?"

"To get this," I said, pulling out the pill Rick saved for me and slipping it into Ben's hand.

His eyebrows rose. "Having trouble sleeping? Experiencing anxiety attacks?"

Well, now that he mentioned it, the whole cruise seemed like one big anxiety attack. I looked at the white pill and was tempted to down it right there.

"Bee," Ben grabbed my elbow and guided me out the double doors and onto the windy deck. "Where did you get this? From your friend Jack?"

"Why do you think I got it from Jack?"

"Because a lot of doctors use this kind of pill to treat his condition," Ben informed me.

Hmm. I really didn't think Jack had anything to do with the pill business so I didn't pursue that angle, although I did catalog it in the back of my mind for future reference.

"You can tell me the truth," Ben encouraged.

I sighed. I should be honest about the pill, but I didn't want him to tell me to butt out of Rick's business because I thought Rick's business was Rawhide's business was

Mahdu's business was Ferris' business but was most importantly my business. As we walked through the lobby, past the Internet café, I told him the partial truth. "Remember Rick, the guy who went missing the first night and turned up later?"

Ben nodded, leaning his elbows on the railing as he turned the pill over in his fingers.

"Well, since then someone saying he's from the ship doctor has been bringing this pill for him to take twice a day for his concussion."

Frowning again, even deeper (new record), Ben shook his head. "No way a doctor would prescribe this after a concussion."

"What is it?"

"A benzodiazepine, like Xanax, prescribed for serious insomnia and anxiety, hence the reason Jack Smack would benefit. However, the downside is—it causes temporary amnesia, called traveler's amnesia, antegrade amnesia or in layman's terms, short-term memory loss. New events that happen when the person is under the influence of this are not transferred to his long-term memory bank, leaving them to exist in a transient world."

I nodded. "That's consistent with the way Rick's been acting and feeling."

"This would be a DEA case. Can he recognize the person delivering the pill?"

I shook my head as Ben smacked his own with the heel of his hand. "Duh. He can't because he's under the influence of the drug. Sneaky bastard who's drugging him. I'd venture to guess it's not the ship doctor at all but the person who attacked him."

"We'll know when it's delivered tomorrow morning because Rick's not taking it anymore," I informed Ben.

A hand slid around my waist and pinned me to the railing.

I felt breath on my neck as he spoke: "What's this 'we'? Rick will know. I will know. And you will be staying out of it."

I stared into a familiar face which stifled the scream in my throat.

Twenty-six

♦ ♣ ♥ ♠

With my surprise firmly caught in my throat, Frank brought his lips to mine and drowned any possible noise with a long, deep kiss. After that I was too weak with wanting to even breathe, much less speak. Frank recognized my state and administered some more mouth-to-mouth, which succeeded in setting every nerve ending in my body on fire. Warm, musky Dove scent washed over me, over and over. Finally, my brain began to be heard over my zinging erogenous zones.

"Honey Bee," he murmured into the hair just above my left ear.

Resisting the delicious shiver, I pushed back from his arms. He looked kind of cute in his cargo shorts, deck shoes and Hawaiian shirt decorated with oversize pink hibiscus. "What are you doing here?"

"How soon we forget. You invited me on this cruise, remember?"

"Don't be a smart ass. How did you get here?"

"He's been here the whole time."

I looked over Frank's shoulder to see Ingrid approaching. Confused, I looked at Frank and saw agreement and then apology in his warm cocoa eyes. I wasn't liking this. What was he apologizing for? I looked back at Ingrid. She was glaring at me.

Maybe it was what I had suspected since I found out they knew each other. Maybe he and Ingrid were having an affair. Maybe they'd been together longer than I'd known him and I was the interloper. Maybe she was the one trying to kill me. Maybe they'd been playing Hold 'Em with each other in our cabin while I was out playing Hold 'Em with cards. Maybe she was his ex-wife.

I thought I was going to be sick.

"This is getting to be an irritating habit, Bee. Why did you ditch me?" Ingrid demanded as she drew up on Frank's right. He didn't look at her. He kept his gaze driving into me.

"I had things to do." I said, jutting my chin up.

"Well," she whispered with a harsh edge. "You have compromised the investigation. You disappeared, and I had to let Frank know in case you'd been kidnapped or killed. Now not only is the investigation probably derailed, but Frank's job probably will be too."

Frank shot Ingrid a warning look. "Enough. She's alive. It's worth it."

"What the hell is going on?" I demanded.

Frank sighed. "I've been on the ship since we left the Port of Galveston. Ingrid and I are working on a case."

"What? Ingrid is a psychology major and a fashionista minor with a degree in public relations, what does that have to do with security?"

"Those are her covers, Honey Bee."

"Oh I see. Clear as mud," I intoned, narrowing my eyes at Frank. He was surveying my outfit, top to toe, proudly. Then, suddenly, I understood at least one piece of the puzzle. "You are the one who gave her money for all those clothes she bought. For the massage and the kelp wrap."

He shrugged. "I was so sorry to have ruined our vacation. I wanted to make it up to you."

"Then you should have sicced someone with better taste on me."

"Hey!" Ingrid interjected, planting a fist on her cocked hip. "I did a good website."

"Okay. I like the website. Stick to dressing up the computer not me."

"I didn't have a choice," Frank explained. "Ingrid had to be your bodyguard. It could have been worse. Joe could have been your roommate, dressing you in Wranglers and button-downs the whole trip."

"Oh, is Joe, Marlboro Man?" Joe—Frank's faceless assistant who'd helped us in Vegas—was my hero on the cruise. I felt myself going a bit weak in the knees.

Ingrid and Frank shared a look, then laughed. "Not a bad description," Frank admitted.

I cocked an eyebrow. "Hmm. Roommates, huh? That might not have been so bad."

Frank's face darkened. His jaw clenched. "That wasn't funny, Bee. You are in enough trouble after cozying up to that Ian Reno creep."

"In trouble?" I said, feeling my back come up at his bossy tone. "What kind of trouble are you in with *me* for skulking around the ship for days, spying on me?" In retrospect, I could now place Frank as the employee with the familiar walk I kept seeing talking to Joe, the Marlboro Man.

"I was working."

"Were you the presence I kept feeling in the hallway outside our cabin?"

Frank dropped his gaze guiltily.

"You jerk. Why did you do that when you had Superwoman here guarding me?"

"I had to make sure you were safe."

"And why would you not tell me you were here on the ship? You think I can't keep a secret?"

"Bee, when I am on a case, no one can know where I am or who I am."

"I don't know where you are and who you are when you *aren't* on a case."

Bingo. Frowning, Frank shook his head in frustration.

"Okay, so tell me about this case. Does it have to do with the disappearances?"

"The disappearances have worked into our case, which means you have worked into our case," Frank said unhappily. He ran a finger along a strand of hair next to my face and tucked it behind my ear. "And you need to get out of the middle of it before you get really hurt."

I looked from Ingrid to Frank and back. "Okay, I'll get out of the middle if you tell me who you work for."

Frank shook his head again, more sadly this time. "It's classified, Honey Bee."

"The government then?"

"Not exactly."

"The military?"

"Not exactly."

"I know! You two are mystery shoppers testing the gambling cruise!"

"No!" They both shouted, affronted, although I swear I saw Frank's eyes twinkle.

"Finally a straight answer," I said. "Although not the one I was looking for."

"Bee," Frank drew me close, kissing the top of my head, running his hand lightly down my back. Purr. "This is what you need to do instead of figuring out who signs our paychecks: stay under wraps for the rest of the cruise. You've gotten into too many scrapes, and it's making me crazy."

"Don't you want to know what I've found out?"

Frank held up a hand. "Stop, Bee. I want you to stay safe. Give up on the tournament. It's not worth it. Go to your cabin. Go nowhere. Don't open the door for anyone. Don't even go out to eat. Missing a meal won't hurt you. Ingrid will bring you something for breakfast."

First, the scrapes weren't my fault, which is how he made them sound. Second, Frank evidently thought I was fat. I could miss a meal, huh? I'd get him back. "I don't think that is a good idea," I said with studied calmness.

He raised his eyebrows, looking down at me curiously.

"Never be a sitting duck. My mother told me once that it was best to hide in plain sight."

Frank glowered. Mostly because we had employed Elva's advice with great success in Vegas with his approval.

He pulled me to him and whispered roughly in my ear, "Listen—"

"Dammit, Miss Cooley," Kinkaid bustled up, paused, and gave me and Frank an aghast once-over. "You certainly do get around, don't you?"

"What does that mean?" Frank asked, letting me go and drilling me with a heated stare.

"I just don't have time to get into it, sir," Kinkaid blew a piece of pinkish kinky hair out of her face as she turned to me. "I've had about enough of your prima donna act, Bee Cool. If it weren't for your fans, I would've disqualified you as a no-show a long time ago, but they were all threatening to mutiny if I didn't track you down for the tournament. If you'd wanted to make a grand entrance, we could have arranged it without all this hassle."

I twiddled a two-finger wave at Frank and Ingrid who stood by helplessly as Kinkaid escorted me to the ballroom, although I noticed Frank kept us in sight until we got to the door.

Ringo, my sunglass hero, was waiting with a pair of sleek rectangular black Chanels as I crossed the threshold.

I waved him off. "I remembered mine tonight," I reached into my bag and felt around. Lipstick, key card, metal canister. Uh-oh. Something was wrong. I looked down. "Damnit. I must have picked up my mom's purse." I stared at her secret weapon, pepper spray. I had that and no glasses. Wasn't that my life in a nutshell?

Still smiling, he slid the Chanels on my face. I gave him a peck on the cheek. "Ringo, you're going to go broke buying me sunglasses. Go to Wal-mart. Make knockoffs chic."

"Don't worry," he smiled. "Chanel will be begging us to wear their shades by next week."

"How do you figure?"

"You're going to win the tournament. It won't be televised for a couple of months which will give us plenty of time to line up all the shades you wore as sponsors.

Kinkaid propelled me toward my table, but was called away by one of her minions waving from the check-in desk. Jack snagged me by the skirt hem. "Hey, dude, don't get fresh," I teased.

"W-where's Ingrid?"

"Working," I said vaguely, wanting to warn him that it was going to be a long hard road being in love with a pseudopsychology educated, fashionista, bodyguard, flack, secret security whatever. But I wasn't quite up to killing his in-love glow at the mention of her name. Humph. I used to be that way, until my lover deceived and spied on me then had the gall to discount any important information I might have, went on to boss me around and call me fat.

"What's wrong?" Jack asked. "Aren't you g-going to fill m-me in?"

I outlined the Rick drug revelation even though I didn't know the whodunit. "You know anything?"

"I found out S-Sam the Man Hyun has been on three other c-cruises over the past couple of years from which people have d-disappeared. All three were p-poker players."

"How did you confirm it?"

"Journalist friend of mine. We've been t-telegraphing each other since the e-mail went down."

"The problem is proving it. We would have to catch him in the act. And, who is helping him? There were at least two people trying to fling me out the window at the spa."

"I have an idea. Why d-don't you go out there and beat him in the t-tournament, then make a point of wandering off alone on this aft d-deck? I'll be waiting out behind that huge j-joker sculpture with a video c-camera."

I shook my head. "All his attacks have been preplanned. Remember, the surveillance cameras are covered."

"Okay, then pass Hyun a n-note that you want to meet with him after the t-tournament at that location."

"He might get suspicious with his target going on the offensive."

"He's escalating anyway if he's wh-whacked three people on one cruise. I imagine he's already at the d-desperate stage. It's worth a t-try as long as we keep you safe. Basically, we only need him to make an aggressive m-move to get the authorities to look into it."

Kinkaid had hustled over and grabbed my arm, dragging me to my table. Speaking of aggressive. "Chatty Kathy is out of here," she snapped at Jack over her shoulder.

As I nodded to everyone at the table, Kinkaid signaled Rhonda to order the deal.

I hoped luck would swing my way. Tonight was the night I needed to catch some cards.

Pocket sevens weren't exactly what I would call the luckiest deal in Texas Hold 'Em, but I decided that I had to come into the game aggressive and raised the big blind by fifteen thousand. It wasn't exactly a bluff, but it was a gamble. And wasn't that the name of the game? I scared off

Ian, Sam and two of the other amateurs; the other three at the table called, so I figured they had enough to stay in the game, which was probably more than I had. Still I hung in, reraising a thousand before The Flop of five of diamonds, two of diamonds, seven of clubs. Boy, was I lucky. I needed to use this as long as the cards fell my way. I raised again and knocked another player out, leaving me Rhonda and a nervous man who I gauged to be a total Mouse. I bet he had a hand and a half. Maybe a straight draw or flush? Damn. Fourth Street was a six of diamonds. Double Damn. I raised ten thousand, hoping to run the Mouse off since I couldn't read Rhonda clearly quite yet and would just have to hope she wasn't the one with the flush. Rhonda raised and reraised. The Mouse finally caved. Rhonda went all in with just a thousand less chips than I had. Holding my breath, I went all in with her.

Seven of spades fell on The River.

It was my night, not Rhonda's. I wouldn't have to worry about getting a solid read on her. Shaking her head in self disgust, she threw in her pocket flush, pushed herself away from the table and stalked off, sparing a hateful glare at me. I really didn't blame her, but it still made me fight off a bit of a chill.

I was in the enviable position now of being chip leader at our table by a long shot, which gave me the automatic psychological advantage. I played the next five hands aggressively, caught the cards I needed and won usually head-to-head with the other player who'd hung in—never the same person. I think I probably had the second-best hand every time—winning with two middle pair, a flush, pocket rockets and once with just a King kicker—but managed to scare off the better hand along the way. I did fold the hand after the kicker win, because Sam decided I'd been bluffing and raised me outrageously when all I had in my pocket was a Queen, a ten and a bad feeling. The next hand, though,

I was dealt pocket rockets with an Ace on The Flop and I rode that out, winning twenty-five thousand in chips and knocking out both the Mouse and Ian.

Ian leaned down to whisper in my ear as he exited, "You are amazing. Sometime soon I'll see into that mind of yours."

Sam was a rigid textbook player, which isn't a bad thing. It allowed him to stay in the game but didn't necessarily allow him to adjust for others' runs of luck or unpredictable behavior. He apparently was in the Annie Duke camp, and didn't wear sunglasses. Still, his face was so unreadable I'd have to say it was an advantage for him to have such a blank slate open for viewing. It was very disconcerting.

It was down to the three of us at our table an hour later—Sam, a Maniac amateur with a wretched temper, and me. Looking around, there were only about a dozen players left around the room, including Ben who surprisingly looked like the tournament chip leader. Kinkaid announced table consolidation after the current hand.

I peeked under Frank's marker at the Jack of spades, ten of clubs. I've folded this hand before, but usually at a full table. There were better draws out there that Sam could have, but it sure cut down the odds that only six of the cards were out instead of twenty. I was the small blind, so went with a modest raise of five thousand. Sam raised. I guessed he had a high pair. The Maniac, angrily smacking his chips into a stack, pushed in a call. I met the bet. I prayed for a great flop.

It came a two of spades (the Maniac moaned), King of spades (I mentally moaned) and a 10 of spades (I looked to heaven behind my Chanels).

We all walked a high wire with our bets. With a semidecent pair and a flush draw, I wanted to scare everyone away but couldn't without depleting my chip stack too seriously. I wanted to be able to play even with Ben in the next hand.

The Turn brought a Jack of diamonds. The Maniac went all in which made me wonder what he had under his marker. Sam and I both met the bet, leaving me with a couple thousand chips and Sam with only a handful. The Maniac swore a blue streak, ripped his earphones out and then I knew he'd been bluffing.

An eight of spades fell on Fifth Street.

Now Sam smiled. He turned over his pocket for a pair of eights and a pair of Kings. His smile faded to a frown when he saw my cards.

Twenty-seven
♦ ♣ ♥ ♠

*T*hankfully, I got to keep my seat. I was superstitious before I became a Texas Hold 'Em player and the game has only made it worse. I really think that if the cards are falling one way on a table, they will keep falling that way the rest of the game. That's why I find HORSE so fascinating. Playing for high cards then playing for low, takes talent and adaptability—throw in the luck factor and it certainly makes for interesting play.

The tournament was down to nine players. The only poker stars left were the Russian and me—by default, certainly, since four of the best players hadn't had the chance to finish. Kinkaid sat Ben next to me, on purpose, I'm certain. With TV cameras rolling for a future telecast the cruise line would heavily promote, the more drama the better. Maybe she thought we'd get in a knock-down-drag-out à la Jerry Springer.

Maybe we would.

I had to fold the first six deals with no suited cards, no

pairs and nothing higher than a nine, and I wondered if I'd used all my luck in the first half of the night. It worked out well for me, however, since four of the remaining players were eliminated in dramatic fashion by Ben and the Russian while I sat hording chips, not even forced to post a blind. Kinkaid swung by and whispered a warning. "You and your bro better not be in collusion. If I find proof, I'll have you punished."

She sounded so anticipatory of the prospect that I couldn't help asking, "Punish me how? By flipping me over the railing like the poor insurance investigator?"

Kinkaid drew back in shock then leaned in, smiling so the cameras couldn't pick up her animosity. "Are you kidding? I'd rather see you tortured slowly as you've tortured me this whole cruise—having to give up all your fancy clothes and money and look out from behind bars for years rather than something quick and easy like being sucked into the Gulf waters or chomped to death by a sharp-toothed shark."

Aw, so warm and fuzzy. I smiled at her. Ben was watching us with eyebrows raised over his John Lennon lenses.

The dealer called my attention to the bet. I peeked at my pocket and frowned at the Ace and King of clubs peeking back. I had a hard time lying, but with shades, I could manage a pretty good poker face. Over the last couple of months I'd been experimenting with opposite reactions and found they not only helped me curb my emotions at the table but also often threw off other players.

I sat at the button but had missed the bets while verbally dueling with Kinkaid, so quickly reviewed them now. Every player had stayed in the game, but conservatively. That meant Ben had nothing in his hand or he'd have hit the felt hard. I didn't know about the rest except Sam, who I guessed from his bet had either an Ace high or a high pair otherwise he'd have folded.

I wanted to milk the hand for more chips so I called all the way to The Turn. Nobody had padded the pot by much, even though The Flop came a four of hearts, ten of clubs, King of hearts. Fourth Street showed an Ace of diamonds. With two pair I had to raise but Sam beat me to it. He had a pair of something, maybe three of a kind. But I had the two highest pairs so I had to hold my breath and go all in. Everybody but Sam ducked out, grumbling.

I nailed the full house on The River with an Ace of hearts and shook my head in amazement. Smiling again, Sam turned over his two pair, Aces and Kings, and cupped his hands around the chips. He'd slid them halfway toward himself when I slowly turned up my cards. His eyes widened, then narrowed to black slits as his grin faded and he lifted his hands up off the felt. He snatched up his jacket, jammed it on and stuck a hand in the pocket where I'd slipped the note I'd written earlier. His brows drew together as he pulled it out. The dealer had distributed our pocket cards, so I peeked at them while watching Sam read my note.

Meet me at the aft deck after the tournament and I'll share some tips on how to win the game of modern Hold 'Em.

—BC

Sam stared at me a beat and then stomped off, anger radiating from him in almost tangible waves. He was mad enough now to kill, that was for sure. I just hoped Jack wouldn't let me down or I was going to be in real trouble.

The tournament ended up being an advertising dream come true. If I hadn't been involved, I think Kinkaid would have been giddy. Ben had been luckier than I'd been in catching cards and despite his wild, overconfident betting we ended up heads up at the end of the tournament. Every now and then I could hear the TV commentators in the corner of the room having a field day with the Hold 'Em twins—Bee Cool and Ben . . . what?

"What are they calling you?" I leaned into my brother.

He shrugged and winked into a camera. "Ben Hot."

Oh gag, his ego had been overblown enough as it was. Instead of razzing him about it, I just nodded, hoping the more distracted he became with his stardom, the more likely I would be to sneak away with the last hand. It worked for a while. I had him down to a third of my chips. It was time to step it up. At the break, he was inundated with giggling women wanting his autograph in and on all sorts of interesting places.

I waited until most of our audience had cleared the room, then escaped to the restroom. Ingrid was sulking outside in the hall and fell into step with me as I went around the corner to a less crowded facility. We ducked in.

"I thought you were working, Ingrid," I observed coolly.

"I am," she sulked. "Frank is my boss on this project. He's decided babysitting you is more important than the real job."

"That's silly. I'm in a public place on film for goodness' sake. I don't think anyone will try to snag me during the tournament."

She shrugged as she pushed into the first stall. "That's what I told him. He said the last time you were in trouble you were shot at on live TV. I pointed out that this tournament is taped, so any bloodshed would be edited out. He's just not reasonable when it comes to you."

I no sooner heard the lock slide on her door than the restroom door opened and in my peripheral vision I could see a figure charge toward me. Before I could cry out in surprise, a hand with a wet handkerchief clamped down over my mouth. My vision went blurry, the room spun. I felt like I was drunk. I started to giggle.

"I don't find this funny at all, Bee," Ingrid said, irritated, from inside her stall. "This is a serious investigation. Lives are at stake and you . . ."

I was dragged by my arms out the door. A woman out in the hall elbowed her husband and sniffed in my direction.

"Pruuuuuuuuude," I slurred as her husband hurried her away.

"She's drunk," my dragger explained. I knew that voice. I'd just heard it, really recently. Tonight? My mind was suddenly so slippery, I just couldn't pin down the information floating around in it.

"Whhhhhhere are weeeeee goiiiiiiing?"

My escort didn't answer and I couldn't seem to get my head to respond to a signal to turn and look at who was propelling me forward. I thought there was something in my purse if I could find it but I couldn't figure out how lipstick would help when kidnapped. Doors opened and I felt the warm sea breeze on my face. It was refreshing and I focused a bit better for a moment.

It had gotten really dark out on deck. I thought there should have been some lights out here, but there wasn't anything where we were but moonlight. Where were we? Better question: Who was the other half of the we? A flash caught my gaze—the video camera hidden in an upper corner of the awning. I peered at it. The lens was covered with black electrical tape. Uh-oh. That realization was enough to fill me with adrenaline, allowing me to twist out of his grasp.

I was face-to-face with Sam Hyun. He pushed me against the cold deck railing. "I thought our daaaate wassssssss after the tournaaaaaament?" My tongue felt thick and slow.

"It was a good idea but I couldn't wait."

"They'lllll beeee misssssing me," I offered.

"They'll get used to it."

I was getting progressively more lucid—impending death does that to you. I decided to let him think I was still half out of it when I was only about a quarter goofy. "Whhh-hyyyy?" I cocked my head at him.

"Because you're done with tournament poker. I told you before I'm going to kill your game and I am." He pulled out a paper and read. "I, Belinda Cooley, admit without a doubt that I cheat at the game of Texas Hold 'Em by collusion, by marked cards, by signaling in Las Vegas tournaments and those throughout the world. Signed on this day—"

"I'm nnnot gonna siiiiiiign that!"

Hyun grabbed me by my ponytail, lifted me off the ground, folded my body over the railing and showed me the churning water below. "Yes, you are, or you are going swimming."

Face-to-face with the churning silver water below, I found my tongue. "I guess Rawhide, Mahdu and Ferris didn't sign it, huh? I guess the poor investigator found you to be the one who's thrown dozens over ship railings over the past couple of years."

"What are you talking about?"

"Don't play dumb with me. And I guess you keep feeding Rick pills like the liquid you just tried to drug me with, to make him forget your attack."

"You're nuts! Why would I feed Rick my cologne?"

"Your cologne?" I shouted.

Sam nodded proudly. "Polo."

No wonder I got nauseous. Toby, my ex-fiancé, used to wear Polo. "You didn't threaten the others?"

"You're the only one I want out of the game." He frowned. "No woman should be able to play poker, especially not like you do."

I relaxed. Sam was all blow and no go. I shook my head

and shoved the paper away, sneezing the Polo out of my nose twice. "Let me go."

"Okay. It's your funeral." He shrugged and loosened his hold on my leg. I slid closer to the dark, shiny water. "Wait. Let me go *after* you pull me back to the deck."

"Sam the Man, slowly and carefully pull Miss Cooley back on deck or I'll sh-shoot," I heard Jack's voice order with barely a hint of his stutter, from somewhere behind Hyun. Where did the Smack get a gun?

"Don't shoot," Hyun begged, eyes widening. "I was just scaring her."

"It's not nice to tease the killer whales, Sam. The SPCA'll get you for that."

I was flipped back up on deck like a tuna. From my vantage point, I could see Jack digging the video camera into Hyun's back as he walked him forward into the deck railing. "Hey, that doesn't feel like a gun," Hyun said.

Scrambling to my feet and plucking Mom's purse out of his waistband, I ran before Sam could figure out he was being held by a social phobic at video point.

❚ nearly ran over Ian as I pushed my way through the doors back into the lobby.

"What's wrong?" He stopped me with his hands on my shoulders.

"Sam Hyun is trying to kill me," I wheezed between huffs.

He grabbed my wrist and pulled me toward the stairs. "Come with me, quick."

We took the stairs two at a time. I paused before we tackled the next story. "I can't abandon Jack. He saved me."

Ian picked up the house phone and reported the chase on the deck to security, then grabbed my hand and we raced down the hallway. Ian pulled out his key card and opened the door, shoving me in.

"But what about Jack?" I asked. "I should go back to make sure they get the real story and arrest Hyun. It think he's the one who threw all the poker stars overboard."

"Not these poker stars by chance?" Ian asked low in my ear.

I turned slowly and my breath caught at the scene before me. "What's going on here?"

"We're having a little game," Ian answered calmly. Mahdu, Rawhide and Denton Ferris sat at a makeshift poker table, all duct taped at their torsos. Mouths and wrists duct taped, they all shot me panicked looks as Ian continued, "And you weren't invited, Belinda. But since you're here, we'll let you play. I've always wanted to bring a woman into our little experiments but I have never seen any that warranted the effort. I wondered after the Big Kahuna whether you might be the one, but you had to prove to be more than just lucky. I've been very impressed by your play during this *Gambler* tournament, but I also liked you a little too much to sacrifice you for information. I'm so glad that you made the decision for me by needing to be rescued."

I waited a beat for someone to cue the Twilight Zone music, because that is what the whole scene evoked. "What decision?" I asked.

Ian blinked at me, surprised. "Whether it was worth losing a hot woman for my science. Men, now they are expendable, but a woman I might want, that leads to a dilemma."

"Wouldn't I have to want you too?"

"Don't you?" Ian asked. "I know I felt some chemistry going on, surely thanks to those pheromones I have been wearing. Another experiment that's working quite well."

"I don't think your pheromones could overpower your personality," I deadpanned. "That tends to matter more to me."

"As I said," he continued, dismissing my barb, or not hearing it at all, "you've chosen your own fate."

"And that would be?"

"To play poker for your life."

"What?"

"Those are the stakes of this particular ring game," Rhonda said, coming out from the bathroom with Paul, who brandished a roll of duct tape. Ian's arm slid down my back and grabbed a wrist. I twisted away as his other hand grabbed my left wrist. I kicked out, bucked my body and screamed. Duct tape slapped down over my nose and mouth. I couldn't breathe but kept fighting as they dragged me to a chair. The fighting thing was probably a bad idea since I was suffering from oxygen deprivation sooner than I would have had I been a limp noodle. Pretty soon I *would* be a limp noodle, I realized, as I went weak. Things started going dim.

All of a sudden Ian reached over and ripped the tape off my face. Let me tell you what, microdermabrasion has nothing on duct tape. I sucked in a breath as Ian sneered at Paul.

"You idiot. Don't kill her yet."

My hero.

Since my mouth was free I decided to use it. "What are you doing with us?"

"No-limit Hold 'Em with more motivation than you will find in any other game. Play for cash, but the one who has the most at the end of the game wins his life back.

"The rest, well, we thank you for your donation to science by removing your brain for further study." He waved at one of the beds laid out with surgical equipment, some jars with formaldehyde standing by on the nightstand. We drank that in for a terrifying moment before he continued. "Then we throw you over the side of the ship because we believe in recycling."

Ferris whimpered. Mahdu's eyes popped out. Rawhide growled. I shivered against my duct tape prison. Being visually adept wasn't always an advantage when I could see so clearly in my mind's eye sharks feasting on headless corpses, mine included. The term card shark took on a whole new meaning.

"If it's not really a tournament table, not a true ring game, then how long is the game?" I asked. It mattered desperately because I played very differently if I sat down to win a little money in a ring game than if I had to long haul it at a tournament. One was a game where the more who played, the more money there was in the pot. The other was a game where the faster you eliminated players, the closer you were to walking away number one.

"That is what you don't know. You can't play it like a tournament, you can't play it like a true ring game where you can get up and leave any time. Therefore you can't strategize or plan, you just have to win as much as you can as soon as you can. I've discovered it's the best way to see into a reactive poker brain."

Paul had walked over. I looked at him. "So this is the offer you couldn't refuse to get yourself out of hock? Killing people?"

Flushing red, Paul ripped off a smaller piece of duct tape and moved to put it over my mouth, his hand shaking. Ian motioned him to stop.

"What are you doing with the probes?" I asked, seeing Ian liked to talk about what he was doing. The longer I kept the tape off my mouth, the better for all of us.

"Seeing into your mind," Ian said, motioning to Rhonda

who had the probes hooked up to a machine that was connected to a laptop computer. "And we are doing little experiments."

Rhonda pressed a button on the machine and Ferris yelped, eyes wide.

"What was that?"

"Denton Ferris got a little shock," Ian explained, eerily calm. Ick. He nodded to Rhonda. "You'd better adjust that. We don't want such a strong reaction."

"Shock therapy?"

Ian shook his head.

"What is your purpose then?"

"We are trying to determine if stimulating different centers in the brain can change one's play."

"Are you trying to run a scam in Vegas?"

Ian laughed and it chilled me to the bone. "I hadn't considered that, actually. Paul, of course, did, which is why he's here. It's funny that it occurred to you too. I'll have to add that to my research. Perhaps your goody-two-shoes gambler's mind isn't as different as Paul's addicted, desperate one."

"This is your study." I said aloud as I realized it. "Is it worth our lives to get tenure?"

"More than tenure, Belinda," Ian said. "I will be gaining worldwide renown and a place in history forever."

I shook my head. Rawhide growled. Paul cuffed him on the back of the head and moved forward to duct tape my mouth again. Ian waved him off. "She's a fascinating conversationalist. It's a shame she won't be around to talk to after tonight."

"You don't think I'm going to win?"

Ian cocked his head and considered. "It's possible but highly improbable. The odds of a woman winning any tournament are extremely low. I think they put them at two thousand to one for the World Series of Poker this year."

"That's the percentage of women who play in the WSOP, so I'd say those are fair odds for a woman like me. Now, Jennifer Harman would have to have a bit better odds."

Ian dismissed my observation with a waving hand. "No woman is going to win the WSOP until my study is published." Glancing at his watch, he motioned to Rhonda and Paul. "We need to get started."

"What happened with Rick anyway? I assume you tried to kidnap him to be here as well." I asked quickly. I still couldn't figure out who the woman was who'd lured him to the closet. Rhonda didn't fit the profile.

"Rhonda is what happened to Rick," Ian said, disgusted. "She has a fatal flaw that I didn't anticipate or I wouldn't have partnered with her in this project. She is sentimental. Who would have guessed? She couldn't stomach feeding him to the fishes once we finished studying him in action."

What a softy, that Rhonda. Besides a stiffening in her spine when Ian criticized her, Rhonda didn't react as she bent over each man at the table, checking the probes, adjusting a few here and there.

"So after Callie bashed him on the head, we just had to leave him. I was really looking forward to making some corollaries between his ability to strategize with headlocks on the mat and bluffs on the felt."

"Callie?" I said, aghast, suddenly worried for my whole family. She was staying in Ben's room, eating meals with Mom and Dad. I had to get out of here.

"She's addicted to benzodiazepine and Valium. Easy to have someone work for you as long as you keep her in pills. She just does little jobs here and there. We really wanted her to arrange to stay with you but that bossy Amazonian goddess is stronger willed."

"But I thought my involvement was accidental."

"No, I'd planned to use you as the subject of the pheromone study from the beginning." Ian smiled and I shivered.

A crisp knock rattled the door. Ian looked sharply at Rhonda who frowned in return. The person on the other end started shouting. My throat constricted. My stomach clutched. I recognized that voice. "If you don't open up right now, I'll report this game to the ship authorities!"

I shook my head frantically. "Don't do it, it's a bluff. Just wait for the guy to go away."

Ian raised his eyebrows. My advice was all he needed to make his decision. "Open up." He nodded to Paul as he slapped a piece of duct tape over my mouth.

Howard sauntered in, still dressed to the nines, brandishing a wad of cash. I rolled my eyes. Did my parents *never* listen to anything I said?! "I'm here to play! Deal me in!" he announced. He faltered a step as he looked around the room. "Hey girlie," he said to me, then to Ian, "What's the tape about? Want a quiet game, eh?"

Ian narrowed his eyes at me. "Why is *he* here?"

I started to shrug, but then realized this was an opportunity. I moved my mouth like I was dying to say something. I was, in fact, because I figured I'd be dying if I didn't. Mahdu and Ferris threw each other panicked looks. Rawhide growled louder. Rhonda nervously hid behind her computer. Paul shifted from foot to foot. Ian studied me for a moment, in which I tried to look extremely earnest and trustworthy, then blew out an exasperated breath as he carefully pulled the tape off my mouth.

"Mom's secret weapon!" I shouted before it was slapped back on, much less gently. Ian knocked me over on the floor next to the bed as he leaped for Dad. Thank goodness for that stunt, because Howard moved quick as lightning, grabbing my purse. Ian knocked Dad down but Dad must have landed right on the trigger of the pepper gas because I heard a hiss and he started coughing.

My throat started to burn like I was breathing in pure acid. The pain was intense. I closed my eyes and put the bedspread over my nose. I could hear everyone else coughing and wheezing. Ian, still trying to function, dragged my chair to the balcony, hacking and moaning. I guess I was going to be the first to go. Ferris had worked the duct tape over those sharp teeth of his and could get his tongue out the hole he made, he started screaming in between bone-rattling coughs. The whites of Rawhide's eyes were bright red as he growled at Ian, rocking his chair loudly. The pepper gas kept hissing.

I tried to brace my feet against the balcony door frame but Ian just pulled harder, ripping the strap off my right Manolo. Man, was I ticked off now! I bucked and writhed, making it difficult for him to get his awkward load to the railing. He hollered to Paul to come help, but instead the blonde lumbered to the door, hand on his mouth, tears streaming, coughs wracking his body. He threw the door open and ran into the hall.

Ian called to Rhonda. After a moment, I felt the chair lift and balance on the edge of the balcony railing. My heart squeezed in my chest. This was it. I couldn't swim duct taped to a chair. I wondered what it would feel like to drown. Maybe I'd break my neck on the impact with the water. I wished for that.

"Put her down."

"It's too late for that."

"If you don't put her down now, I will cut your hands off and throw them to attract the sharks so you can see them waiting for you as I pitch you over the side."

Wow. That was pretty mean. I knew Frank had a temper, but I didn't know he could be this cruel. Cool.

Since I was facing the ocean, I could only hear and feel Frank. For some reason, although I hung precariously five floors above the unforgiving sea, I was comforted by the sound of his breathing. I wondered why he wasn't coughing and gagging like the rest of us. Maybe he was really Superman. I could see the lights from the shore twinkling on the far horizon. I wondered where we were. What normal people were doing behind those lights. Which of us was going to feed the sharks first.

Ian looked back at Frank, and then at me. "I must continue my work."

He lifted his hands off the chair seemingly in slow motion, slithered over the railing and into the blackness. I waited to follow him but was jerked back instead. A splash sounded below. I shivered and sniffed, my nose running from pepper spray and fear. Other damsels in distress gasp winningly, and I get snotty. It's that karma thing all over again.

Frank dabbed at my nose with a handkercheif and put his knuckle under my chin as he lifted the face mask he wore to the top of his head. Slowly he peeled the duct tape off my mouth. His brown eyes warned and warmed simultaneously. How did he do that? "You are in big trouble, Honey Bee."

"I keep hearing that."

"And it's done no good, I see. You ditched Superwoman again."

"I didn't ditch her. I was kidnapped."

"By Ian?"

"By Sam Hyun."

Frank drew his eyebrows together and glanced back into the room. "Where is he then?"

"He doesn't have anything to do with this. Ian saved me from Sam."

"And you ended up taped to a chair dangling over the

Gulf." Frank shook his head. "Honey Bee, only you would be rescued by someone more dangerous than your attacker."

I sighed. "I know. I guess I disproved Richard's theory. I didn't even get to win the tournament."

Frank leaned down. "Ah, but you might just win at love." At first his five o'clock shadow scraping across my duct tape–treated lips burned, but then when his kiss made me burn other places, I didn't notice the pain at all anymore.

"Break it up, would you?" Ingrid called from inside. "We've got better things to do."

Frank slowly pulled his lips from mine. "Speak for yourself, Superwoman."

Ingrid snorted behind her mask, as she held Rhonda to the floor with a knee to her back and an arm up around her shoulder blades.

"Where did you guys get masks? How did you know we even had pepper spray?"

Frank shrugged. "We come prepared."

"Who's we?"

"FBG Enterprises." Frank grinned. He knew I already knew this. Dammit. "Now you can't tell me you don't know who I work for."

I shook my head, glaring. "Cut me loose."

"Nuh-uh," Frank said. "Not until I get all the rest of these creeps taken care of and can keep an eye solely on you." He motioned to someone behind me. Joe lifted me off the ground and walked through the cabin and out the door. "Hey! Hey! What about my Dad?"

"I'm right here, girlie," Dad said as we made it out into the hall that was swarming with the playing-card shirts of cruise security. I thought I was going cross-eyed from all the red and black—spades, clubs, diamonds and hearts. Dad called as Joe weaved through the crowd, "Listen to these guys, they know what's best for you."

Grr.

"I need to find Jack," I informed Joe.

"Jack's fine. He marched Sam Hyun at video camera point to the ship security. He's being debriefed right now."

"Where are you taking me?" I asked Joe.

"Where Frank says you belong."

Twenty-eight

◆ ♣ ♥ ♠

I heard the door open and I didn't even look around. The morning sun was rising, casting a golden sheen on the water that I had been watching for so long I'd become nearly hypnotized. When you're almost thrown off a ship three times in as many days, it's time to trust that fate will step in if it's not meant to be.

Fate or Frank, that is.

"You know," I said to the sea. "It's not a safe idea to tell a woman where she belongs and leave her to think about that for hours."

"Is that right?"

"Yes. It leaves her a long, long time to plan."

"Plan what?" His breath ruffled the hair at my nape.

"Her revenge," I answered as I felt his hands wrap around me, diving into the parting of my robe.

"Will it be painful, her revenge?" he asked, his fingers exploring lightly.

"Oh very."

"Will it be cruel?" He nuzzled my left earlobe.

"The worst." I pressed my backside into his Levi's zipper.

"Will it be inhumane?" His baritone caught as he drew in a sudden breath. I smiled. Slowly.

"You are going to be out of your mind," I assured him as I turned around and began.

And we both were. For hours.

And hours.

"I think I've changed my mind about cruises," I told Frank later as we lounged, legs stretched out, intertwined, sun warming our damp bodies on the balcony.

"Hmm?"

"They're not so bad after all."

"As long as you don't seek out murderers and mad scientists, I think they can be relaxing."

"Who knocked off the insurance investigator?"

"Rhonda says it was Ian, because he was connecting the dots. We'll know more when they examine his notes. If they find them."

"There are still some things I don't understand. Why did Rhonda, Ian and Paul go into Cozumel?"

"They were trying to see if they could arrange to get their brains off the ship at the next port. That's been their MO. They bribe someone to take them or mail them to their secret lab in the mountains above Oaxaca. The authorities there located it."

I shivered. "Glad I wasn't there to see that."

"You ought to be glad you weren't there to *be* part of that." Frank shook his head. "You almost were. The winner of the ring game was going to be drugged like Rick and walked off the boat at Tampico and kept for further study. Honey Bee, you have to learn to avoid this kind of danger from now on."

"Frank, how do I avoid it? Danger seems to find me. I mean, how many people go on cruises and have the excitement we had on this one?"

"You know, Bee, very few people on the ship were aware of any of that 'excitement' otherwise known as danger. You, on the other hand, were right in the middle of it."

"But it's not my fault!"

"Okay," Frank said with a patient sigh. "Let's say it isn't your fault. After all, your life was pretty dull and drab before a year ago, wasn't it?"

Now I was dull, drab *and* fat. Humph. I didn't answer.

Frank continued. "So, let's find a common denominator. Your brother is one. Poker is two."

"And Frank is three," I added.

His eyes darkened dangerously. Ominously. Sexily. I untangled my legs from his and crawled on my hands and knees until I was lying on top of him. "You have to admit, you are a common denominator amid the trouble. Now if I knew more about you, I might decide that you are just a coincidental offshoot of the danger, but not knowing every detail of your life . . ."

Frank shut me up by kissing me, long and hard. When we came up for air, he whispered, "Promise me, Honey Bee, you'll give up poker."

"Promise me, you'll tell me who Frank Gilbert really is."

"Hmmm."

We docked back in Galveston hours later. As we stepped onto the dock, we saw Rhonda, Paul and Sam being loaded into separate FBI rides. Reporters and cameramen swarmed around them, held back by uniformed Galveston police.

A woman approached us on our left. "Hi, I'm a producer

for Eyewitness News in Houston. My reporter was called off with our other cameraman to cover a bomb threat at the Galveston city hall. Can I ask you a few questions about what happened on the cruise?"

I nodded toward my companion. "This is the guy you should talk to. Jack Smack is a freelance investigative reporter—he's the one who broke the case."

Jack started to shake his head and I whispered in his ear. "This could be your big break. Be focused. Report!"

Stepping away, I nodded in encouragement as the producer shoved the mic into Jack's face. He started talking, only stuttering a time or two before he got a rhythm, and I could tell he was in journalist mode. He'd spoken for about a minute when he was signaled to stop.

"I just got word, the producers are taking the feed live on *Good Morning America*," the producer shouted as the camera man gave him a three-two-one countdown and cued him to speak. I couldn't have been more proud of my own child. Jack was awesome, rocking with his report—stuttering only twice and sweating in rivulets down his back where the cameras couldn't see. Frank, ultrasexy in his Levi's, Luccheses and Ray-Bans, drew up next to me, tucking a strand of hair behind my ear as Jack wrapped it up.

The monitors showed the scene back in the studio in New York City, the anchors all giving a thumbs-up, one saying, "Good work, Jack. It sounds like Jack Smack is on his way to being a household name. Watch out—looks like *GMA* has their own man in the trenches at the felt tables!"

"A star is born." Diane Sawyer chimed in.

Ben had sidled up beside me, watching the TV monitor. "Are they talking about me again?" He said, meaning it, of course.

I raised my eyebrows. "Not this time. Sorry, I think the mad scientists have eclipsed your tournament win."

"You'll do anything to make sure I don't get all the attention," Ben whined, giving me a noogie. "But you won't be able to steal it away when I go to the WSOP."

"You're not going to fork out ten grand to be on the World Series of Poker," I chided.

"I don't have to. I just won a seat."

"What?"

"When you abandoned your seat, I won the *Sea Gambler* tournament by default," Ben grinned. "And the first prize money and a seat at the WSOP."

Frank wore his great stone-cop face. I knew what he wanted me to say—that my brief and checkered career as a pro poker player was over.

"I guess I can't let you go alone," I heard myself tell Ben. "Besides, it's time for WSOP's first woman winner."

Ben grabbed my hand and twirled me around. "World Series of Poker, here we come!"

Frank shook his head as he walked away.

Bee's Buzz

The Softer Secrets of Texas Hold 'Em . . .
What I've found to be the top ten tells

1. SIZE MATTERS

By far, the number one most important tell is the bet, not
the batting of eyes or the tapping of fingers while dishing
it. *What? The bet's size?* you may be saying. This from a
self-proclaimed intuitive player? This from a woman who
hates calculating probabilities? Yes! Yet, it still takes intuition to interpret the bet. Let me explain: You have to frame
your interpretation of each bet according to the player who
makes it. The Mouse sitting next to you who only calls the
big blind if she has pocket rockets is scary if she raises on
The Turn. On the other hand, the same move by the Maniac to her right is less scary, because he probably has
nothing better than a two and eight off-suit, also known as
a royal flop. Got it? Don't try to pinhole players at first, just
watch and feel. You'll know when their bet means something.

2. GAUGING THE CARAT OF THE DIAMOND

You know the type . . . the people who keep studying their cards like they've changed since they last touched the felt. Wishful thinking. Nope, those cards are the same sad off-suit couple they were dealt to begin with. Too bad for them. Too good for you.

3. BODYGUARDING THE POCKET

Watch out for this one. Someone who is keeping a finger on their cards, has a hand inched out a little farther on the table than usual, or maybe even has leaned over the felt a bit more than they had been usually has a hand that is damned good. I even had one gal who scooted her chair up just a fraction closer to the table. Red flag. I folded. She had a royal flush.

4. ANTS IN HIS PANTS

The player who is bouncing out of their chair, unable to wait for you to fractionalize your probabilities and shove your chips forward, is usually reason enough for you to raise your bet. This guy has a weak hand and is just trying to freak you out. Let him dance for entertainment's sake and get ready to rake in the chips.

5. MAKING WHOOPEE

No, not that kind of whoopee. The ha-ha kind. This is the guy who can't hide the smile when he hits another set of trips on The Flop. This is the gal who is giggling at every stupid thing the dork next to her says because she is already holding a full house on Fourth Street. This is the luckiest person at the table, and he or she, more likely, is loving it. She can't help it. Who doesn't love finally having it her way? Get out of her way until her smile fades a bit.

6. THE ICE MAN

Now, I know they are sexy, those mirror-shaded men who look like they're thinking of all the ways they would like to rip your clothes off. They are really thinking of how much money their three and nine off-suit will lose them if you don't buy their bluff.

7. BETTY BLASÉ

Don't confuse her with the ice-in-the-veins player described above. This one isn't cool, she's bored. Or rather, acting that way. This one looks like she could yawn at any moment, that she would rather be changing the oil in her car than playing cards. This one is dangerous. This one has a throne room in front of her with the rest of the court on The Flop.

8. SPLASHING THE POT

I know some grandstanders and fish who tend to do this all the time. They don't last long at the table and soon learn their lesson. For the most part, when done irregularly, this is an actor's move. Cavalierly flinging your chips into the pot is a cover for a weak hand. Don't get psyched out unless the bet size tells you otherwise (see #1).

9. I WONDER IF SHE'S MARRIED?

The guy who is watching the woman across the table three seats off the bet like he'd like to ask her on a date is trouble for you, and not because you want him to buy *you* a drink. He can't see her cleavage from over there so this is an obvious hoax. He is taking his eyes away from the action to hide his thrill over his strong hand. Otherwise he might do a backflip or start chortling hysterically at the bettor going all in when the guy we're talking about already has a full house on The Flop.

10. ADVANTAGE DENTISTS

You really wouldn't think dentists would have a natural advantage, now would you? They do, though, because dentists automatically want to check everyone's teeth. If you can't see a player's mouth (okay, if not teeth, at least the lips), then feel free to raise on her. It's a phenomenon I can't explain—I really don't know why people press their lips together when they're dealt bad cards. Maybe they're afraid the devil on their shoulder will make them give away the trash in their pocket.

Heck, I'm feeling generous. I'll throw in a bonus . . .

11. WHERE'S THE HOURGLASS WHEN YOU NEED IT?

The player who takes forever to make a bet usually has a decent drawing hand, so keep an eye on this one. If, after The Turn, she starts acting like Betty Blasé, you probably need to fold unless you've got something amazing. Of course, temper all of this with what you learned in #1. Hey, I never said Hold 'Em was cut and dried. If it were, winning would be easy!

Really, though, who wants to hear from little old me? I found some tips from the real experts . . .

"Women like to play because poker is heavily based on instincts. Women like to follow their gut." —Jennifer Harman

"You have to be very patient to win this tournament (WSOP's Main Event) and get really lucky." —Annie Duke

"I have a very aggressive style of playing that disturbs people."　　　　　　　—Isabelle "No Mercy" Mercier

"It's got to be controlled aggression. There's no point in all in, all in, all in. That's not aggression. That's kamikaze."

—Lucy "Golden Ovaries" Rokach

"I would suggest to most women who play regularly with men to think about how they perceive you and play deceptively."

—Kathy Liebert

"A pretty young thing can take advantage of getting men to check when ordinarily they would bet. It's OK to play helpless if it saves your money."

—Cat Hulbert

"When you show a negative attitude, you set yourself up for more defeat. Players who possess a positive attitude play better."

—Debbie Burkhead

"Money management can be the difference between a winning day and a losing day, or a winning week and a losing week."

—Susie Isaacs

". . . men never think women are bluffing, so this makes it easier for us to get away with a bluff once in a while."

—Evelyn Ng

"I still think there's a lot of men that don't really want women to be at the poker tables. If you open any poker magazine or all the websites, everything is advertised by scantily clad women. So a woman in this business is like, 'Do I join the scantily clad women or do I try to be more like a man?' I think that's sort of the struggle."

—Jennifer "Unabombshell" Tilly

"Someone once asked me why women don't gamble as much as men do, and I gave the common-sensical reply that we don't have as much money. That was a true but incomplete answer. In fact, women's total instinct for gambling is satisfied by marriage."

—Gloria Steinem

"Self-control, skill, and luck are all factors you have to have to win this game. Study, learn, and practice. Play poker. Don't let poker play you. Know why you are playing the game."

—Sharla Lehrmann